Delh

Krishan Partap Singh is a former banker who now lives and writes in New Delhi. He is the author of *The Raisina Series*, a three-book series set in the political village of Lutyens' Delhi, India's seat of power.

He can be reached at raisina.series@gmail.com

THE RAISINA SERIES:

Young Turks
Delhi Durbar
The War Ministry

Krishan Partap Singh

Delhi Durbar

hachette
INDIA

First published in 2010 by Hachette India
An Hachette UK company

Copyright © Krishan Partap Singh 2010
Krishan Partap Singh asserts the moral right to be identified as the author of the work.

ISBN: 978-81-906173-4-5

All rights reserved. No part of the publication may be reproduced, stored in a retrieval system, or transmitted in any form or by any means without the prior written permission of the publisher, nor be otherwise circulated in any form of binding or cover other than that in which it is published and without a similar condition being imposed on the subsequent purchaser.

This is a work of fiction. Any resemblance to real persons, living or dead, is purely coincidental.

Hachette India
612/614 (6th Floor), Time Tower,
MG Road, Sector 28, Gurgaon-122001, India

Typeset in Minion Pro 9.5/12 by
InoSoft Systems, Noida

Printed in India by Manipal Press Ltd, Manipal

*'Corruption, the most infallible symptom of
constitutional liberty.'*

EDWARD GIBBON

Prologue: In My Father's Shoes

THE TALE THAT follows is neither a personal confession nor an apology – for which it can very easily be mistaken – but something much more substantial. It is an explanation or, to be more precise, an elucidation of the excesses that were committed within my knowledge by men of power.

As it turned out, it took only a handful of days for the great altruistic hopes of our forefathers to be trampled upon by the naked greed and self-interest of the few, among whose number, I concede, I must be counted. It all happened so stealthily that everything we once held sacred as a nation became a memory without any sort of public outrage or mourning in this so-called largest democracy in the world. And I witnessed the unfolding act of our disgrace from a front row seat. This truth marks the highest point as well as the deepest regret of my life; the paradox irrevocably entwined in my memory.

I had returned to India confronting a dilemma of destiny, and voluntarily choosing to be Indian once again. The dark blue passport would be my umbilical partner till death do us part. Unlike many of my generation and class, I had never, in my youth, been convinced that if I was to have a great future it would by definition preclude returning to my motherland.

Living abroad for most of my early adulthood only helped me further cement a deep bond with my country. I understood more deeply what it meant to be Indian, away from India. The irony is not lost on me – it proved to be a sort of Nehruvian passage of illumination, shining its torch on the darkest depths of myself. My return turned out to be more than just an end of a journey; it became the beginning of another more enlightening one – my re-acquaintance with Delhi.

Prior to my abrupt homecoming I had spent a fairly enjoyable and professionally satisfying few years in Dubai, working as a private banker with a multinational bank. After graduating from business school in the United States and working four years on Wall Street, I had, with some encouragement from my father, strayed from the beaten path. I was hired by an exclusive and relatively anonymous Swiss private bank for their Dubai branch office. Officially, I was supposed to be targeting the affluent non-resident Indian community of the Gulf. But the specific reason I had been hired was to use my contacts to prospect for the ultra-rich of India who had ample surreptitious reserves of foreign exchange to invest; the Government of India being, or pretending to be, oblivious of this fact.

Indian foreign exchange regulations, still unnecessarily schizophrenic about a run on the controlled rupee, did not allow the rich to freely invest their fortunes abroad. Laws, obviously, had not and did not stop these worthies from getting to the promised land of western real estate and capital markets, even if the end result was ultimately to their detriment. Though, in a hard-to-miss historical irony, the money increasingly found its way back into India disguised as welcome foreign investment, the India story coming full circle with the investment needs of our clients mirroring global capital flows. And financial consultants, or account executives or, if you prefer, private bankers like myself, knew nothing better than how to cater to their every need. It was a tricky dance, especially if you met the client in India, because then you had to approach the subject obliquely and could only get to the point after the client's suspicions were fully assuaged and trust built. The signing of the account-opening documents – always in Dubai or somewhere else outside India – was the other hurdle. Only then did the actual investing begin.

I had been given carte blanche by my superiors, with no one overseeing me, mainly because of the money that flooded in thanks to my labours. As long as the stigma of terror-funds did not taint the bank's image, my Swiss bosses had no interest in knowing the antecedents of my clients; that was a problem only the regulated American banks were forced to surmount. Even when other governments got tough with the Swiss for their banking secrecy, the Indian Government, whatever it might say for public consumption, could be relied upon to never delve too seriously into the secret wealth of its elite citizenry. Too many skeletons lurked in those Alpine cupboards. If Hawala dealers, bullion traders and dodgy exporters often were conduits for feeding the pipeline at the source, it was with me that the money trail ended – after a decent bit of laundering at various dhobi ghats in the most scenic parts of the world, of course. For the right fee we provided a full array of services for our precious clients.

International private banking was a perfect fit for my talents, and my lineage. I proved to be a natural when it came to the delicate art of client servicing. Yes, I admit, it was not dissimilar to being a whore in an expensive suit. You just had to remember that the client was always right. I was – undoubtedly – their seducer, but there were no innocent victims to be found here. Very little of the money I handled over the years had been earned through above-aboard means. But that was no concern of mine. They gave me the money to make them wealthier – or, at the very least, to maintain their net worth – and that is exactly what I religiously went about doing.

I kept my morals and my conscience (such as they were) locked away – a small rule of business I had imbibed from my father – and concentrated on meeting my targets for assets to be gathered and commissions to be produced from the ensuing investment of these assets. Numbers ruled supreme; they were all I had to worry about.

Life was relatively simple, quite black and white, really, that is until I was abruptly summoned back to good old Delhi a week after my thirty-fourth birthday.

MY FATHER, SARDAR Gurcharan Singh Sidhu, to give it to you straight, had made it his life's work to bring some of the efficiency and procedures of a commodities market to those behind-the-scenes activities in the nation's capital that are generally clubbed under the heading of 'governmental corruption' – an accomplishment that had earned him his place as one of the most influential public servants of his generation. But he was neither a politician nor a bureaucrat; he was really a hybrid of the two. He made his place in the space between these two worlds and took advantage of the mistrust and lack of communication between them.

My father knew more about the intricacies of administration than most politicians and was better-versed in the uncertainties of politics than most bureaucrats. He played one against the other and using this advantage made sure every decision of the particular department or ministry that he happened to be attached to had his stamp on it. Three decades of statecraft had honed his instincts and allowed him to perfect this role to the full.

Father had grown up in Chandigarh and had gone on to study law from there, but he hadn't really practised for very long as he'd found his true calling fairly early in life. Starting off as a Private Secretary to a Cabinet Minister in Punjab – the father of one of his closest friends – he first learned the secret of harnessing borrowed political power for the purpose of bringing the bureaucracy to heel. My father became steadily more powerful. His modus operandi was to attach himself to influential politicians using any means necessary and then to quickly go about making himself indispensable. While his basic strategy didn't change very much, his realm of power expanded. He spent the first quarter of his career in Chandigarh and then moved on to bigger and better things in Delhi.

In both cities, he became so renowned for his special talents that each new government found it could not do without him. In all his career, he never once suffered the inevitable eviction from office and influence that other political appointees suffered after becoming the orphaned legacy of previous regimes. He graduated from the role of Private Secretary to more senior roles that provided him with the garb of exalted titles like 'Officer on Special Duty' and 'Adviser to the Government'. The longevity of his almost continuous service made him a singularity. The politicians could not live without him; the bureaucracy hated and feared him in equal measure.

Most of my friends had seen my father in a government position for so long that they'd just assumed he was a career civil servant; I hadn't bothered to correct their mistaken impressions. He wielded consequential power and yet the common man didn't know his name or recognize his face. Talk about democracy at work.

And what exactly was it that he did so well?

In each ministry that he worked – and he had served in more than most bureaucrats – he unerringly identified the areas in the ministry that could produce the kind of deals that would net the maximum amount of cash, for the powers-that-be and himself, with minimum risk of disclosure at the time or, more importantly, later, when the Opposition inevitably came to power.

You could say he was a sort of financial consultant too – maximum reward for minimum risk. Like father, like son. He didn't exactly hide what he did from me or my brother. Quite the contrary. Father shared the fine details of how he'd masterfully plotted and crafted each transaction as if it were an exalted art form. Perhaps, in a messed up sort of way, it was. He could make the levers of power move when they seemed frustratingly intractable to others, the rich and powerful included, because he knew how the matrix of government reacted to even the slightest stimuli and for that reason his services were highly prized, and highly priced.

I was brought up in this environment of moral ambiguity, so I dearly hope that will be taken into account when I am judged by the big boss in the sky for my part in subsequent events, of which I was a key and more or less voluntary participant.

I was taught to take everything I could by any means possible without feeling any sense of remorse and this necessarily coloured the way I saw the world, a world where the strong stomp on everyone below them and doing good is for the naïve; for bleeding-heart idealists who die the worst kind of death, one of heart-aching disillusionment.

I had been accidentally groomed to meet the requirements of the economic miracle that hit India in the early nineties, where the needs of the individual finally began to be addressed and seen as important, even necessary. Capitalism started seeping into our very marrow and the socialistic gangrene was cut away, having only found a place in history as a well-intentioned failure. Nehru's dream was finally dead and I think I helped deliver its death knell. I had been summoned back to Delhi to fulfil the destiny for which I always subconsciously knew I was meant – to be a wheeler-dealer in the capital of sleaze, corruption and hypocrisy.

Sardar Gurcharan Singh Sidhu – *mera baap* – had just gone through another round of shamming retirement, which he enacted whenever a change of government took place as he waited for someone in the new order to come pay obeisance and go through the motions of convincing him that his talents were badly required by the establishment, yet again. This time he had been approached by the head honcho himself, the Prime Minister.

Prime Minister Paresh Yadav, the current overlord of more or less the entire cow belt with his backward-caste-plus-Muslim voting coalition, had appointed my father as his Senior Domestic Adviser. His job, as you may imagine, was as always, to fill the prime-ministerial coffers as quickly as possible. Yadav was heading a Third-Front coalition government, sans the Congress or the BJP, and he knew better than anyone, having brought down more than one government in the past, how brittle they tended to be.

Now, five months after Father's ascension to the summit of power, I had received a call that changed my life forever.

I had just arrived back at Dubai airport after a business trip to Beirut. But I never made it out of the airport.

You see, Father was dead. It was up to me to take over the family business.

My period of apprenticeship was over.

RULING CASTE

Chapter 1

INDIRA GANDHI INTERNATIONAL Airport is the first warning sign to any visitor arriving from abroad to run back home, for they will soon enter a city and country that lives in many different centuries at once and those used to the certainties and niceties of modernity, particularly the sanitized tranquillity of Dubai, may not survive contact with this reality. Beware, the airport seems to say with its manifestation of barely controlled chaos, you have no idea what you are getting yourself into. I should have listened.

The landscape, both physical and mental, of the capital had changed in the years since I had last resided in Delhi; the great economic miracle was at work, or at least Delhi believed it to be. I had kept visiting during the intervening period, of course, but then you really don't get the full blast of the transformation in snatched visits in which meetings with clients take precedence. Now I was back for good.

My father had been aboard a helicopter with the pilot and an aide, when it had developed 'technical difficulties', and had crashed in the middle of farm land in western Uttar Pradesh. His body was unrecognizable. He was said to have been on his way back from Bareilly, but nobody could ascertain what he had gone there to do. There was some unsubstantiated talk that foul play may have been involved, but that was to be expected considering Father's profile as a power broker. Unfortunately, aviation accidents had become part and parcel of the narrative of Indian public life; figures far more illustrious than Father had been lost in the air.

On a personal level, it was naturally a brutal blow to the family. Mother, obviously, had taken it the worst. I arrived home to a house spread with white sheets and Mother's sisters forming an anxious coterie around her. She looked dry-eyed and composed, but when she saw me she broke down all over again. My elder brother, Manbir, was flying in as well, from London where he worked as an advertising man and kept an arm's length from the family business. He was the good brother, but a bit on the dour side. I think he envied the connection I had always shared with Father. He didn't let it show but I could tell it bugged the hell out of him. Nor did I particularly care, it was his problem to deal with.

After the initial shock of Father's death had passed I reacted emotionlessly, no tears or overflowing grief for me; Father would not have approved. I repressed my grave sense of loss at the passing of the most important man in my life and carried on with a stiff upper lip. Fate had decreed it, he was gone, and with him went all his secrets – a fact that lay at the centre of the turmoil that was about to ensue.

Funeral rites were completed in a rush when Manbir arrived. At the cremation, even I was surprised at the dizzying array of political personalities who attended despite the excruciating summer heat. Every member of cabinet was present, apart from the PM himself who was away touring Europe. Present too was the Vice President of India and the ex-chief of army staff, the formidable General Dayal, who watched me balefully as I assisted my older brother perform the final rites. The General and I shared a long and strained history, so I was sure his attendance hadn't been a voluntary act. Looking at the large gathering I couldn't help wondering if those present had come to pay their respects, or to look for assurances that their dark deeds would not be revealed to the world by his heirs, namely me.

To my brother's great irritation, even though I was the younger sibling, I was treated like the belle of the ball. I am ashamed to admit it but, even with my father's body lying a few feet away, I was having a memorably good time. I'm sure Father would have been proud. His legacy had seamlessly passed into my hands.

Actually, I was already well entrenched in Father's affairs as my private banking expertise had been increasingly used in recent years to cater more to his clients than mine, all done off the books with my employers unaware of my freelancing. I knew much and they were well aware of the knowledge I possessed. But the period immediately following the funeral was a dicey one, because there was a lot of unfinished business that needed to be dealt with before I could truly become my own man. And the unfinished business, as it turned out, had a mind of its own.

Father's appointment as adviser had sent shock waves through the corridors of power. Nobody had been fooled about his role as Senior Domestic Adviser. In this last appointment he had achieved his most cherished ambition: to avail himself of the powers of the PMO, armed with which he had been in a position to bend every sinew of government to his will. He had been in office for only a few months but that had been more than enough time for him to use the long arm of the PMO to the benefit of all stakeholders, particularly the PM and his family. Deals had been inked, percentages agreed upon and the illicit monies deployed in appropriate areas of the economy where they could come back laundered and smelling like daisies. Sitting in Dubai, I had been handling less and less of these funds as opportunities in India grew with the increasing sophistication of the economy. In fact, my main business was to reroute the money back to the homeland through Mauritius or Singapore after the requisite lag. That was the reason why Father, a couple of days before his demise, had already asked me to move back to Delhi as soon as I could. Alas, the father and son team had not been fated to be.

OVER THE NEXT few weeks I got busy with the umpteen necessary things that require to be done when a person passes on, some legal and some not. One of them was clearing out Father's South Block office. Nobody had asked me to do it but I thought it the right thing to do. I entered his office half expecting him to be there, appearing Houdini-like, out of thin air. Father had always seemed so indestructible to me that it would be a long while before I would fully comprehend his loss. I imagined him sitting erect behind his desk with his sharp features, his grand wazir's beard and his proud turban.

I hadn't worn a turban since cutting my own impressively long hair just before setting off for college. Often, looking at my father, I had felt a tinge of regret at having relinquished some of my heritage. Though we may not have had much in common when it came to our appearance, there was a strong bond that always held us together. You could say greed had ruled us both and ruled our relationship. Love was present, of course, but largely in the form of a secondary emotion.

It had taken me about a month to finish the housekeeping of my father's affairs and provide the results to the PM. I had not dealt directly with Paresh Yadav yet, and had been taking my orders over the telephone from his son Shitij, a less than charming character about whom I have more to say later. When someone like my father, the wizard behind the political funding machinery of a bigwig like the Prime Minister, abruptly exits from the scene – as he certainly did – there is an unavoidable amount of pilferage that takes place. Baser instincts were involved in all these dealings, and it was to be expected that those who could, would take advantage of a situation where no documents or legal tenders stated the exchange of government acquiescence for monetary payment. Since the interests in this case involved the Prime Minister, the leakage was of a lesser order, though it did still touch the twenty per cent mark. Father had not made a list of where he had deployed all the incoming funds, at least I could not find one, for understandable reasons of security. No doubt he had the crucial information in his head and could not have been bothered about what would ensue if something happened to him – with Father you could never tell which explanation fit the truth.

The money was normally allocated to the companies of friendly industrialists looking to take on easy money, or else it went to the old favourite – real estate. Both of these types of investments were made in the name of a front organization or person who was not likely to reveal the true ownership of the assets under their stewardship if the middleman, say my father, was not there to hold them to the bargain they had struck. The Prime Minister had trusted Father to such an extent that he was largely oblivious of the identity of more than half of these assets. If I had not had some idea of my father's maze of investments, the losses to Mr Yadav's bottom line would have been much more damaging. He was still none too happy that he had lost twenty per cent of his recently ill-gotten wealth.

And this state of mind on his part is where our problem started.

I HAD JUST finished sorting out all my father's personal effects (and shredding a pile of incriminating documents) when one of the PM's private secretaries entered and informed me that Prime Minister Yadav was asking for me. So I put away the documents I had begun to pack, locked my father's office, and walked into the famous wood-panelled interior of the Prime Minister's office.

Whatever nervousness I had felt at the prospect of meeting the PM to talk business, so to speak, for the first time, was quickly neutralized by his comically underwhelming physical stature. When Paresh Yadav got up from behind his desk to greet me, it was as if he had stepped off a platform. The PM was a midget; television sure can play games with reality. He couldn't have been more than an inch or two over five feet tall. I am only of medium height myself, but I could look right down the PM's nose and this gave me an instant feeling of superiority over Yadav that never left me – I suppose it was the dormant martial side of my Sikh identity making a passing visit. The Prime Minister wore a dhoti-kurta and walked with a jaunt in his step. The only feature of consequence in his visage was a prominent forehead that protruded forward like a ship's hull and seemed capable of ramming anyone or anything in its path.

'Jasjit beta, I'm really sorry I wasn't able to come to the funeral or meet you sooner. You must forgive me, but sometimes I feel like a hapless prisoner to the whims and fancies of this job.'

'No, no, nothing to apologize for, sir. There was nothing for us to discuss until now,' I assured him.

'Ah, what a loss, your father leaving us as he did. I feel so helpless without him. He was not only my confidant but my friend,' he said with genuine emotion.

'Thank you for saying so, sir. It means a lot,' I replied.

Then I noticed another person in the room – a man my age, only of a more substantial size, who did not bother to get up on seeing me. It was the heir apparent, Shitij Yadav, who had so far only made an impression on me as the voice that had barked instructions over the phone. He had all of his father's physical imperfections with nothing of his charm.

The PM appeared lost in thought for a moment – probably observing a two-minute silence for all his lost treasure – but he recovered soon enough and turned to his son: 'Get up, get up. Where are your manners? Come here and meet Jasjit.'

The reprimand worked. Junior waddled his way towards me and greeted me with a distinct lack of enthusiasm. No charismatic leader of the masses this one, for sure.

'Forgive him, Jasjit. He is my only son and I fear I've spoilt him rotten. But he will learn,' the PM explained sheepishly, his criticism clearly displeasing the recipient.

We took our chairs and the customary tea was poured.

Taking a long sip of the sweet chai, the PM looked at me and came directly to the point: 'You have to somehow try to take the place of your father. And remember, you will not have the luxury of making mistakes while you learn.'

'I'll do my best, sir.'

'Good. Now let me be frank, you are being given an opportunity here that doesn't come very often, if ever, to a man your age, so make the most of it.' He arched an eyebrow and examined my reaction very carefully.

I didn't flinch. 'What do you require of me?'

'Be my eyes and ears in Delhi and handle any special projects that I may require you to do. Not from an office in the PMO, you understand, but in a behind-the-scenes role.'

'What about the funds and assets – ?'

He cut me off with alacrity: 'No, no, beta. Don't worry yourself with those mundane matters. The second generation needn't dirty their hands, you must concentrate on larger matters that require vision and energy. I have other people who will take care of those interests now.' In one swoop he had finessed me and neatly reclaimed control of his wealth. I suppose he had learned the risk of relying too greatly on one man. I was not surprised by his move, but I would be lying if I said I was not disappointed.

'As you wish,' I muttered.

'But we still require your expertise for external matters,'

Yadav offered as a consolation, cryptically referring to his foreign accounts. He knew I knew too much about them for everything to be taken away.

I figured it was something to be grateful for. 'Is there any special project you need me to take care of straight away, sir?' I fished – in troubled waters as it turned out.

'Well, I want Shitij and you to form a team, let him watch you at work for me and let him learn how this town works. Getting elected is one thing, but unless you know how to make practical use of electoral power there really is no point, is there? Take him around, introduce him to the people you know, or your father knew, get to know each other,' the PM decreed. 'Okay?'

I nodded. He was the client and the assignment he picked for me was his prerogative.

THOUGH IT HAS a staid reputation in comparison to flashy Mumbai, the city of Delhi more than ably provides for its elite, so long as they are able and willing to finance their deepest, darkest fantasies. And for those of us who have grown up in the city it is easy, if we spend more than a reasonable quantity of time back home, to quickly revert to type.

I'm not sure how I got roped into a night-out with Yadav Junior a week after officially joining the PM's brigade, but I think his constant moronic presence and my lack of sleep over the previous days had left me a little less deft-footed than normal. Besides, I figured, if the oaf was going to shadow me for the foreseeable future, I had better try and humour him like the big client that he, ultimately, was.

We started off at a new bar in Greater Kailash and then showed up at the launch party of a new luxury watch. A curvy, former Miss India-turned actress – a breed that has overpopulated showbiz of late, this one with especially large hooters – was doing the honours; but nobody even gave her a look. The Page Three socialite crowd – only in India did Page Three signify the over-dressed rather than the undressed – was too busy wagging its tail at the sight of my new pal, the Prince of Yadavland. The past few days had been so full of surprises that I had forgotten who he was and what he represented to not just the common man but even to the most connected social butterflies – pure unadulterated power.

I met a few old friends at the party and when they found out I knew the prime ministerial brat they insisted, indeed begged, on being presented before him. I figured that if I was going to have to play the role of Yadav Junior's nanny, I might as well indulge the sense of power the position ensured. After witnessing the desperate reaction of the normally self-important crowd, I rather liked the idea of being able to broker the needs of others for a fix of power. I could feel the aphrodisiac of power working on me 'the gatekeeper' too – as women fluttered their eyelids and tossed their hair in my direction; not quite at the level of flashing their tits at me yet but it wasn't bad for a start. And for this suddenly elevated position in the social hierarchy I had to thank the fat piece of cowdung who was trying to impress two young things by making funny shapes with his stomach! I was selling my soul, if not to the devil, then at the very least to some other dark force. I quelled my misgivings with a huge gulp of Scotch, entering the bargain with only a moment's fleeting repentance. You do not argue with destiny

A couple of drinks later, on the insistence of my pals, after an impossibly long evening with the Prime Minister's plump papoose, I tore myself free from the clutches of Yadav Junior. He looked sullen as I left. I would deal with him later, I thought, as I headed out with my chums to a party at the south Delhi farmhouse of a friend of a friend. Exactly who the friend was and where the farmhouse was situated were details that do not concern one at that point of the night; everybody is your pal and if someone wants to provide their residence as your evening playground, it is hail-fellow-well-met and you go with the flow.

It was a Friday night. I was exhausted. I was grieving for my father, and more than a little pissed with the Yadav family. So I was really looking to let off some steam after all that had happened in the last few weeks. By the time we arrived, the party was in full swing, a phenomenon that I think is directly relatable to the quantity of alcohol and other stimulants being imbibed. I can tell you that there was no shortage of either at this shindig.

I sat in a corner with my group of seven or eight, evenly divided between men and women, and decided on a whim to do shots of absinthe. Immediately, a bottle materialized. As most of humanity's drinkers well know, there is no drink worse than the devil's spirit. And it is especially so for me. Not only does absinthe make me extremely rude and boorish but I cap this by getting somewhat paranoid.

I had done about five shots in quick succession and had brazenly started grabbing the two women sitting on either side of me, who had emerged, like the absinthe, seemingly out of nowhere and could only have been the highest quality East European call girls. Anyway, these subtleties were beyond me by now. In my fog I just thought they were other guests, very pretty and friendly ones, to be sure.

Suddenly, there was a commotion across the room at someone's arrival. I couldn't immediately see who it was because the large drawing room in which the party was being held was slightly sunken, with a bird's-eye view of the entertainment area from the elevated entrance.

Her appearance by itself would have been enough to give me a coronary but the accompanying look that Neena gave me in my compromised situation was of a kind I will never forget for as long as I live. It was contemptuous, hateful, disappointed and sad all rolled into one. And then, having shot the arrow off, she grabbed the arm of the army officer with her and moved on with a regal elegance that is the birthright of only a few.

Since Neena's grand entrance had grabbed the attention of the entire party – almost a hundred people – they had also witnessed our little silent exchange.

Seeing her now I grew angry and emotional, irrationally so, but then I was imbibing the green devil. And absinthe makes the heart grow fonder. I took a last swig from the bottle, flung the bimbettes off me as if they were cushions, and charged in the direction of the arriving princess.

There was a history between us, one of extreme passion, which made it impossible for me to react any other way. For every man there is born a woman who will be his surrogate mother, his nemesis, and everything else in between – Neena was mine.

I yelled her name as I barrelled my way through the crowd.

She stopped short and turned around.

Luckily for all concerned, I tripped and fell, knocking myself clean out, right at my estranged wife's feet.

Chapter 2

I HAVE ALWAYS considered my greatest strength to be a brutal self-awareness of my limitations. I have never fooled myself into believing that my looks are anything but plain – I have sharp features but they are marred by a pair of beady eyes that have spoilt every picture taken of me since birth. My hair is thick but I am blessed with a forehead that is much too large. The only saving grace is that years of following a harsh daily regimen of pull-ups, push-ups and sit-ups has given some heft to my otherwise disappointing body. A girl is not liable to give me a second glance but I am known to be able, if allowed the proverbial foot in the door, to grow on a damsel.

Neena Dayal, with her striking good looks, had always been out of my league. Not that this fact had stopped me from ardently pursuing her from the moment we met; though truth be told, she did make the initial move.

The first time I spoke to her she was sitting at the Gymkhana Club bar. I had just walked up to the counter to order another whisky when this woman on a barstool turned away from a guy looking forlornly at her, and grabbed my hand. 'Oh, here he is now,' she'd exclaimed. 'Well, I would have loved to stay and chat about old times, Pradeep, but… erm… um…'

'Jasjit,' I had supplied helpfully.

'Yes… um… dear Jasu here is taking me for a film.'

Then Neena had looked right at me and smiled a smile that had made my heart stop. It may sound soppy and I may be accused of rewriting history with the benefit of hindsight but I swear to you I'd realized then and there that this stunning woman was the one for me. Though I'd winced at her distortion of my name, I'd crocked my arm gallantly. 'Jasu awaits,' I'd said. I had escorted her out of the bar, rescuing her from her lovelorn admirer, but not before I had managed to extract an introduction and the promise of a compensatory drink in lieu of the one I had to forfeit to rescue her, at the nearest available hotel bar.

Several drinks later, the official car in which Neena had come was dismissed. I kept her out all night and got her home only at six the next morning. This earned the immediate ire of her early-to-rise father; a first impression that endured in his mind. Neena, as it turned out, was the daughter of General Brajesh Dayal, the then chief of the Indian army. I must say her formidable father's designation did make my knees buckle a bit but I gritted my teeth through the transitory pangs. I never did get to find out why she'd chosen me out of all the eligible young bucks at the Gymkhana bar that night. A combination of proximity and chance, I would think.

I was taking a break from my job in Dubai, and with Neena newly in my life, I just didn't want to go back. The days went by and my departure date for Dubai loomed closer. I extended my vacation by an extra few weeks despite the disapproval of my employers. It was love, or at least an infatuation that bordered on it. Ever since her father had been appointed the chief of the Indian army she had been serving as his official hostess. Her mother was the sickly sort and stayed most of the year in Dehradun. Neena was also an artist who had just held her first exhibition in Bombay. She found the army chief's official residence the perfect place to pursue her passion.

Soon we were inseparable. We went everywhere together,

to eat, to shop, to parties, to the bars, to the nightclubs, to my favourite monuments, and to the other places where lovers go. I told her everything about myself. I promised there would be no secrets between us and she did the same. At the end of those blissful weeks I asked her to come with me to Dubai. She didn't even pause to think before impulsively saying yes.

The General, needless to say, was not pleased with these developments and seized every opportunity he could find to belittle me in the hopes of getting his daughter to change her mind. But Neena was the one person he could not push. He had no choice but to surrender to her wishes. Once he knew there was no talking her out of it he insisted on a proper marriage ceremony before allowing his daughter to join me in Dubai. My father, I must admit, was not thrilled with our marital plans either. The General and he were wary of each other. The General often voiced his disapproval of Father's Machiavellian ways to Neena, while Father expressed nothing but contempt for the General's holier-than-thou facade to me.

Three weeks later, we had a splashy Delhi marriage, with both sets of parents smiling fakely together for the wedding pics. It was quite an event – the daughter of a four-star army general marrying the son of the country's most respected, and therefore feared, political operative. The power elite showed up in full force for the wedding – after all we all belonged to the same caste. We were marrying, in a way, within the power caste of Lutyens' Delhi. Ultimately, I think our relationship became a casualty to this new form of endogamy.

Neena and I reached Dubai and tried to settle into our new life. But the sterility of Dubai and the sameness of its shopping malls and villas soon began to suffocate Neena. Like me, Neena was a child of parental renown. The anonymity of being among Dubai's super rich just didn't appeal to her. Wealth didn't give her the kick that privilege and power afforded. She would pounce on me the minute I returned from work, telling me how much she had missed me, but I think what she really missed was Delhi and her position of authority as the handsome army chief's gorgeous daughter. Her painting suffered. She blamed me for the vacuousness of her life. I discovered she could be shrill and hurtful. She discovered I could be aloof almost to the point of coldness when perhaps she was looking for comfort and emotional support.

Some married couples stop fighting after a while and settle down to a life of closed-off co-existence, but that was not the case with us. The bitter fights continued with brief interludes of relative peace. Neena left me a couple of times and only came back after I followed her to India and begged her to return. Then, soon after General Dayal's term as army chief ended, he was appointed Governor of Rajasthan, and shortly thereafter he was elected Vice President of India. The handsome and aristocratic General Dayal, with his cravats and his sideburns, made such a welcome change from the usual crass and ungainly sort that populates Indian politics that Page Three newshounds followed him around zealously as he went about inaugurating buildings, launching books and proudly attending as chief guest at annual college functions.

The last time she left me was almost a year before my father's helicopter crash. By then she was tired and so was I. Neena went back, happy to play her part at the Vice President's side and revel in the limelight that life in Dubai with me had denied her. I was no match for my father-in-law in terms of giving her the status and celebrity on which she thrived, so this time I didn't go back to cajole her home.

She'd filed for divorce six months later.

SOME YEARS AGO, soon after we were married, the good General had acquired for himself a large estate in Uttarakhand, near Dehradun – a tea estate he liked to say he had inherited, but which he had actually bought with the proceeds of an arms deal that had involved the collusion of all the protagonists of this tale. It went back to the time when the midget PM had served, for one year, as Defence Minister in a previous coalition government, and Dayal had been his army chief. I had helped set up the mechanism for how all the payments were to be made to each party's offshore accounts as beneficiaries of the deal. My father, who'd naturally engineered the whole thing as adviser to the Defence Minister, had gleefully filled me in on the details and I'd dutifully filed the information away for later use.

It seems, the Indian army had been in the market for a series of high-technology acquisitions like missile defence, enhanced electronic warfare capability, networked communication and information systems, anti-aircraft and fire-finding radar, thermal sensors, unmanned combat air vehicles, special forces gear and the like. The Israelis were in a position to provide every item on the army's shopping list and were more than willing to grease palms if Dayal could have the defence deal grouped in a multi-year omnibus package and cleared through government machinery in one go.

The deal was approved at a pace not seen since the purchase of the Bofors howitzer; the file in question had flown in a single day, from desk to desk. Such was the combined competence and power of Yadav, Dayal and my father that the trio had pushed through the deal and all the usual vested interests that were likely to cry foul and cause a furore in the media had kept their mouths shut. There was no mystery to this; everybody who could have been a nuisance had been paid off, including some nosey journalists on the defence beat. The defence deal had been structured in such a way that, as and when the Government paid upon delivery of the different equipment over the course of the years, the key trio would get their cut from the Israelis with the largest sum being paid in the end.

But there was more to the story of General Dayal yet to tell.

After spending a very brief stint in retirement he had been made Governor of Rajasthan and transported to the cushy environs of Jaipur. Then the midget PM had come to power at the head of a rickety minority government, with the unstated outside support of the Congress party. Two general elections in as many years with three fallen governments – the result of splintered verdicts – had ensured that no party, particularly the Congress and the BJP, was in any mood to return to the hustings anytime soon. Paresh Yadav's hold on his vaunted caste-coalition was weakening but it had still given him enough seats to finally be sworn in as PM in a government formed in partnership with other regional and caste parties, united only by a common venality and the lack of any national vision.

Such was the state of our polity.

Soon after Yadav became PM, a vice presidential election was held in which no one political grouping was able to elect its candidate to the post as the fractured electorate consisted of Members of Parliament from both the Lok Sabha and Rajya Sabha. The days of the dominant ruling party or even the dominant coalition appointing a lackey to the post were long gone. The names of several doddering geriatric politicians were put forward but even their smallest enemy had the power to nix their nomination. The parties then tried out the names of economists, scientists and even, good lord, bureaucrats, but nobody seemed to approach electability. And then a newspaper article mysteriously appeared on the front page of one of Delhi's leading papers announcing that General Brajesh Dayal was rapidly becoming the leading consensus choice for the vice presidency.

Up till this point no one, especially the leaders of the main political parties, had thought of General Dayal as a possible contender; the political class being allergic to the thought of any senior member of the military brass gaining civilian power even of the largely ceremonial vice presidential kind. But, desperate for a resolution to the electoral impasse, the General's name began gaining currency, with the PM masterminding the campaign, until he became the longed-for consensus choice.

The idiots elected my father-in-law, a man whom I had surreptitiously nicknamed General Bastard, as the Vice President – positioning a heartbeat away from the Presidency, the supposedly nominal but constitutionally designated Supreme Commander of the Indian Armed Forces. If I ever needed proof, this settled my opinion that the current crop of politicians did not have a clue about what was good for the country, or for themselves. They had managed to instal in the second-highest constitutional post arguably the most cunning man ever to lead the Indian army.

Having never really been anything more than a mediocre field commander my father-in-law had gained and maintained the aura of a hero thanks to the trumpeting of a highly dubious war story. A story that claimed that as a young paratrooper, he had been the first officer to enter Dhaka, during the victorious 1971 war after being daringly paradropped behind enemy lines with his unit, the 2nd Para battalion. Don't ask me how I can recollect these details of his career, I can only explain it by saying that anything to do with General Bastard tended to concentrate my mental powers. His claim of entering Dhaka first was unverifiable and, knowing him as I did, probably a complete fabrication. But the story had been repeated so many times in so many news publications that he came to be called the 'Hero of Dhaka'.

In the army it was well known and joked about that he knew as much about military strategy as a camel knew about snow. But, like Eisenhower, he was a politician among soldiers, the best man manager in the business and he assiduously built political contacts at every opportunity. This was done most flamboyantly when he started getting senior field commands that allowed him to put on a show of hospitality, of the kind only the army can, for his political masters. The politicos never had anything but good things to say about their favourite general. He had curried favour at every level and beaten stronger candidates for the job of army chief by pulling all the considerable political strings at his disposal. His reputation for being an arch-manipulator had only grown during his tenure as army chief.

In addition to his many gifts, Dayal looked liked an Indian Caesar – tall, trim, with a face chiselled by the gods. Standing side by side with the midget PM he looked like a bloody king and he was only too well aware of the impression he made.

Neena, unscathed from her failed marriage to me, had also become the toast of the country, standing by her father's side in vice presidential splendour. I often wondered how the Neena I knew reconciled to this showy image of herself. Surely, deep down, she knew what her manipulative father was up to? Why had she walked out on me for him? I had suspected all along that after General Bastard got elected any hope of her returning to Dubai would be lost. She had found Dubai culturally antiseptic and understandably so. Why would she have stayed with me any longer when Delhi and her newly crowned father beckoned? I suppose I had made it easier for her to make the choice by not asking her to come back.

When I moved back to Delhi after the death of my father, her face was plastered everywhere – in magazines, newspapers and on television. Reminded of her so often, my dormant wounds began to fester. A degree of self-loathing played a part as well. That her rise to national prominence took place at the side of the man whom I detested more than most, added to my sense of grievance. My relationship with Dayal had been a frosty one from the very beginning, and there was ample repressed animosity on both sides. I knew from Neena that he felt that she had married beneath herself, a clear slight at my father. And I suppose he had a point.

I, in turn, had always considered him the lurking third presence in our marriage; always forcing Neena to choose between him and me with his constant phone calls and pleas for her to visit him. By the end of our marriage I had convinced myself that as long as he was a strong presence in our midst, Neena and I didn't stand a chance. His being elected Vice President and her setting up shop as his hostess, with the enigmatic Mrs Dayal cloistered in Dehradun, was something that was destined to happen.

So, on that night of all nights, when I finally saw Neena in the flesh, and being totally under the influence of Satan's drink, I had only needed the merest of excuses to allow my resentment to burst forth.

THE DOORS OPENED and Neena walked in followed by two bearers holding aloft two trays. The insignia on their uniforms left me in no doubt about where I was.

I was a guest of the Vice President of India.

Lying in bed, I wondered if General Bastard knew of my presence and felt a need to take my leave as soon as possible. I didn't want to be around when he found out about the previous night's events. Even the bravest private banker was not conditioned to mess with dastardly four-star generals and, far worse, their vengeful daughters. Daylight and sobriety tended to transform me into a meeker creature.

Without a word, breakfast was laid out on a table. The smell of food did my stomach no good at all. The bearers retreated on madam's silent command. We were alone.

I looked at my wife and felt a pang of real loss. Neena wore a tightly draped sari that revealed more than it hid. If there is a part of a woman's body I have a fetish for it is the hips. And Neena reigned supreme in that area – an asset that was accentuated when she wore a sari. She knew this weakness of mine well so I couldn't help but notice that she had tied her sari lower than normally acceptable around the waist to reveal that tantalizing part of her figure where the waist dipped and then swelled. There was no way the Vice President's daughter was going out in public like that. I had to assume the extra skin was for my pleasure.

'We must be the talk of the town today,' I said tearing my eyes away from her midriff and going in search of the orange juice and the coffee.

Neena fixed me with a level gaze: 'What do you think you were doing, running at me like that?'

'Yeah, sorry about that. I wasn't myself.'

A perfectly fluffed omelette was eased onto my plate. 'Looks like you haven't been yourself for quite a while now,' Neena said with the maternal disapproval that was prescribed to irritate me.

Wanting to avoid any form of antagonism, I steered the subject away from her opinion of my lifestyle. 'How in bloody hell did I get here?'

'Well, after your little accident you passed out on the floor which led your little band of companions to run around screaming hysterically, in their supremely intoxicated state, that you had been murdered. Since there was obviously no one among your chums who wished to claim your body, I was compelled to take charge.'

The memory of falling on my face flashed vividly in my head and I instantly ran my fingers over my key facial areas to check for any major rearrangement of my features, but I appeared to have escaped unscathed; of course a mirror would be required for a closer examination. 'I assume your burly army officer boyfriend lugged my sorry carcass out of there? Thank him for me.'

'He isn't, as you put it, my boyfriend, but one my father's aides, his military officer on special duty, to be precise. Father prefers someone to escort me to functions ever since... you know...'

'Yes, I know,' I didn't feel I could say much more.

'Some things aren't meant to last,' Neena said, after a small silence, rather unnecessarily, according to me.

I looked up from my now empty plate – the lure of the omelette had overcome my queasy stomach – and our eyes met. She smiled at me for what seemed like the first time this century and it made all the difference. She was the girl I had fallen for at the Gymkhana and who stalked my memory, all over again.

'The General hit the roof when I told him that you were here. Luckily, he had to fly to Ahmedabad or he would have greeted you himself,' said Neena, making an attempt at joviality.

'I'm sure I would have absolutely enjoyed his company again. It's been so long since our last delightful encounter.'

She sniggered. Yes, we could finally laugh about it a little.

'It took a long while for me to forgive you for what you said that day,' she said.

I was really in no mood to get into another argument over the underlying, intractable reasons for our estrangement. 'Let's not – '

'Why? So that we can keep hating each other for the rest of our lives and making scenes in public, that is when we're not skulking around the same city trying our best to avoid each other?'

'I think you made it pretty clear you wanted nothing to do with me.' She hadn't even bothered to put in an appearance at my father's funeral.

'Words spoken in anger, Jasjit, just like yours that day. Can't we forgive and forget everything?'

'Everything?' She was willing to wipe the slate clean. But as far as I was concerned she had less to forgive. Alongside the monster hangover and a stomach now suddenly in full revolt against the newly ingested omelette, this offer added confusion to the mix.

'We went about it all wrong. It was a mess in the end, for sure, but you cannot deny what we felt for each other. Maybe we've learnt from our mistakes and become different people now. Maybe we deserve to be…' She groped for the right word.

'Friends?' I helped her out.

'Yes, why not? We skipped that part, didn't we?'

'We went from strangers to lovers to strangers.'

'Come to think of it, we only really liked each other for a total of a few weeks, most of which took place years ago,' said Neena.

'But we shared more in those weeks than most people do in their entire lives,' I said, not allowing her to underplay it that far.

Neena was sitting across the table from me and the sun was blazing through the window onto her. The years had softened her hauteur; there was a vulnerability now that allowed her beauty, with defences down, to make its full impact. An intense hunger to repossess her overcame me. The presence of a bed nearby became hard to ignore. But I knew my instincts could no longer be trusted in a situation like this, especially not when it came to her. Things had got much too complicated.

One thing was patently clear to me, though. Despite my mixed feelings at the prospect of a reunion there was no way I could deny that I craved the taste of her mouth and the smell of her hair again with an intensity I had thought beyond me. She saw the way I was looking at her and she shook her head, smiling ruefully. 'This friendship idea isn't going to work with us, is it?'

'I'm afraid you and I are destined to either make love or make war.'

'And which way are you leaning towards at present?'

'I wish I knew, because I no longer trust my heart when it comes to you. That memory has a permanent veto,' was my honest answer.

She covered my hand with hers. 'I really didn't mean what I said that day. I will always love you, even though I try my best not to.' She looked into my eyes then, her own filled with sorrow.

I acknowledged her revelation with a cold stare. A part of me wanted to hold her close and surrender to her declaration of love, but then paralysis set in at the thought of how short moments of love like this one, led to long, unbearable periods of heartache.

Neena waited a few moments, in vain, for a reassuring word or gesture from me and then left the room with a stifled sob.

Fresh starts were easier said than done.

AS SOON AS I got dressed I departed from the vice presidential residence – not the Vice President's official residence on Maulana Azad Road, which was being refurbished, but a temporary lodging in one of the large bungalows located within the grounds of Rashtrapati Bhavan, usually allotted to senior presidential staff members. Neena had considerately arranged for one of the many cars at the Vice President's disposal to give me a lift home. I did not have to worry about fetching my own car from the farmhouse as I had taken the precaution, as usual, of getting a friend to provide my transportation the night before. After living in reasonably civilized places like New York and Dubai I'd limited my driving to a minimum on the Darwinian streets of Delhi where only the largest and most brutal survived. I was lucky that our family had for more than a decade employed a reliable chauffeur by the name of Karnail Singh. On moving back to Delhi I had doubled his salary but I had told him that I expected him to be always available, at my beck and call.

Karnail Singh was a former army man so he knew how to take orders and was enthusiastically efficient, which was a good thing since nothing irritated me more than a surly employee. He also met my most important requirement of being loyal and knowing how to keep his mouth shut about what he did or did not see – a trait not easy to find anywhere nowadays.

It was mid-morning by the time I reached home. Over the years my parents had continued to stay in our modestly-sized house in Jor Bagh, no matter whether Father was in government service or not. I suppose it helped that its address within the bounds of Lutyens' Delhi was as good as any government residence.

I checked my phone for messages and found that I had an afternoon appointment with one of India's leading corporate lawyers, which by definition also meant that he was a fixer par excellence for various corporate houses. But the appointment was not to be, as Shitij Yadav phoned just then and loudly demanded my presence at the Prime Minister's residence at noon. He sounded like he meant business.

It was possible he was throwing his weight around to show me who was boss in revenge for my having brushed him off the previous night. If that was indeed true, I had to let him have his little victory so he could save face. It would be a small price to pay for the exceptional night I'd had.

AFTER NOT RETURNING home at night I was hoping to leave the house without running into Mother and having to offer an explanation, but some days just nothing seems to go right. Like all mothers she seemed to have a sixth sense about what I was hoping to pull and was lying in wait for me as I tried to escape. The poor girl had grieved for Father terribly in the immediate aftermath of the incident but after the funeral she had returned to her normal routine quicker than I had expected. Perhaps she had always known her husband would disappear in a cloud of smoke one day.

Anyway, she was on my case now.

'So, where were you all night?' In her eyes I would always be a guilty thirteen-year-old.

'You wouldn't believe me if I told you.'

'Try me.'

I figured the truth would make good copy for once. 'I was the honoured guest of our dear Vice President at Rashtrapati Bhavan.'

'Were you with Neena?' I could see eager thoughts of my return to the marital bed and a happy brood of grandchildren swimming in her thoughts.

'Not in the same room, if that's what you're asking.'

'Any man in India would give his right arm to be with her, and my son is the only specimen who can't bear to,' she grumbled, returning her errant dupatta into place with a sharp flick of her wrist.

'I always did have trouble going along with the rest of the flock,' I grinned, and exited before I got my ear yanked.

YADAV JUNIOR HAD telephoned me in a most excitable state. I had a fair idea of what it was all about; in all probability a moronic investment idea some hanger-on had fed into his hollow head, as had been the case on the previous occasion that he had wasted my time. But the client was the client and I had to go see him.

The fellow really had the most rotten manners. I was made to wait for ten minutes in the prime ministerial sitting room before Shitij arrived with much fanfare, accompanied by an entourage fit for a prince. I, of course, showed my usual disdain and told him to make them wait outside the room if he wanted to talk business, or he would not get a word out of me. The brute glared at me for what seemed like a full minute before acceding to my request. I was not sure that being alone with the short-tempered and hefty Yadav Junior was such a great idea on the whole. I mean, if he decided to bash my head in right there, the cover-up would be quick and efficient. Nobody would ever know what had become of me. I tried to put that macabre prospect out of my mind and concentrate my attention on the crown prince; not the most pleasant sight.

'How was your election meeting?' I attempted polite conversation. I knew he had been deputed to represent his father at a political rally in some far-flung part of Delhi earlier that morning. I preferred not to ask about how he had gotten on after I had ditched him the night before. Wouldn't do to refer to it directly; that would just be asking for more trouble.

'How do you think?' was the less than good-natured reply. I'm sure the hangover that he certainly suffered couldn't have made it a pleasant trip. I could definitely not picture him giving a cogent oration in any language, that's for sure.

Despite being educated in all the right places, at home and abroad, Shitij had garnered all the wrong lessons from his years as a son of privilege. Power may corrupt but, less conspicuously, it arrests the self-development of a person. Shitij, like other maladjusted children of the powerful, was stuck in this stage of personality freeze, unable to grow in the harsh glare of the spotlight. In Shitij's case in particular his diagnosis was an overdeveloped sense of entitlement meshed with a proclivity for violence, the latter well documented over the years, though so far at least, he had avoided jail. Only his father was able to keep him in check.

'Doesn't sound like fun from the sound of it.' I tried my best to maintain my equanimity and not get provoked into having words with the beast.

'You don't have a clue, do you? You and your lot just sit here and see this side of our lives, not realizing the places we have to go and the things we have to do to keep our position.'

I didn't endeavour to ask which lot he was referring to. Though he did make a valid point, it would have had more weight coming from Yadav Senior and not the son who was reaping the rewards of his father's toil. 'Ah, the great public servant sacrificing his comfort for the people,' I responded with a healthy dose of sarcasm.

'Will you stop talking rubbish and listen to why I called you over?'

Though it might not have appeared so from his words and his demeanour, Shitij was trying his best to be civil; or at least his version of it. So I decided to hear out the shit. 'Very well, you are currently my most important – and only – client; go right ahead and speak up.'

'Jasjit, are you a cricket fan?' he asked me out of the blue, disconcerting me by calling me by my name for the first time ever.

I admitted that though I followed the game with less than the requisite passion of a normal Indian fan, I was not oblivious to its charms. I was one of a dwindling tribe of traditionalists who preferred the longest form of the game: Test cricket. You could be sure Shitij did not share my view, he was clearly a T20 man.

Yadav Junior looked me in the eye. 'I have decided I want to be the Chief of the Cricket Board.' He pronounced this with the Zen-like calm of someone who had found his path in life.

'Which state's cricket board? UP's? Or Bihar's?' I named the two states that comprised his father's political empire.

'You misunderstand. I want to be the President of the Indian Cricket Board.'

I strangled the laugh that was building up halfway down my gullet because I caught Yadav Junior looking serious as sin. 'I'm sorry but you've gone bonkers,' I blurted out.

'Not at all. The election is in six weeks. There is more than enough time for me to sail through. To get elected you need political clout and money; I have both in spades.'

I really did not understand how I was supposed to help out; nor did I have the faintest idea how to deal with the bizarre request. The money I had been left to handle was abroad and I didn't have access to his father's political clout. I shrugged: 'So go and get elected. Why are you sitting here telling me about it?'

'Because you're going to arrange it for me,' the brat declared with supreme confidence as he lowered his rump into a chair.

'Sorry, but I know nothing about this kind of thing. You'll have to find someone who has some experience with these kind of elections.' I was as firm as I could manage.

'Now be sensible, Jasjit. I'll have to go to my father if you force me. He has already told you that he wants the both of us to work together. This is a test of loyalty for you. You must prove yourself. If you don't, then you will not be rewarded. Your father clearly understood that, why can't you?'

Where his own interests were involved Shitij could be as slippery as his dad. I knew he had me but I was not going to like it or make it easy for him. 'Fine, you want plain talk, I'll give you plain talk, Shitij. Let me explain a little rule of political survival to you. Family members of Prime Ministers, if they know what's good for them, are expected to make their cash quietly and stay well away from the limelight. The minute you get into the limelight you become fair game for every one of your father's political enemies and, trust me, they are to be found at every street corner in this town.'

The plump hand waved away my concerns. 'Don't worry so much, I have it all planned out. I just need the use of your skills to execute my master plan.'

I pleaded with him to see reason: 'Why in God's name do you want to become President of the Cricket Board? It will be a constant pain in your ass. Only, in this case, the pain will include the whole of India cursing you each time the team shows its true colours, as indeed it tends to do rather regularly these days.'

'I'm glad you care so much for my welfare, Jasjit, but I can take care of myself. I'll have you know that I have been the President of the Bihar Cricket Association for the last few years.'

That explained the sorry state of cricket in Bihar. 'That's politics. What I want to know is if you give a shit at all about the sport itself?'

'Can't live without it, yaar. I bet on every match that is played anywhere in the world.'

Aha. I knew there had to be some lowly and despicable reason behind this plan. I could already see the younger Yadav threatening the captain of the team to do his bidding, forcing him to deliberately throw a game so that he could make even more cash than he already possessed.

A sense of impending doom overtook me. The absurdity of the situation I was in was now replaced in my thoughts by the certainty that there was no possible reward for me in this caper – only the sure face of disaster. I was being forced to take on the exact task for which I had no expertise. Nudge by nudge, the Yadavs were elbowing me away from the task I was skilled at performing and pushing me into an area where I was totally out of my depth. What the hell did I know about breaking the hold of the oligarchy of high priests that controlled India's most revered faith, a.k.a. cricket?

This venture had disaster written all over it, but I didn't have a choice if I wanted to stay in the game.

And that I sorely did.

Chapter 3

SATINDER DHILLON, MY father's oldest and closest friend, came from an influential and landed family of Punjab. He had, at the outset of his career, initially tried his hand at electoral politics, but then he quickly grew bored with it and took it upon himself to indulge his passion for cricket in a more direct fashion. For three years he had served as the President of the colonially named Board of Control for Cricket in India – better known by its acronym BCCI, which always got me thinking about the similarly named infamous Pakistani bank. The coincidence appeared like a really bad omen to me and only made me more jittery about the entire venture Shitij was hoping to pull.

Satinder Dhillon was an uncle of mine in the Punjabi way Delhiites respectfully promote anyone of a certain maturity to that familial relationship. So naturally I went running in sheer terror with Shitij's outlandish request to Dhillon Uncle, who had spent half his life in the cut-throat world of Indian sports politics.

The politics of India's numerous sports bodies is the one sphere in which politicians, bureaucrats and businessmen meet in electoral battle, with each one having an equal chance of success. Only the elite are allowed entry. The ambitions of an upstart like Shitij Yadav, despite his present position, would no doubt be looked upon with disdain. And the biggest and most commercially successful of all these sports bodies was undoubtedly the BCCI.

Cricket was the country's favourite sport. Not, I believe, because of any intrinsic special quality the game possessed but because we had some of the finest players in the world. This was not the case with the majority of the other sports. True, there was the odd chess or tennis player who had gained some international recognition but these were elitist sports that had no chance of catching the imagination of the masses.

In the cricket world it was India's fans that kept the sport alive with multinationals pouring in ad revenue to catch the attention of the large Indian middle-class. A tour by the Indian cricket team was capable of saving a foreign cricket board from bankruptcy. So when you combined the clout of power with money in an organization, as was the case with the BCCI, the queue for its leadership would rightly be long and competitive. Elections for the top jobs in the cricket board resulted in such manoeuvring and ruthless power play that Machiavelli himself would have been impressed. All democratic, legal and rational norms were set aside by these men of national standing, tycoons and Cabinet Ministers among them. The high they got from controlling the source of India's passion could not be quenched even in their impressive professional lives. They were prepared to do whatever it took to obtain their goal.

And little old me had six weeks to figure out how to inflict defeat on these sharks.

Dhillon Uncle was a large man with an unkempt beard and a clumsily tied turban. Father had long believed it to be an intentional ploy to trick strangers into fatally underestimating his skills. Sitting in his drawing room, we began by awkwardly discussing my father in the past tense; a subject neither of us was still comfortable talking about for any length of time. Thankfully, we quickly moved on to the business at hand. On hearing me out, Dhillon Uncle did not, surprisingly, pass an immediate remark of impossibility on my quest; instead he began by patiently spelling out for me the details of who constituted the electorate for the election of the BCCI presidency and other senior posts.

There were around thirty votes in all. The electorate comprised of state cricket associations plus three Government votes for the departments that had national level teams, which were the Universities, Railways and Defence Services. The Government votes were good news since I knew the midget PM would use whatever means necessary to ensure that at least all three of those were in the bag. The thirteen other votes needed for victory I would simply have to beg, borrow and steal.

The state cricket boards were not always run in the most democratic and efficient manner. Some were monopolies of an individual who made sure he (there were no shes in this world) manipulated the electorate so that it comprised of diehard supporters and removed any danger of an ouster.

There were a few boards that were controlled by the government of the particular state and could therefore be amenable to political favours, come election time. I liked the sound of that. At the other extreme were state boards, like Delhi's, that were constantly in strife, with rival factions going at each other's throats. These kinds of boards were the reason why, during some elections, two representatives from the same state showed up with completely different voting intentions. Then the courts had to get involved and elections were settled in the Supreme Court.

Hearing Dhillon Uncle drone on, I grew more and more disheartened and drank my single malt quicker than I should have. After a point I couldn't bear hearing any more horror stories. 'Then, Uncle,' I interrupted him, 'how do I get my man elected?'

He stopped and considered me expressionlessly. Satinder Dhillon could always be relied on to speak with clarity and candour even if the answer was not the one the advice seeker wanted. 'Okay, the good news is you have a lot of firepower at your disposal if, as you say, the Prime Minister is fully behind this campaign. I'm surprised that he is, though, since he can only lose prestige in this kind of contest, which should be peanuts for him, but then he wouldn't be the first PM to lose his political bearings for the love of a misguided child.' He made a flicker of a face to show his displeasure. 'As for the election itself, you don't have time to canvass each of the state boards themselves; they'll drive you around the bend. You need to go directly to the kingmakers who control groups of these votes.'

'Like who?'

'Like me,' he exploded in bellicose laughter.

The old master still had life in him after all these years. I grinned: 'You have my solemn oath that you will be suitably compensated for each of the votes you deliver, Uncle.'

'That's an important inducement because otherwise I would find it very difficult to live with supporting a detestable cowherd like Shitij. But you will still need to get the support of the other big men and they may not be as considerate as me.'

'I'm sure. Would you please talk to them for me?' I pleaded.

'The Yadavs will have to pay extra for that service.'

'Of course, Uncle, and deservedly so.'

'Good, then leave it with me for a day and I'll get back to you.'

'For my information, who are the main candidates in play right now?'

'There's only one; it is assumed to be a coronation. The sitting President Vikas Pande has completed three years, which is the maximum term allowed at one go, and now he's trying to get a puppet to succeed him.'

'Who?' I really should have paid more attention to the sports news.

Dhillon Uncle's smile just got broader: 'The one and only Ramesh Rawat.'

Super. Pande had picked the perfect puppet – a cricketing legend and national god. Not only had he been an ace spin bowler but he had been India's cricket captain for almost a decade and was revered for the unaccustomed string of victories he had overseen. Though some uncharitably remarked that the team had been so good even a half-wit could have led them to victory; and in fact, had. It was commonly known Rawat could not communicate coherently in any language known to man. I had made the mistake of playing nine holes of golf with him once in Dubai and it had been the longest half round of my life. Fluency of tongue in real life obviously had no positive correlation with fluency of action on the field of play.

'It just keeps getting better and better,' I opined in genuine anguish.

'I hope you like a good old-fashioned bust-up. The press will just lap up a story that has the PM's son up against the nation's favourite son for the Holy Grail of Indian sport.'

'Uncle, I have just had a minor stroke here and you're making fun of what could be a calamity for everyone involved! What PM wants to go up against a beloved figure like Rawat, even if he is an imbecile?'

'Cheer up, you have me on your side. Rawat's popularity won't count for anything in this election. I'll guide you through it, just don't lose your nerve because it's going to be a roller-coaster ride till the very end.'

'Great, just what I need in my life, more excitement.'

'Excitement will keep you from growing old.'

'Sure it will – by ensuring my early demise,' I said, only partially in jest. 'The stakes are very high. If we lose, the PM will suffer a grave political embarrassment and then he may want to find someone to blame. Lord knows, it's not going to be his fat lump of a son.'

Dhillon Uncle glanced at me disapprovingly, but so subtly that nobody other than I who had known him all my life, would have spotted it. 'If your father were here, he would have told you to concentrate on your job and handle the future as it comes. You have nothing to worry about at the moment – the PM is petrified that you may run off with all his money, or worse, tell the whole country where he hoards it. He has as much to lose from ending this relationship as you do.'

But I sensed the barest tremor of doubt in his speech. He knew as well as I that the midget PM, master of corruption that he was, could always make more money but I would end up either in jail or dead when I became a liability. The latter eventuality was not such a far-fetched idea, considering my dealings with Shitij Yadav.

People like the Yadavs played the game without any sense of remorse or undue emotion; only personal survival, at any cost, mattered.

THE DAYS THAT followed were filled with frantic activity. I spent them criss-crossing the country as I cajoled and threatened state cricket heavyweights, trying to gain support for my candidate, who himself had added nothing further to the process after that first day. I might as well have been campaigning for myself.

Suitcases of money were delivered, political favours exchanged, and muscle deployed where reason failed. The politicians were the easiest to deal with since those who were against us were in the Opposition and unreachable; and those who were with us were part of the Government and eager to curry favour with the PM. It was Dhillon Uncle's so-called 'kingmakers' who drove me up the wall. I made contact with those kingmakers who had, at worst, neutral inclinations towards the enemy camp. These gents turned out to be a slimier group of individuals than any politicians I had ever met. They postured, lied, and generally succeeding in wasting a lot of my time. Since they were already men of considerable means I found that bribery was not always effective in gaining their allegiance; only the threat of an income tax raid brought some of them to heel. It was all done very quietly, of course. The media obsessed about Shitij and his candidacy while I worked away behind the scenes.

In a matter of days, I found I had started to master the art of threatening quietly, like the best of political musclemen. But, despite making use of all the money and threats I had at my disposal I could not be sure that any of these sons of bitches would deliver when it came to the crunch. For all I knew – and in some cases I *did* know – they could still be making more lucrative last-minute deals with the other side. I was somewhat assuaged by the knowledge that most of them would not double-cross me for fear of retribution from an irate PM, however short the expectancy of his tenure. But, still, there were always one or two chaps, enough to change the end result, who proved the rule that common sense was not that common.

THROUGH ALL MY wheeling and dealing I had managed to completely avoid Neena, physically if not mentally. I was never one to take the initiative to solve a problem whose resolution it was possible to defer for another day and a month had passed with me still at square one. Neena's declaration of love had thrown me more than I cared to admit. Expectedly, Neena made the move for me.

I was on a conference call with the President and the Secretary of the Orissa state board, who were not inclined to go along with backing Shitij as I had been assured they would by one of the kingmakers. What had happened was that the kingmaker was aligned with a rival faction in the state board that had recently lost its hold on the board and was contesting the election of the new office-bearers in court. Naturally, the kingmaker had been disinclined to spread the wealth that I had provided with his opponents, and these functionaries wanted their payment for delivering the state's vote in case the court ruled in their favour.

I was, of course, happy to meet their demands but it took some haggling to get a final figure out of them. Whatever the courts decided, I wanted the state's vote in our bag; paying twice was not a problem. I had already done the same in three other states. It reduced the amount of fiddling Pande, the outgoing President of the board, could manipulate from the chair by ruling in favour of giving a state's vote to a faction that was in his pocket. Or, failing that, invalidating the vote of the entire state, sure to be a supporter of ours, due to disputed representation. Even if the courts failed to make clear in time who was eligible to represent a state at the election, our money certainly would.

So, while these reptiles from Orissa were talking a mile a minute into my ear (using carefully coded terms for the monetary sums involved), one of our maids came to inform me that Ms. Dayal was waiting to speak with me on the land-line. I had asked not to be disturbed in my room all afternoon but the domestic help assumed, incorrectly but understandably so, that my instructions did not apply to my soon-to-be former wife.

Since my last conversation with Neena, I had spent all my time blatantly corrupting and intimidating some of the most powerful men in the country. Yet, somehow, a mere phone call from this woman was scaring the living daylights out of me! Neena had been out of my life for a year, and the two years before that had hardly been blissful. I just didn't understand how or why she still had this effect on me. I hastened the settlement process with the greedy duo and then switched to the other phone for my punishment.

She didn't give me a chance to say hello: 'I am going to assume for your sake that you've been too busy buying votes for your friend to call me even once.'

'Don't say such scandalous things on the phone, woman, you have no idea who could be listening.'

'My oh my, dear old Jasu is becoming a full-blooded wheeler-dealer.' She was the only one I had ever tolerated a nickname from and it now appeared she had reclaimed her right to address me by that foul corruption of my name. Her intentions were nakedly clear to me. I was back in the game, so to speak.

'How did you find out about the cricket election?' It was a stupid question to ask someone whose father had made it his business to know what everyone else was up to at all times, but I couldn't think of anything else to say at that moment to distract myself from the subtle implications that her calling me Jasu carried.

'I talked to your mother,' she revealed.

'You spoke with my mother?' This was an unexpected development and I went into full-scale panic mode. The ladies were making common cause.

'Is that a problem? She seemed quite relieved to know a decent, respectable girl like me hadn't completely given up on her idiot son.'

'So she says to you. If you only knew how she's itching to get me re-married off to the first blue-blooded cow of a sardarni she can find after the divorce,' I blustered, a bit too obviously.

'You should have informed her that your tastes have regressed to a much baser level.'

'That's only because the decent, respectable girls just seem too hot for me to handle,' I said, letting down my guard, happy to flirt with and tease Neena again.

'You're the one who's too hot to handle nowadays, darling.'

'I couldn't possibly disagree with India's sweetheart.'

'Very funny. But since you're in such an obedient mood it seems like a good time to ask a favour.'

'Let me guess. You want to be the first female President of the BCCI?'

'Maybe later. Right now I need you to rescue me from Rashtrapati Bhavan and take me out as soon as possible.'

'I'm headed for Calcutta in an hour,' I lied.

'Can't you go tomorrow? I'm going crazy in this regal isolation,' she pleaded sweetly.

It was almost more than my senses could bear. The dilemma reached its ultimate hurdle. To hell with it, I decided finally, she had paid her penance; let's give it another whirl. Maybe Delhi would help us remember our lost love.

'Fine. What do you want to do? Should I book a hotel room?'

'Junglee! Dinner will be enough. Let's see how it goes.'

'Your face is splashed everywhere, there is no way we're going to get any privacy and I'm not so sure I want our dear Vice President to know that we are seeing each other again.' The last words slipped out before I could bite my tongue.

'I'll handle the Vice President. But I didn't realize we were "seeing each other again".'

'What else would you call it? Whether you like it or not, you are still my wife in the eyes of the law.'

'Then why does it seem like a first date?' she wondered.

'New beginnings always do.'

'If you say so. Now, where are we going tonight?'

'Somewhere discreet… I know, we'll go to the Gymkhana.'

She giggled in approval and my heart expanded in pride at having evoked that response.

'All right. What time will you pick me up?'

'Pick you up? You have a hundred cars at your disposal and you want me to pick you up?'

'Don't be a pest. I really need to escape from my security

detail for a night and feel like a normal human being again. There will be instructions to let you in at the gate just past the Dandi March statue on Willingdon Crescent. I'll wait for you at the first tee of the golf course.'

The presidential estate had a decent-sized golf course within its confines, although I couldn't think of a single President who had played golf. General Bastard played religiously almost every day at daybreak. I'd have paid good money to get a chance to thrash his ass on the links, at least once. As might be expected, he was not the most magnanimous of losers. 'Knowing your beloved father, he'll have me arrested for kidnapping inside of an hour.'

'You're getting paranoid in your old age. I'll see you at eight. Bye for now, idiot.' And she hung up, leaving me totally distracted and sapped of any interest in pursuing the small matter of the BCCI election.

I MADE IT through the day without allowing myself to get too distracted by my evening rendezvous. Karnail Singh was missing, so I had to drive myself – never a good idea when you combine my lack of co-ordination with Delhi's vicious traffic. Somehow I arrived at the gates of Rashtrapati Bhavan, and as Neena had promised, I was given access and directions to the pick-up point. The presidential estate was a miniaturization of the rest of Lutyens' Delhi with bungalows of various shapes and sizes and tree-lined avenues with roundabouts at every intersection. It was a marvel of British ingenuity and Indian manpower. I doubt either race could have constructed such a wonder without the partnership of the other. I found the golf course with surprising ease, at least for me, and there Neena was as she had promised, standing amidst the darkened greenery, bathed in moonlight.

The acrimony between us was momentarily forgotten; our rose-tinted glasses were firmly on.

I was summarily evicted from the driver's seat without so much as a by-your-leave, being told that I was likely to get us both killed. The lady had a point and I meekly surrendered the steering wheel. The car screeched to a start as Neena gunned the engine, keen on leaving the estate in the minimum possible time.

'How's the cricket thing going so far?' she asked, as we tore out of the estate, more to ease my mind off her competent but recklessly high-velocity driving than any real curiosity on her part.

I discreetly clutched the edges of my seat. 'Two weeks left and it could go either way. Every day I wake up and have to make sure my herd is still intact. Most days, somebody has strayed over to the other side and I have to compensate by stealing one back. It's extremely exhausting.'

'I'm sure it is,' she flashed me a brilliant smile before dangerously muscling in ahead of a bus that had the right of way on the Teen Murti roundabout. I thanked God that the Gymkhana was close by. 'Where is the election being held?'

'Chandigarh. It's a Union Territory and centrally administered. So we've got the local machinery on our side, which is important if things get ugly.'

'What does ugly mean?' she asked distractedly giving a dirty look to an autorickshaw driver who was taking his own sweet time getting out of the way.

'Ugly means that if the other side decides to resort to the use of intimidatory tactics, we'll be ready for them.'

'Scandalous!' she exclaimed, finally showing genuine interest. 'I knew these things got boisterous but this isn't cricket.'

'No, it isn't, this election is set to be the dirtiest ever.'

'What is this Shitij Yadav fellow like?'

'A combination of too much food, too much money, too much power and too little judgement.'

She laughed and I turned to look at her. She looked radiantly beautiful. Her skin sparkled, her long hair shone. This was our first, guards down, regular, face-to-face conversation in years and it felt so comfortable, so right.

She caught me staring at her.

'What?' she queried as we turned into the Gymkhana.

I reached for her hand. 'I was just thinking how nice it was chatting with you again… like normal people do…'

'Yeah, normal people…'

Neena found a parking slot and expertly reversed the car into it. I released my seat-belt and was about to open the door when she put her hand on my arm to stop me. I looked towards her and saw that we were going back into the past one more, hopefully last, time. 'We have a little way to go yet,' Neena said in a whisper.

'Meaning?' I knew exactly what she meant but wanted her to bring it up on this occasion.

'Meaning, I owe you a full explanation of why I left and… uh… escalated the situation…' She obviously could not bring herself to directly mention her filing for divorce. 'You didn't come to get me, and you didn't even call. Your indifference hurt.'

I couldn't see because it was dark but I was sure she was crying. I took hold of her hand. Her pain brought me no pleasure. 'I tell you what, let's get this over with and then make a pledge never to mention it again? What better place to bury the past than here at the Gymkhana where we met. Deal?'

She nodded. 'I just keep thinking about all the wasted time.'

'Hey, don't think of that time as a waste. Without our enforced separation we would never have understood what we had and what we could have again. For all you know, by now we might have turned into a bitter divorced couple like so many of our peers. Broken marriages are a dime a dozen. We've always come back and tried to make it work. Whatever they say about us, Neena, they will never be able to call us quitters.'

'That does make me feel a little better.'

'Other people's misery is always good for that.' Now I had something to get off my chest as well. 'If you had waited a little longer, I might still have come back for you.'

'How was I to know that for sure? When you didn't come to Dehradun my heart broke and I lost all hope. You didn't call or email or anything. I was at my lowest point when I agreed to file the papers.'

'I was angry that you left again.' I decided to leave out my animus for her father, the unmentioned but obvious initiator of the divorce proceedings.

'Are you still angry?'

I leaned over, cupped her face in my hands, and kissed her. It is not easy to describe what it felt like; touching Neena again evoked emotions of a depth that were beyond my comprehension. We had said and done things that should have caused irreparable damage but here we were, in each other's arms again. Neena and I shared a bond that refused to break despite everything. Not having come close to experiencing anything similar to this with anyone else, I was compelled to reach the conclusion that whatever force ruled our relationship, it was so strong it could only be deciphered as that mystical phenomenon people called love. Surprisingly, this realization was not accompanied by sirens of mortification on my part, as I had expected, but instead felt to me like the arrival into port of a ship that had long been given up as lost at sea.

A CAR BEARING two noisy couples drove into the empty slot next to us and brought an abrupt end to our special moment. We were forced to disentangle from our passions and actually reach the Gymkhana bar as originally planned. There, to my considerable dismay, I found the bar teeming with people despite it being a Monday. The mystery of the unusual activity was solved when Neena was engulfed by a large group of elderly ladies and gents. I soon figured out that the President of the club was throwing himself a birthday bash. The President also happened to be a retired general who knew the Dayal family rather well, as did his circle of friends, many of whom were retired army officers themselves.

I was just glad that General Bastard's social calendar had him busy elsewhere, though it was a certainty that he would find out about Neena and me from one of his buddies or their gossipy wives. We managed to escape from the clutches of the old fogies after a great deal of effort, but by then we had tired of the Gymkhana and wanted to be alone again. The Rashtrapati Bhavan was the only place we could think of that would provide us any privacy so we returned there. It was the peak of summer and so was not exactly the perfect day for a stroll but we didn't care. After parking the car at the spot where Neena had waited for me earlier in the evening, we walked arm in arm around the green, wide-open spaces of the estate talking about everything and nothing, revelling in our renaissance.

I AWOKE THE next morning with a renewed zest for life.

'You have a visitor,' proclaimed Mother as I ambled out of my room, not bothering to wait and see if I had registered her announcement as she scurried into the kitchen. I was not particularly surprised to hear this since people had always come to our house at all hours to meet Father, and I suppose I had inherited this obligatory role as well. Admittedly, I normally discouraged any early birds but I was disposed that morning to be charitable towards all.

It was the Vice President's military aide, one that Dayal was not entitled to, but had insisted on installing anyway, who awaited me downstairs in the drawing room. I displayed what I thought passed for genuine befuddlement at the appearance of such a high and mighty personage's aide at my doorstep. Patting my stubborn hair into place, I proceeded towards the drawing room. There I found awaiting me the same square-shouldered piece of work who had transported my drunken frame to Neena's home from the now infamous party. I thought it best not to mention the events of that evening with Mother hovering within earshot.

His name was Captain Chavan and he turned out to not be such a bad sort after all. Neena had told him quite a bit about me, confiding in him as she would in a friend. He was sympathetic to my cause and the two of us got along surprisingly well – so much so that he only got to the reason for his visit after I reminded him about it.

As expected, General Bastard had got an early morning call from one of his old chums at the Gymkhana, no doubt informing him about whom his daughter had been consorting with the previous night. The call had caused the honourable Vice President to suffer a violent outburst of anger. Soon thereafter Chavan had been summoned and told to invite me for a round of golf at six the next morning at the presidential golf course. I, of course, cheerfully accepted and walked the good captain out to his car during which, now safely out of earshot of my mother, I apologized for my behaviour that absinthe-loaded night and complimented him on his strength.

We parted on the verge of becoming friends.

DELAYING MY CRICKET-RELATED travels for a day, I went the same afternoon to the Delhi Golf Club to put in a bit of practice to tune my rusty golf game for the next day's encounter. My dearest wish was coming true. I was not going to miss a chance to give my father-in-law a thrashing he would remember.

For most of my life, the golf course has been the one place that I have always felt unbeatable. Clients, bosses and elders have all been forced to acknowledge me as the senior partner when chasing that little white ball. I command an authority on the golf course that is evident to them. After playing a game of golf with me my superiors invariably let some of the deference earned on the golf course seep into their professional dealings with me.

I'd started playing golf when I was very young. There was a point in my teens when the only friends I had were those who played golf, so complete was the sport's influence on me. Even the extremes of heat and cold that dominate Delhi's climate could not prevent my band of brothers and me from our mission to spend every waking moment in pursuit of the perfect swing. And we had got good at it; extremely good. My fever for the game, however, had never risen to the level of delusion. I knew I would never be able to cut it professionally, but I could definitely hold my own against most part-timers, and our dear Vice President was one of them.

I had played some golf since returning to Delhi but ever since the BCCI election was thrown into my lap there hadn't been much time to indulge in this most time-consuming of sports. My handicap varied in the low to mid single-digits depending on the amount I got to play. After hitting a few hundred balls on the range and gaining my confidence, I returned home hoping to relax and turn in early for my duel the next day. Unfortunately, Mother would not delay her questioning for another second.

General Bastard's friends had done a great deal of gossiping during the day and my mother had been receiving inquisitive calls from half of Lutyens' Delhi wanting to talk about Neena and me. I was convinced the newspapers would not be far behind, after having announced our split in banner headlines a year earlier.

'How can you keep such important news from your own mother?' my mother asked as soon as I entered the house, pinning me with her most effective look of injured hurt. The voice was lowered, the eyes moist.

'There was nothing to talk about till a few days ago. Besides, when have I ever discussed something like this with you before?' I was not about to plead guilty to a bogus charge.

'But we are talking about the Vice President's daughter, Jasjit. The whole world appears to know what my son is up to before me.'

'The whole world has not found out about it so far. You have.'

'No thanks to you.' She made a valid point. Then she beamed at me changing her stance: 'In case you're curious, I approve.' The matriarch had re-emerged.

'That's well and good but I should warn you that we are nowhere near returning to a fully functioning marriage.'

'I never said anything about the state of your marriage,' brazenly lied the woman who had hectored me on the subject for years. I must have inherited my ability to subvert the truth without blinking an eyelid from her.

'You don't need to, I can see it in your eyes.'

'I would just advise you not to keep her dangling too long, Jasjit. A girl like Neena doesn't come along very often.' She didn't know the half of it and I prayed that she never would.

'Thank you for your words of wisdom, Mother. I thought you were looking forward to going out and finding me a nice sardarni after the divorce.' It was the perfect opportunity to needle her on the subject; an opportunity I could never resist.

'A good family is a good family,' said my mother sagely. 'And they are among the country's most prominent and admired families. One can't always have everything.'

Neena's not being a sardarni had rankled when we'd first married. But Mother was well aware that in the caste of power Neena had the highest pedigree now and as a result Mother would again be able to strut in front of her friends and relatives. I began to worry that once the public found out about Neena's suddenly reappeared husband, a new dimension would be added to our relationship. A lot more would be at stake. I wondered if our relationship was ready for that kind of pressure at this stage.

Not to mention how it would affect what I did for a living.

When I went to bed an hour or so later my mother was still in the most jovial of moods, fielding phone calls from acquaintances of all shades. I called Neena from my room. She knew about the golf game I was supposed to play with her father and she begged me to be on my best behaviour even if there was provocation. I gave a noncommittal reply and began instead to tell her about my conversation with my cantankerous mother, always a good topic to lighten the atmosphere. She laughed a bit but I could tell she was very worried about what would happen the next day.

I, on the other hand, was actually looking forward to it.

I ARRIVED AT the presidential golf course at a quarter to six the next morning and found the villain there already hitting balls in what was still pleasant weather, but which would soon give way to sweltering heat. He must have had two hundred balls piled up beside him and close to a dozen caddies picking up his shots in the fairway since there was no practice range. Any passer-by would have been in no doubt that a big shot was at play. As I got closer, I witnessed one of the most hilarious sights I have ever seen on a golf course. The caddies collecting the practice balls in the fairway were obviously not regular caddies but army jawans who were making the act of collecting their lord and master's shots as hazardous a proposition as possible. An experienced caddy would have stood a few feet away from where most of the player's shots were falling to make sure the ball came to him as it rolled to a stop. The jawans, keen to impress the Vice President, were running towards the ball while it was in flight and trying to catch the ball on one bounce. The consequences were brutal as they were clearly unaccustomed to tracking the ball against the sky. As everyone knows golf balls are lethal weapons when in motion and General Bastard's shots were taking their toll. Every shot had a jawan keeling over like a bowling pin, but the brave loyal fools kept getting up and chasing the next shot. The entire group of jawan-cum-caddies chased each and every shot, converging on the ball like cricketers trying to catch a skied mishit that was about to fall in no-man's land.

While this farce continued, His Excellency went about his practice regimen with a serenity and seriousness befitting Tiger Woods, unaware of the happenings around him, which included my arrival. My new pal Captain Chavan, dressed in his golfing kit, was on hand to greet me and present me to his boss. I won't lie to you, some of my earlier swagger failed me at that moment but I was still firm on not allowing my father-in-law to push me around again. Captain Chavan whispered into His Excellency's ear and he nodded but continued hitting balls. After about ten minutes of this, he finally deigned to turn around and greet me.

'Well, Sidhu, glad you could make it.' He had always referred to me by my last name. I imagined that was how he addressed all officers of negligible rank.

'I would never dream of turning down an invitation from the Vice President,' I replied, which, of course, left open the possibility of my not being so kind to him in his capacity as my father-in-law. I got a displeased stare for my impertinence. There was no way to deny it, the man had presence and was as intimidating a personality as I had ever been confronted by. Even now, in his golf shirt and trousers, he managed to look like he was surveying a battlefield. It was as if there was a magnetic field surrounding him that induced servitude and, being caught in it, I had to stop myself from almost apologizing for my snideness.

'That's good to know. How's your game?'

'Haven't had much of a chance to play recently.'

'Yes, I've heard you've been *very* busy in the last few weeks.' He gave me a knowing smile. 'What handicap do you think you can manage?'

'Seven would be fine.'

'I play to an eleven. You can give me two shots since we are only playing nine holes. Chavan will join us but he is just a beginner.' The ADC's golfing skills were dismissed with a contemptuous wave. Chavan seemed used to the General's deprecatory tone and displayed no reaction.

We headed towards the first tee which was just a couple of strides away. I noticed that along with the jawans in the fairway we had a crowd of helpers following behind us as well. There was an orderly in military uniform, a couple of presidential bearers carrying large bags, and some serious-looking security personnel whose pedigree looked more military than police to me.

The caddies lined up at attention along the length of the fairway. My opening tee shot almost managed to decapitate one of them. After all three of us had hit our tee shots, General Bastard jumped into a golf cart and zoomed off, leaving Chavan and me to catch up on foot. The golf cart, which was chauffeur-driven, had the vice presidential seal emblazoned on all its sides. No assassin would have ever confused his target.

I was geared up for a high-tension contest of sworn enemies like the famous James Bond–Goldfinger golfing battle of wills where rules were of no consequence and victory was all that mattered. What I got instead was nine holes during which my opponent spent ninety per cent of his time on the phone in his cart, completely ignoring me. So I spent the round having an extensive chat with Captain Chavan and giving him some basic tips that vastly improved his ball striking. The golf course, if you could call it that, was a cute little fourteen hole layout that made up what it lacked in difficulty with its imposing setting and amenities. The course was laid out to the south of the great building and involved surmounting obstacles in the form of roads, walls and trees that were directly in the player's line of sight. It may not have been much of a test but it was a fun little course. I played pretty well too and did thrash General Bastard, though he was too distracted to notice and that just ruined it for me.

The golf was undoubtedly a damp squib but the information I got out of Captain Chavan was fascinating and invaluable.

WHEN IT BECAME apparent that the Vice President was more interested in talking on the phone than playing golf, Captain Chavan thought I deserved an explanation.

'He's talking to the new army chief.'

'I thought General Das detested him.'

'Oh no. That was just a story the Vice President made up to get him appointed. A few months ago, when the shortlist of candidates for the post was sent to the PMO it became clear that the race was really between General Das and General Sengupta – '

'And General Sengupta had served as a staff officer under the Vice President.' I knew this part of the story.

'Precisely. So the PMO thought Sengupta was too close to the Vice President, which made them uncomfortable, and instead tapped Das for chief.'

'Except he also has a connection with our friend here?'

'When the Vice President was chief he had gone out of his way to promote Das to lieutenant-general, even though his fitness reports were not up to the mark.'

'Why did he do that?' General Bastard wasn't known for his altruistic nature.

'Mrs Das is a very beautiful and persuasive lady,' said Captain Chavan with a twinkle in his eye.

I urgently turned around to check the whereabouts of our host and was relieved to find he was on the other side of the fairway cursing to high heaven after hitting a shot two inches behind the ball.

'Isn't having an affair with a fellow officer's wife a court-martial offence?' I remembered reading about a similar incident in the newspaper that had ended with the implicated officer being drummed out of the service.

'If the husband of the woman involved is complicit in the act for the sake of his own advancement then I hardly think he would be likely to file a complaint.'

'You're a brave man to be telling me all this. You do know that I am the long reviled lover of his precious daughter?' I motioned with my head towards General Bastard.

'I know the history between Neena and you. She told me about it. It could make for a good romance novel. But I'm not telling you anything that wasn't common knowledge at the time among the higher echelons of the army.'

'Is Mrs Das still his mistress?'

'No, it's ancient history. His Excellency has moved onto greener pastures,' said Chavan in the most matter-of-fact way.

'The horny Vice President. Hmmm. I love the sound of that.' The mental picture of the great General with his pants around his ankles during an afternoon quickie cracked me up. 'But I can't comprehend how the PMO never found out about this connection if it was gossiped about in the army. Doesn't the IB put together a detailed report on each candidate for army chief?' I put a wet towel on my head as relief from the sweltering sun.

'They do, but the affair happened a long time ago. Not as many people recall it now and those that do are not the type to blab about it to vile IB agents. As you can imagine, the IB is not held in the highest regard within the army.'

We took a break to hit our approach shots to the green. I pulled mine to the left, rotten shot. 'So he has his own army chief?' I surmised to Chavan.

'Yes. And as the Senior Defence Officer in a government post he has asked all three chiefs to keep him informed of all developments. They all call at least twice a week, always early in the morning, like General Das did today, to avoid even their staff from finding out.'

'Isn't he afraid the IB will find out? I'm sure the PM has directed them to keep an eye and ear on him.'

Chavan looked at me and shrugged. 'You have no idea the amount of state-of-the-art anti-surveillance equipment we have had installed here. Look closely at that box attached to the back of his cart.' I did as advised and noticed that indeed there was an electronic black box attached to the cart with a small antenna and wires emanating from it.

'Army issue?'

'What else? The Israeli technology we have deployed is driving the IB crazy and there's nothing they can do about it. Even the plain mobile phone the Vice President is talking on right now is protected inside a zone of absolute privacy.'

General Bastard hit a good recovery shot and his retinue dutifully gave him a full ovation.

'I still find it hard to believe that the Air Chief Marshal and Navy Chief would agree to report to a former army chief. The Vice President has nothing to do with the Armed Forces, or any real power whatsoever.'

'Nobody in this government is paying attention to the needs of the Armed Forces. The Defence Minister is a buffoon and is more interested in spending time in his home state of Bihar. And as for the PMO, as you may well know, national security is not high on their list of priorities. The Vice President has used his influence and contacts to help each of the chiefs in this regard on an ongoing basis.' Chavan seemed truly incensed. Indian politicians had always been short-sighted when it came to defence planning.

'So all the chiefs are gravitating towards the one man in high office who can understand their problems?'

'Do you blame them?'

'Can't say I do, but it still scares me.' It was not only my nightmare scenario, but the nightmare scenario of the entire civilian establishment.

'You're referring to the unmentionable.'

I nodded grimly. 'A military coup.'

'I don't think things have deteriorated anywhere near that far yet,' Chavan said, only half in jest. 'But I promise if it does happen I will make sure you aren't sent to the gallows.'

Our enlightening conversation came to an end as we reached the green where the General waited impatiently. After five holes the bearers had set up a table for us. They served light refreshments. This was the only point in the game when General Bastard attempted conversation with me. We talked about everything except Neena. Clearly, Neena had also had a no-nonsense talk with her father about not misbehaving with me; Neena being the only person who dared to do so without risking major injury. Then the short interlude ended and Dayal was back in his cart and on his phone.

THE ROUND ENDED and I found that another spread of eats awaited. Breakfast seemed to be the favoured hour for both the Dayals to have it out with the likes of me. Chavan took the hint and departed after making some lame excuse about chores he had promised to do for his wife. The bearers served us with impressive expertise and we ate in deathly silence. I'm not much of an eater, especially at breakfast, so I was done quickly. General Bastard took his sweet time and ate a mammoth amount of grub. I have endured few more uncomfortable experiences than watching my father-in-law stuff his face. If that was his normal appetite it definitely didn't show on his physique. I was sure he was doing it on purpose; some kind of psychological warfare. Mercifully, he finally had his fill. The bearers served coffee and were then shooed away out of hearing distance.

'So I hear you've been fucking my daughter again.'

I cannot fully explain to you the impact of that sentence on my psyche. The man was a master. First he had put my nerves on edge with the silent treatment and now he was jarring me with this crass accusation. Interrogation at its best. To hear the Vice President of the country use a four-letter word only added to the effect he was trying to make. I was speechless for a few seconds; my mind went blank. Only the memory of his constant interference in my marriage got my juices flowing. I snapped out of the meek role I had been stuck in over the previous couple of hours.

'With due respect, sir, that's none of your business.' One of the lessons I had learnt as a banker was that even if you were planning to be rude it was always best to feign respect by tacking on a 'sir'. It tended to mask some of the venom.

'When it comes to my daughter, you rodent, everything is my business.' His eyes raged fire and his upper lip curled with contempt.

'That is a matter of opinion,' I defied him.

'My opinion is all that matters on this subject and you would be well served to remember that. And understand this, Neena is doing very important work right now and has a great future ahead of her. I will not allow it to be jeopardized by scum like you. She deserves somebody who is worthy of her.'

'I don't care what you say about me. The fact remains that your daughter loves me and I will not allow anyone to tear us apart again.'

'Don't make me destroy you, Sidhu, because if you don't walk away from Neena that is exactly what I will have to do. You are a ticking time bomb that is going to explode sooner or later and I am going to ensure you do not destroy Neena's life as well. You have continued in your family's long tradition of being a bag-man for lowlifes, and I cannot be associated with anyone like that.' The jibe at my father and Yadav, his business partners, was new and a bit unsettling.

'Try and remember, sir, who helped elevate you to the office you currently hold before you start judging others,' I warned.

'Let me be clear, Sidhu. I may not have respected your father but I did appreciate his professionalism. He knew who he was and what role he had to play in the scheme of things. Most importantly, he knew his limitations. I was saddened to hear of his death, a suspicious death I might add,' he smiled, raising his cup for a refill; it was poured instantly.

'I don't know what you mean,' I stated neutrally, though I was startled by what he was alluding to.

'Find out what your father was doing in Bareilly and you'll find out the answer to that riddle, Sidhu. What I'm concerned with right now is that little shit Yadav taking from me what I have rightly earned! Yesterday he told me that my share of the remaining Israeli commission funds would no longer be honoured. Then he had the temerity to tell me that I should consider it as payment for becoming Vice President. That's a steep price for a job that mainly involves sitting like a circus monkey in the Rajya Sabha or interminably attending the birth and death anniversaries of every second-rate leader this country has ever produced. I will not stand for such underhandedness!'

There it was writ large. The midget PM had gone back on his crooked deal of deals and General Bastard was bathed in righteous indignation. And I was being appointed arbiter between two individuals neither of whom trusted nor particularly liked me. 'That's unfortunate,' I had to concede, our personal disagreements compartmentalizing for the moment. This was business. 'But I should forewarn you that my influence with the PM is limited.'

'In that case you will all be made to pay in kind for this duplicity,' he thundered.

Mercifully, the vice presidential tirade was cut short with the arrival of a most colourful personage. Karan Nehru had cut through the golf course and was striding towards our table. Dayal stood up and greeted him as if he were a conquering hero returning from battle. In Karan Nehru's case this was not far from the truth. This bearer of a famous political name was also a war hero, having fought and been wounded in the Kargil War. His limp left arm was a constant reminder of his sacrifice, not that the redoubtable Mr Nehru let anyone forget it. He bore his name with pride and had a larger than life personality to match, which had come in handy when he decided to enter the family business.

Karan Nehru was a member of the Congress party, but it was his misfortune that he did not belong to the main line of the Nehru family that bore Prime Ministers at the turn of every generation. His cousin ran the party as its national President, and Karan had to make do as the state President of the ramshackle Uttar Pradesh unit.

It was an open secret that Karan thought poorly of his cousin's leadership abilities, and his cousin felt threatened enough by him to keep a wary eye on Karan's activities, as he gained in political stature with the Congress slowly but steadily reviving in the home state of the Nehrus, something once thought unimaginable.

Karan Nehru held Dayal in high regard as the General had pampered the young man when he had briefly served under him more than a decade ago. They were good chums now. I, on the other hand, shared nothing more than a chatting acquaintance with the always-animated Nehru scion.

'Ah, Jasjit, how have you been, Surd?' asked Nehru in his usual vociferous way, his broad neck bulging with energy. I assured him I was well.

'Good, good. We must get together one of these days and have a chat,' he said, meaning it was not going to be happening today. I was more than happy to take this as my cue to depart.

'Don't forget what we discussed. Both topics,' Dayal shot a reminder as I retired from the battlefield. 'And in the meantime I would watch my back if I were you – starting with your little trip to Chandigarh.'

With that ominous threat General Dayal turned his back on me and entered into a serious conference with Major Nehru, leaving me to weigh the possible consequences of his last words in solitude.

Chapter 4

THE CITY OF Chandigarh was envisioned by Nehru and made into a reality by the French architectural master, Le Corbusier. You'd expect a city with such an esteemed parentage to be an oasis of refinement but you would be disappointed. I say this despite the fact that I was born there and most of my family, including my surviving grandparents, still reside there. Whatever novel character it once may have possessed, Chandigarh is losing out to the forces of progress and Nehru's vision of an urban utopia is well on the way to the scrap yard. So, if you strip away its pretentious history, Chandigarh is destined to remain the city that was told when it was young that it would one day outshine the likes of Delhi and Bombay but failed to live up to those lofty expectations or, worse, to forget them.

I kept the latest case of unpleasantness with General Bastard to myself, and he seemed to have done the same, because Neena took the cessation of the routine bad-mouthing between us as a sign that an entente had come into force. The poor soul didn't realize that it was merely the lull before the storm, which is an apt analogy because the monsoons made their advance onto Chandigarh, just as all of us arrived there for the BCCI election.

To get back to the cricket elections, very little had happened in the last days of campaigning as a vast majority of those involved had hardened their loyalties to either of the two camps. Vikas Pande had made very apparent that this would be a free-for-all contest and we had taken suitable steps in preparation of all eventualities. Earlier in the year – when it had looked like a cakewalk for Rawat – Pande had advanced the elections by a couple of months, saying he didn't want the elections to coincide with the Australian team's tour of India. This had been a bogus excuse used to hide his real agenda, which was to string his puppet into the Presidentship of the board before any other contender appeared on the horizon. He hadn't accounted for us.

There had been another slight ruckus a week before the election, when Pande had threatened to move the elections to another city. Before the election had become a genuine contest, Chandigarh had been picked as the hosting city at the suggestion of the Secretary of the BCCI who was a Pande acolyte and was also President of the Haryana cricket board. Dhillon Uncle, who was dictator for life of the Punjab board, had offered the impressive facilities of Punjab's world-class Mohali stadium for staging the elections, and the offer had been happily accepted.

But when it became apparent that Dhillon Uncle had taken sides, Pande went to battle stations. Uncle settled the issue by getting his pal the Punjab Chief Minister to give Pande a call to tell him how disappointed he would be if the election were moved from Chandigarh. Pande was an industrialist who had considerable business interests in Punjab. He knew he couldn't afford to 'disappoint' the Chief Minister and, taking the hint, backed down. He then tried to use the judiciary to indefinitely delay the election, as he had managed to do in the past, by accusing us of buying votes. Pande demanded that the election be held only after a criminal inquiry had been conducted. This was especially rich coming from a rat like him; he was just pissed off that we had outbid him at every turn. Once again, we were successful in stonewalling him after easily winning over the presiding judges. Yadav Junior was perhaps the only opponent that Pande didn't have the required influence and resources to steal the election from. Considering the array of forces lined up against him, I was quite impressed that Pande kept plugging away and held his ground against our onslaught. In his place, I would have certainly thrown in the towel.

Anyhow, as the elections approached, I was considerably distracted by the antics of the media, which acted as ravenously as I had predicted, the minute they got wind of the details of my love life.

DURING THE COURSE of the reforming nineties and the burgeoning power of television news, the parameters of news reporting were seismically altered; this introduced a manic element to the way stories were covered.

In the weeks since our reconciliation, I had accompanied Neena to some large social events and we had succeeded in causing a riot everywhere we went. My face was splashed in all the newspapers; my anonymity was a thing of the past. So far the reports had resisted the urge to write about my actual occupation, identifying me instead as a 'financial whiz kid' perhaps because it made better copy. The attention scared me because I had lived in Delhi long enough to know that fixers like myself normally met their end when they came out of the shadows and showed themselves. I hoped I would be the exception but a dull ache in my stomach hinted otherwise.

For once I had looked forward to going to Chandigarh, thinking I would be able to get out of the spotlight for a little while. I was made starkly aware of my misjudgement when I went to visit Dhillon Uncle at the stadium and was greeted by a wall of sports reporters, each of whom was completely aware of my role in Shitij Yadav's candidacy. The candidate himself was kept under lock and key at my maternal grandparents' house (the grandparents having been shipped to Delhi for the duration) and was only allowed to give some media interviews to trusted journalists the night before the election. In one case, the blubbery buffoon took twenty re-takes to correctly get out a simple sound-bite.

Members of my voting camp began arriving the night before the election. I had made arrangements for them to stay at the houses of relatives, as well as in government and corporate guesthouses. I was not going to allow them to stay in hotels where they could fall prey to the machinations of the rival camp. All their mobile phones were confiscated on arrival, which caused a bit of a hullabaloo, but they had taken my client's money after all, and I made them very plainly aware of what they had set themselves up for. I was going to own their ass for the next twenty-four hours. They were not allowed to move out of their rooms without my permission. Local police were posted with every one of them. A small army of highly paid private bodyguards was hired to make sure the cops didn't stray. Money was no object. Only the kingmakers were allowed some form of independence but they were under the constant supervision of Dhillon Uncle who didn't let them out of his sight, so I wasn't too worried.

The three Government votes were secure as the PM had ordered the senior-most bureaucrat from each of the concerned ministries to be present at the election to personally place the vote. The Defence Secretary, Railways Secretary and HRD Secretary grumbled mutinously but showed up. It was overkill on the midget PM's part but excusable because by the eve of the election the media was covering it as the lead story of the day. People around the country were following the run-up to the cricket board election with all the seriousness of an event of national consequence. I understood more than ever that the repercussions of failure would be dire for all those involved, and for none more significantly than me.

THE DAY OF the election dawned like any other, except I shuddered when I awoke and remembered what lay ahead that morning. The contest was tied with only the Himachal Pradesh vote left to fight over. The Himachal contingent was still threatening to abstain despite diligent attempts by both Pande and me to buy the state's vote. The entire Shitij Yadav camp, Dhillon Uncle downwards, had assembled at my grandparents' house for a final meeting. Most people would have been amazed to know that up till this juncture only a handful of the electors had met their candidate – the hands-off President of the Bihar board, who understood his role to be of a ceremonial nature, had never before bothered to attend the BCCI's annual general meeting. I had given Yadav Junior stringent instructions to speak only when absolutely necessary and to stick to nodding and smiling as much as possible. If we did win the election, it would be Dhillon Uncle who actually ran the show, so I didn't feel too guilty about installing an ass like Shitij at Indian cricket's helm. The opposing team was doing the exact same thing with an equally big idiot as their candidate, though his cricketing credentials were indisputable.

But by the day of the election the distinction in the backgrounds of the candidates had become irrelevant and the only thing that mattered was which side would prevail.

We took a roll-call of allegiances for the last time and then the group made its way towards the stadium, ready for the fireworks to begin. The media was cordoned off, restricted to an area from where they could see but not jostle us. We ignored the questions that came flying at us as we walked past them on our way to the boardroom. Pande and his gang hadn't arrived yet so we twiddled our thumbs for a few minutes. Just as we got news of their arrival I got a phone call that sent our spirits soaring. The midget PM had reached a last-ditch agreement with the Himachal Pradesh Chief Minister, whose party was part of the Opposition in Delhi, to vote for Shitij in exchange for certain political favours from the Central Government. I guessed that funds from the Central Exchequer would flow a little more liberally than before in the direction of the mountain state. The Himachal cricket board was headed by the Chief Minister's stooge, who would obviously do as his boss dictated.

The Himachal vote now put us one ahead. This late in the game I didn't think anything could stop us from victory. The representative from Himachal made an entrance a minute or so later and the first thing he did was to give Shitij a warm hug. Pande's face fell to the floor.

Our feeling of superiority didn't last very long. As Pande was about to bring the meeting to order, the Defence Secretary had to leave the room to answer a phone call. I didn't think anything of it as I was sure he was a busy man with lots of national security-related issues to deal with on a daily basis. Five minutes later, I was also pulled out of the room by one of my privately hired bodyguards. I was flabbergasted to find the Defence Secretary in tears. He sat clutching a mobile phone to his chest, on whose screen I assumed was writ the reason for his sudden loss of composure.

'Sir, what's wrong?' I still didn't suspect it had anything to do with the elections.

'What's wrong? I'll tell you what's wrong: I am two months away from an honourable and well-earned retirement, but thanks to your bloody election my life is about to go down the gutter.' He then went from whimpering to bawling shamelessly. I directed a bodyguard to bring in Dhillon Uncle. This was too much for me to handle alone. I then proceeded to question a reticent Defence Secretary on what had happened and I gathered that the mobile phone in his hands contained some incriminating material regarding corruption, or photos of trysts with a paramour, or something else equally scandalous. I didn't care to know the details – he could gladly keep those to himself – but how this would affect the soon-to-begin election I demanded he reveal at once.

'The man on the phone said I should abstain from voting if I cared for my reputation.'

'And what do you propose to do?'

'I propose to do exactly as he says.'

'The PM will not be pleased,' I threatened, knowing full well that short of death there was nothing of consequence with which one could threaten a bureaucrat set to retire in two months.

'The hell with him, he's the one who got me into this mess.' His decision was final.

'So you're not going back into the boardroom?'

Dhillon Uncle came in and I briefed him on the current state of play. The old man's face did not register an iota of surprise as I got to the punch line of my tale.

'What should we do?' I prayed to God he would come up with some miraculous plan.

'If the Services abstain then the score is tied and you know who has the tie-breaking vote,' Satinder Dhillon said.

In the case of a tie, the BCCI President cast the deciding vote. With Pande still sitting in the President's chair we were as good as sunk. While I despaired and the stupid shit of a Defence Secretary continued to wail, Dhillon Uncle calmly put his mind to work, going through all the permutations and combinations possible: 'Is there anyone in Chandigarh who can take the Defence Secretary's place as a representative of the Services?'

Dhillon Uncle looked at me and I turned with a questioning gaze towards the spineless maggot responsible for the crisis.

'In Chandigarh, there is General Balbir Singh Kohli

who is GOC-in-C, Western Command and is close by at Chandimandir. I can depute him, but he isn't the kind who is amenable to this sort of thing,' the wretch snivelled.

'I don't care! Call him *right* now,' I ordered the Defence Secretary, imagine that. 'Uncle, can we get the election delayed for a while?'

'The election is the fourth item on the agenda so, anyway, we have some time before the voting is set to begin. I know of enough procedural ploys to cause a further delay and keep them tied up for an hour or two,' Dhillon Uncle boasted and set off purposefully towards the boardroom.

The Defence Secretary, still sticking to protocol, asked his PA to have General Kohli call him at the stadium. Once a babu always a babu. The PA called back fifteen minutes later to inform us that the good general and his entire staff were unreachable for the next thirty-six hours as they were in the middle of a war game and therefore in the field. I started to smell a certain vice presidential hand in all this. My father-in-law's threat started to ring in my ears. I couldn't ignore it as bluster any more.

'Jasjit, I bought us ninety minutes. Did you make contact with the Western Army Commander?' Dhillon Uncle returned from his sabotage mission.

'No, he's out on manoeuvres somewhere in the wilderness.'

'You know, while I was employing delaying tactics I got the strangest sense that Pande was quite shocked at what I was doing. I swear to God I think he still believes we're in a position to win.'

That was enough evidence for me to pronounce General Bastard's guilt. 'It isn't him. I'm afraid this is the handiwork of the Vice President.'

'Which Vice President?' asked the confused Defence Secretary.

'The Vice President of India,' I clarified.

'But why would he get involved in this?' Even Dhillon Uncle's shrewdness couldn't make sense of this vendetta.

'He hates my guts and has made it his mission in life to destroy me.'

'But you're married to his daughter,' exclaimed the harried Defence Secretary in disbelief.

Dhillon Uncle had caught on by now. 'He hates him *because* he's married to his precious daughter, Secretary sahib. Embarrassing the PM must be an added bonus.'

'Two birds with one stone,' I added. 'He threatened me a few days ago about the election but I didn't think he could actually follow through on it.'

'That wasn't a smart move. Brajesh Dayal is a very dangerous man,' said Dhillon Uncle, not knowing how well aware of that I was.

'Do we have any avenues of escape left?'

'It depends. How badly do you want to win this election?'

'Very badly,' I admitted.

'If retreat is not an option then I suggest you call the PM and tell him to instruct the army chief to order General Kohli here for the vote.'

I knew that would only result in digging a bigger hole. 'That's no good. The Vice President will be sure to find out and he'll gladly leak it to the press. I can see the headlines now – "Senior Army Commander Pulled Out of War Game to Win Cricket Election for PM's Son". Political suicide.'

'Then I can't see any quick way out of this as of now. We have to push the election to the afternoon so that we can fly someone down from Delhi to replace our friend here.' Dhillon Uncle indicated the Defence Secretary with a jerk of his head, not bothering to hide his obvious disgust.

'And how do we do that with Pande chairing the meeting?' I had felt one step behind events from the moment I had taken on this task.

'Bomb scare,' he declared nonchalantly.

'You have to be joking,' piped in the Defence Secretary.

'Just watch me.' Dhillon Uncle went to the phone and had a short conversation with someone I presumed to be high up in law and order circles. Twenty minutes later the bomb squad arrived and the premises were forcibly vacated. Everyone was asked to stand in the parking lot in pouring rain, with rabid reporters close at hand. The temporary shelter erected for the media would have been the perfect spot to save us from the downpour but going there would have required us to undergo some very hostile questioning – a fate much more severe than getting drenched. The only option was to take cover in the parked vehicles. Pande's people, less media-shy than us, hastened towards the cameras to accuse and abuse us. They were the least of my problems.

In the meantime the police were searching for nothing except their appetites, with an extensive array of snacks and sweets, originally prepared for us, being served to them. Pande, the last time I saw him, looked like he suspected some hanky-panky but obviously couldn't quite put his finger on it. I knew we couldn't rely on his staying confused for very much longer.

DHILLON UNCLE, THE Defence Secretary, Shitij (whom I had put on a leash) and I jumped into my car, which an alert Karnail had waiting for us near the entrance so we wouldn't get wet and could not be spied on by the media, even with their fancy zoom-lens technology. I sat in the driver's seat, Dhillon Uncle took the front passenger seat, and the other two settled in the back. I quickly brought Shitij up to speed with recent developments. On hearing the news, he instantly turned to the man sitting beside him who posed the only obstacle to his triumph.

'What is it that they have on you?' Shitij turned on the Defence Secretary and made a grab for his phone.

'I'm not going to discuss it. Let go, you scoundrel!' The Defence Secretary held on to his mobile with the desperation of a man who had everything to lose.

They looked to me like two overgrown ten-year-olds. Shitij mercifully didn't persist with a second snatching attempt. Instead he snarled, 'You damn well will discuss it if you know what's good for you.'

'Your threats don't scare me. There's nothing you can do to me. I have two months of service left and after that I will be rid of you,' the Defence Secretary retaliated.

Then, as I watched with my mouth agape, Shitij slapped the bureaucrat twice across the face, the second time viciously with the back of his hand. I almost shat in my pants, and I think the assaulted babu might actually have done.

Shitij took hold of the Defence Secretary's collar. 'Let me explain something to you, chodu. Unless you're planning to leave the country you will never be rid of either my father or me. And if you continue to refuse to vote for me, I can promise you that you will not live out the year. I'm sure you'll find that nothing in your precious phone will compare to what I have in store for you.'

Suddenly Shitij's true nature was crystal clear to me. What had earlier only been alluded to had become living, breathing actuality. He was a vicious goon who would use every possible tool to get his way; a goon with the power of a Prime Minister to back him. That's the way he had been brought up and had got used to operating. I had sensed the monster in him from the very beginning, but bearing witness to his demonic actions shook me to my core.

I thought the Defence Secretary was going to drop dead from a coronary right there and then. The poor chap was stuck between this overt threat, and the doom of whatever was hidden in the phone that he continued to hug like it was life itself. I wanted to put him out of his misery. Dhillon Uncle went quiet and merely stared at Shitij impassively as if he had mentally transported himself somewhere far away from this distasteful scene. I was silent as well, having come to the sudden conclusion that I would now have to find an urgent way out of my relationship with the Yadavs as soon as possible or I would surely find myself, sooner or later, at the other end of a no-win negotiation like the one I had just witnessed.

THERE WAS NOT much more excitement to be had after that. The bomb squad came out of the building on Dhillon Uncle's signal and we reconvened in the boardroom. Then it was Pande's turn to delay the vote. He demanded to know in what capacity I was present. I didn't see any purpose in arguing the fact and removed myself from the proceedings. I was actually relieved to have a chance to be alone after having endured a truly traumatic day.

The vote took place and, as expected, Shitij was duly elected. Indian cricket had a new tsar.

After having done more than any man to have made this possible, I could not have cared less.

Chapter 5

I RETURNED TO Delhi right after the vote and asked Neena to meet me as soon as she could get away. I needed to see her to regain my sanity. Neena was my antidote to the toxins that entered my system from supping with the Yadavs. I felt like the world was closing in on me. General Bastard was spending his waking moments planning my disgrace and the Yadavs, I knew now, would one day ask of me something that I could not or would not deliver and then they would gun for me as well – I knew too much about their affairs to just simply be allowed to walk away. There had to be a way out.

My mother was visiting my brother in London so we had the house to ourselves. But Neena arrived with a full retinue. From the look of her bodyguards, similar to those I had seen with General Bastard, I was certain that the civilian police was not allowed anywhere near the Dayal family's inner perimeter of security. These fellows looked like they were from some kind of elite Special Forces unit. The team leader had arrived in advance and only after he had made a thorough check of the premises did Neena leave Rashtrapati Bhavan. I was impressed. My lady was better protected than the PM.

For a change she was casually dressed in jeans and a loose red shirt. I was tempted to stick my hands up her shirt when I kissed and hugged her in welcome but I thought it better to act like a gentleman for a little while longer. No point getting a dressing down in front of the staff. We had dinner and she kept congratulating me for the win in Chandigarh like I was some kind of conquering hero returning from a famous victory. In the eyes of the outside world I had pulled off an amazing win. But I was not in any mood to be continually reminded of the events that had led to the result. Neena sensed this as well.

'Why the long face, Jasu? I thought you would be over the moon; you've been working on this day and night for weeks.'

'Actually, in gaining that win I've had to do and see things that have made me loath myself.'

'Come on, we all feel like that on certain days.'

'No, Neena, this is different. I'm not sure you know what role I play in the current scheme of things in this city.'

'I have some idea.'

'That's not enough, Neena. I should have discussed this with you earlier, before news of our reconciliation went public. Your father is right, I have no business putting a woman of your position at risk.'

'You spoke about us with Papa?'

'Yes, and it wasn't pleasant. I didn't want to tell you earlier because you seemed so happy and anyway I'm fine with your father despising me. You are the most important thing in my life right now and I would do anything for your sake.' I reached out a hand to caress her cheek and she tilted her head in appreciation.

'Mmm. Is that your way of saying you love me?' she asked.

'Was there ever any doubt?'

'No, but there are some things a girl has to hear. I love you too.' We were sharing a sofa and she moved over to my side, sat in my lap, and kissed me deeply. But there were too many questions still hanging in the air for it to last.

'I'll talk to Papa in the morning.'

'Don't bother, I don't want you to start a fight.'

'Why? Are you afraid I'll pack my bags and appear on your doorstep again?'

'Don't be silly,' I said, though I knew that was not a great idea right now.

'Relax, my father and I don't shout or lose our temper with each other.'

'Unless yours truly is the subject. I bring out the best in him.'

'On that you're right. He threw his breakfast tray at the wall after getting a call the morning after we went to the Gymkhana from one of his cronies who saw us there.'

'Chavan didn't tell me about the tray.'

'He didn't find out. I had the mess cleared before the staff reported for duty.'

'Chavan has turned out to be a solid guy. I like him.'

'He was raving about you too after the golf game. He said you were some kind of golfing wizard who had vastly improved his game.'

'Did he? We had a long chat about your father as well. The way he's going about positioning himself, you could be a dictator's daughter sooner than you know. After which you can put me in irons and make me your sex slave.' My fingers finally did make their way under her shirt. She shrieked in surprise and her bodyguards came charging in. Neena turned red with embarrassment but I found it fascinating that they'd entered simultaneously from three different ends of the house. They cleared out rapidly on realizing it was a false alarm.

'See what happens when you say rotten things,' she complained only half-angrily after having retreated to another sofa.

'Are you saying our Vice President isn't up to the job?'

'He's smart enough to know that the last thing this country needs is a dictator.'

'A large chunk of the middle-class is liable to disagree with you,' I said, eyeing her lecherously.

'Behave or I'll scream for my bodyguards again.'

'All right, no more teasing. Come here,' I pleaded and she complied. I put my arm around her.

'Do you enjoy doing what you do?' she asked suddenly.

'I did for a while but I'm not so sure anymore.'

'Then you must stop,' Neena concluded.

'It's not that simple.'

'Yes it is. Just pick up the phone and call the PM to tell him you're through being his and his son's lackey and that you are quitting.'

'I know too much for him to let me go without a fight.'

'What do you mean?' My response alarmed her.

'Once you get mixed up with this crowd, either you flee to a place where they can't find you or you are suddenly made to disappear.' I told her about the cricket elections and Shitij's decisive use of coercive tactics. I thought it wise to excise her father's role in the affair. There were some things a doting daughter like Neena would not believe about her father, and there was no denying he had been a good father to her.

'What are you going to do?'

'I'll think of something.' She held me closer and I buried my face in her divinely fragrant hair. You could never put a price on a moment like that; even I, who made a living pricing the intangible, had to admit that.

I asked Neena to spend the night. But she had her bodyguards to think of. Before leaving she informed me that she was going the next day on a week-long official visit to countries in Southeast Asia with her bloody father. What did a man have to do to keep his wife in the same goddamn country?

WITH NEENA AWAY, my mother in London, and only Shitij to spend time with, Delhi seemed a lonely place. I decided to make a day's visit to Dubai to meet a couple of my private bankers, who had flown down from Geneva and the British Virgin Islands to finalize some overdue decisions for maturing long-term investments that had been delayed by my BCCI election diversion. I arrived in the morning and got all my work out of the way by noon, which left the rest of the day for meeting friends, since my flight out was only at three the next morning.

That evening a close friend of mine threw a dinner party for me at his lavish villa in Jumeirah and invited more or less everybody that I had ever met in the emirate. Even though he had only been given short notice of my arrival he had managed to turn it into an event by getting it impressively catered. All the invitees showed up and those that weren't invited called to wrangle an invitation out of the host. Clearly, my infamy had traversed the Arabian Sea; this was a crowd that could fully admire my position, since they shared my mercenary morality.

The hours flew as I laughed and drank among people who knew how to have a good time. Dubai was a paradise for those who wanted to make money and spend it on material pursuits. Thinkers, especially of a political breed, were not welcome to ply their trade. If you followed the rules you could make a lot of money and spend it with the maximum possible degree of enjoyment. I was once one of them but now I had started to pity them a little. That however didn't stop me from enjoying their company, and their largesse.

The party was still going strong as the time for me to leave for the airport approached. I went to the guestroom to freshen up for the flight ahead and when I came out of the bathroom I found a familiar face staring at me. It was Dinesh Parmar, one of the original barons of the telecom industry, with very deep pockets and an accompanying zeal to buy his way into new pastures; a man whose life my father had played an important role in destroying.

I HAD NEVER met Parmar before but I recognized him immediately from the numerous television interviews he had given, six months ago, when he had been intent on raiding Bharat Spectrum, a company better known for its large real estate holdings than its business productivity, which therefore made it a perfect takeover target. He had gambled and failed. He had never stood a chance once the government had decided to back Bharat Spectrum's management. Manish Jain, the owner of Bharat Spectrum, had also used his money well – to buy retribution – and Father had dealt it out in spades during his first days in the PMO. All the major investigative agencies of the Central Government had swooped down on Parmar and his fledgling business. The government's rules and regulations with regard to the private sector were still so stringent and archaic that every company was probably contravening a dozen rules at any given moment, so it wasn't too hard to frame various cases against Parmar; cases that ranged from tax evasion to foreign exchange violations. Parmar was no angel, already being the target of multiple ongoing government inquiries. Father knew how to turn up the heat and did so in no time at all. The new charges against Parmar were carefully designed for lethal effect to target his person and obstruct his business. The last I had heard of him, he and his family had fled abroad to escape the government's persecution; I hadn't realized he was in Dubai. Given the seriousness of the cases against him, he must have had to pay some judge good money to keep his passport. Or maybe he had secretly possessed another country's passport as an insurance policy.

Parmar was a tall, sturdy gent and the guestroom was in a quiet corner of the large house. It was the perfect place for him to beat the living crap out of me. I only hoped that his beating wouldn't leave me impotent because that would be a real shame, having waited so long and come so close to being with Neena again. I swear that was the one thought that monopolized my thoughts as I stood staring guiltily at Parmar.

'I heard of your father's death. I'd waited a long time, hoping to run into him some day. I guess running into his son and successor will have to do,' said Parmar, sitting down in a chair and stretching his legs on to the bed.

'It's a small world.' I could barely speak. Fear had contracted my vocal cords.

'So they say. You must be wondering what possible reason I could have for following you in here?'

'I admit the thought had crossed my mind.'

'I wanted to meet the progeny of the man who was responsible for not only my downfall but also for stomping to death an embryonic revolution that would have brought accountability and efficiency into the incestuous realm of Indian industry.'

'That's a bit much, don't you think?'

'Not at all. If I had taken Bharat Spectrum out of the hands of that vile Jain family and brought it under professional management, it would have set off a chain reaction of raids on other similarly bloated and inefficiently managed companies. The entire landscape of corporate governance in India would have changed overnight.'

His passion was infectious and I couldn't argue with him because I basically agreed with his capitalistic philosophy. But it was a mistake to follow instructions from a Harvard case study and assume it would take you to victory anywhere on the globe, without studying the lay of the land. Especially in India, where Government poked its nose in everything. I was relieved to see that Parmar only wanted to debate with me and not assault me – or at least not immediately.

'You may be right but you didn't go about it in the right way,' I suggested.

'Meaning, I didn't go to your father?'

'We could have made a deal and he would have swung it for you just as he swung it for Manish Jain. But at that point you thought market forces would be enough to get you to the chequered flag. In India you take the government for granted at your own peril.'

'I agree. I misjudged Jain's resourcefulness and your father's influence. Is it too late to make remedies?' We had both been bankers and knew that everything was cyclical. You could be down now and up the next day, you just had to keep your eyes open for all possible opportunities.

'What are you suggesting?'

'My associates and I are willing to pay you what Jain paid you plus a healthy risk premium if you call off your hound dogs and watch benignly by as we finish our job.'

'Who are your associates?' The poor fool didn't know he was negotiating with a man who could no longer deliver.

'They do not wish to disclose their identities at this juncture,' he parried.

'I don't make deals with people who are unknown quantities.'

'I assure you they are men of highest credibility and trustworthiness.'

It was getting late. Parmar looked like someone who was desperate and desperate people made me nervous. After the government had gone after Parmar, Jain had felt safe enough to start dumping his stock in the market and the stock price of Bharat Spectrum had tanked. Realizing they had been decisively defeated, Parmar and his associates were compelled to sell out their stake at a great loss. I didn't think Parmar's consortium any longer possessed the resources to launch another hostile takeover of Bharat Spectrum and that was that as far I was concerned.

'Look, Mr Parmar, I like you and am truly sorry your family had to go through such a traumatic period. The truth is, it is easy to get the CBI and Enforcement Directorate after somebody, but next to impossible to call them off. Once the courts get involved it becomes a whole different proposition as I am sure you are finding out at present. In fact, I'm still trying to figure out how you were allowed to fly out to Dubai.'

'I am not completely bereft of influence in Delhi.'

'I'm sure, but I cannot help you. I will try to do what I can to get the agencies from causing you any more difficulty. If you come up with another deal make sure you call me – that is, if I'm still in a position to help you.'

'After having worked internationally, I was sure you would have some sympathy for my cause.'

'I do not fight for anybody's cause but my own, Parmar. That's the common lesson both my father as well as my exposure to the world of capitalism have taught me. Causes are for politicians. My job is to take all the emotion out of the decision-making process and swing the best deal possible for my client.'

'You're so full of yourself right now, aren't you, Sidhu? My associates are powerful men and they will not be happy with our conversation today.' He tried to threaten me but his heart wasn't in it; the required menace was missing.

'If they want to come after me tell them to be my guest. They'll be in esteemed company. Well, Mr Parmar, if that's all, I'll be pushing off because I have a plane to catch.' I moved forward and waited for him to get his legs off the bed and out of my way. He did so but at a leisurely pace and then he leant forward, placing his face directly in the beam of the only lamp in the murky room. The negotiator's mask had come off and it revealed a man devastated by the realization that he had no more moves left to make. The stench of his failure and desperation filled the room and repelled me.

'A day may come when you come to me for help,' he said sombrely.

'I don't doubt it and I would expect you to protect the interests of you and yours just as I am doing today. Charity is a luxury our kind cannot afford. Good night.'

The talk with Parmar bothered me all the way back to Delhi. He was a proud man who was plainly on his last legs but refused to beg and lose his self-respect. He had been driven to this by my father's actions. Undoubtedly, there were countless other faceless, decent people my father had steam-rolled over on the directions and payment of the rich and powerful. I wondered how many professional lives and those of their families my father had destroyed as collateral damage of his actions. The sins of the father were for the son to bear, and I did so without complaint, but it did not mean it was easy.

Damnit, what was wrong with me? It wasn't just about numbers anymore; I was growing a conscience. That was the *worst* thing that could happen to a person who did what I did for a living.

I RETURNED HOME to the news that Shitij's slapping of the Defence Secretary had been leaked to the press and was the main topic of conversation in the whole country. There would be hell to pay. An emergency meeting of the Yadav kitchen cabinet was called into session at South Block. The midget PM, Shitij and I took the same seats that we had occupied when we had first met, soon after Father's death, some months before. This was a crisis with definite political ramifications; the question was how best to contain and defuse it.

The Prime Minister, his voice heavy with barely controlled anger, came directly to the point: 'I have ascertained from my son that the incident did, in fact, take place, so there is no need to get into the authenticity of the news report. I want to know who leaked it and how this could have been allowed to happen?' The midget fixed his accusing eyes on me.

'I don't know, sir, maybe somebody was walking by and

witnessed it. Maybe the Defence Secretary leaked it. There could be many possibilities. What difference does it make?'

'I'll tell you what difference it makes; if there is somebody in your operation who is untrustworthy I want him stopped now before he starts leaking more important aspects of my dealings. Do you understand?' The PM's voice rose a decibel.

I nodded obediently. 'Yes, sir. But you can rest assured that those who were part of our team to get Shitij elected have nothing to do with any financial dealing you have with me. I am a team of one in that department.'

'So you say,' said Shitij sullenly, quickly surfacing from his downcast demeanour to try and stick it to me.

The PM ignored his son's statement. 'My people have decided that the best thing to do at this stage is to deny the story completely.'

'What if they have a photograph or video?' I asked, knowing that General Bastard could have leaked the story to get us to deny it. Then he would merrily release the picture soon after, making the PM look like a bold-faced liar.

'He has a point,' admitted Shitij.

'In this day and age you can never know when someone might have used a cell phone to capture an incriminating image. That would be a disaster,' I pointed out.

'Could the car have been bugged?' asked Shitij.

'No chance. Our security people swept all our vehicles for surveillance devices every morning while we were in Chandigarh,' I replied. We had been well prepared on that score. If someone had been watching us it had to have been externally.

'Maybe our solution should be of a different kind. My coalition allies are saying they would like Shitij to take a lower profile with immediate effect. I'm inclined to agree.' The PM cast a baleful eye on his fat son. 'I think a little hard work and discipline is what is required for you, Shitij. Important

Parliamentary and Assembly by-elections are due in UP and Bihar after the monsoons and I've decided that you will take charge of the campaign with immediate effect.'

'What? I'm too busy with my cricketing responsibilities to go anywhere right now,' Shitij the Shit wailed.

'Don't worry about that. Satinder Dhillon will take care of things while you're away,' I said helpfully and got a glare for my efforts. I smiled. The decision was made and there was nothing fatso could do about it.

'In the meantime, we'll try to stave off the press with carefully worded, conditional denials and hope no visual evidence shows up. Is there anything else we need to discuss regarding this subject?' asked the PM.

'Yes, there is,' I volunteered and then told them about how I believed that Vice President Dayal had tried to thwart Shitij's election in Chandigarh.

'How can you be sure?' asked the PM, his face tightening with anger.

'Before I left for Chandigarh he threatened me with dire consequences in relation to the election. And to anticipate your next question, he is not happy that you have cut him out of the Israeli money. Can I ask you to reconsider that decision?' I asked gingerly.

'What is your honest opinion of your father-in-law?' asked the midget PM. I was being tested again.

'The man is a fiend, sir,' I said unequivocally, but I decided to keep the Vice President's increasing influence over the Armed Forces to myself. The Yadavs did not need to know every secret, and I did not want to be the one responsible for precipitating a constitutional crisis in which the midget PM and General Bastard were at war. They were sure to get to it on their own, in due course.

'Jasjit, I think we need to come up with a plan that brings His Majesty down to earth. He must have more than a few skeletons in his closet. I want you to find them. Will you do that for me?'

When the Prime Minister of India, whoever he might be, asks you in honey-dipped words to join in his scheming, however dastardly the object, only men of the highest moral fibre can find it within themselves to deny him their co-operation. Let's just say I did not disappoint Yadav Senior. Now it was official – Neena's father and I were about to go toe to toe. I was not exactly pleased with how things had turned out but, given General Bastard's attitude towards me, I did feel some sense of comfort in knowing that he was being counter-attacked and that the PM was leading the charge. Another repercussion of the feud was that it had allowed the Yadavs to align their interests more securely than ever with mine.

AFTER MY MEETING with the Prime Minister I went to see Dhillon Uncle. Ever since the story about Shitij's slap had leaked, something that had been nagging me. I couldn't believe that General Bastard, even with the army's help, was so resourceful that he could have spotted – in torrential rain – a violent encounter that had lasted no more than two minutes in its entirety, at a location that no one could have expected to find us beforehand. And we were definitely inaccessible to the media. So it just made sense that either someone accidentally stumbled upon the scene, which I found hard to believe since Karnail Singh on my instructions wasn't allowing anyone near the car, or someone in the car had leaked the information. I didn't think the Defence Secretary, after having his life threatened, was enough of a man to defy the Yadavs in such a blatant manner. That just left my dear old Uncle and I knew that on this he wouldn't lie to me; it wasn't his style.

'Well, if it isn't my partner in crime,' Dhillon Uncle greeted me, answering the door of his ground floor apartment in the wonderfully quaint Sujan Singh Park apartment complex –

though without its prime location it might have easily passed for something closer to a British tenement. It was early evening and, it appeared, the cocktail hour had already begun at the Dhillon residence. Uncle poured me a Patiala peg and we settled down for a serious talk.

'What scheme do you have in mind this time?' he inquired less than enthusiastically.

'I have come not to speak about the future but the recent past, dearest Uncle.'

'Elegantly put.'

'Thank you.'

'What do you want to know?'

'Did you leak the slapping incident?'

'Yes.'

Bingo. If all else failed I could make a living as a private detective. 'May I ask why you did it?'

'I did it because that brat needed to be put in his place. How dare he lay his hands on a man who, despite his shortcomings, has given decades of his life to the service of his country? What has that fat son of a pig done, apart from being born to a powerful father and abusing inherited privileges? And we, may God forgive our greed, got this creature elected as head of the sport that is perhaps the only pleasurable facet of the miserable lives of a vast majority of this country. I couldn't stand for it and I will not apologize for my conduct.'

Dhillon Uncle fixed himself another drink and silence prevailed in the room. I had never understood before how people could be so rich and powerful yet claim to be unhappy. I realized that everyone paid a price for success and made a deal with the devil in order to gain their dreams. The only way I could get out of this mess now was if I was prepared to put it all on the line, every single thing that I cared for, including Neena. I wasn't sure if I had the will to take that road.

Instead, I told Dhillon Uncle about the recently concluded kitchen cabinet meeting. I hated my place in it. 'I need to get out of this racket. The trouble is I'm one of the ringleaders,' I rued, staring at the ice in my glass.

'Your father always saved himself because he stayed in the shadows, you've made the mistake of becoming too high profile over the last month. Forget everybody else, from now on just worry about your own welfare. That's the only way you can survive when the Yadav show comes to an end. You'll be the first target of any succeeding government.'

'What option do I have left?'

'You can go abroad.'

'Unthinkable. There is no way I'm going to give my enemies the pleasure of seeing me flee like a coward. Besides, after living in Delhi like a king I am going to find it very difficult to live anywhere else. And there is Neena to think of.' Actually Neena was the only reason that I was thinking of. She had placed her trust in me once again and I was not about to let her down by bolting from the scene.

'In that case you are only left with the path of survival by confrontation.'

'Which involves what?'

'You wait for this government to reach its tipping point and then make a deal with the Opposition. Give them the ammunition that'll knock out Yadav and gain you a free pass. But the key is to wait patiently until the opportune moment arrives.'

'What you propose is a very political scheme and I don't think my skills go that far. Also, you don't fully understand how inextricably my activities are linked with everything Yadav Incorporated does. If I bring them down, I do myself in as well.'

'Explain that,' he said, placing his drink on the side table and coming to full attention for the first time that evening.

'My name is on more documentation than either of the Yadavs is. It's easier to connect me to the foreign accounts than it is my clients. I do my job extremely well.'

'Then spend some time unearthing a scam the PM has pulled off that doesn't directly connect to you.'

'But which will almost certainly have the fingerprints of my father, and your best friend, all over it.'

'He can handle it, he's dead.'

'Well, I can't.'

'When it came to outfoxing politicians, your father was the master. I've no doubt he would have had some innovative way to help you out,' Dhillon Uncle said admiringly.

'Don't sell yourself short, Uncle. You were masterful over the last month.'

I could tell from his eyes that he was pleased by my compliment. He didn't bother denying his own genius: 'I learnt the tricks of the trade early like you. Did I ever tell you about my stint as a politician?'

'Only in passing.' I settled back in my chair, eager to hear his story.

'My father as you know was a big-time Congress politician in Punjab. He's the one who gave your father his first job in government when he made him his Private Secretary.'

'Father always remembered him with great fondness and often said that if he hadn't died he would have certainly become Chief Minister.'

'Such are the vagaries of fate. Anyhow, I went through a phase, around the time I met your father, of wanting to become a neta. I got myself a cupboard full of kurta-pajamas and everything.' Dhillon Uncle smiled at the memory.

'So what happened?'

'I came to the realization that no matter how hard I tried, I would never get as good as my father; knowledge that helped me decide on finding another field of endeavour for myself where I could be the best without any qualifiers.'

'Too bad no one else thinks that way.'

'They want to take the easy way to the top, not understanding that the easy way doesn't toughen you up enough for the battles you will face when you reach the summit. We can thank Indira Gandhi for this mentality in politics.'

'I would have thought Nehru was to blame,' I said.

'No, Jawaharlal Nehru may have promoted his daughter's career but he never interfered in his succession. Sanjay Gandhi was our republic's first crown prince and the Emergency was a direct result of this undemocratic strain of politics.'

'Nobody talks about the Emergency anymore and all those who were involved with it, seem to have been forgiven – even by those whom they sent to jail for several months.'

'The leaders who went to jail, whose ranks include the PM, owe Indira Gandhi and her cronies a great debt of gratitude – she made them all heroes. Too bad for the Indian people that the heroes were a bunch of crooks. The Emergency was a low point in Indian history but I still have one happy memory from it – you were born right bang in the middle of it.'

How strange, I thought. I had never connected my birth date with the duration of the eighteen-month period of Emergency that India's only empress had thrust upon the country. A giant chunk of my generation had been born during independent India's only tryst with – for lack of a better word – non-democracy. So maybe we had been infected by it in some way. The Emergency had ended not because the people of India had stood up in revolt but because, according to some, Mrs Gandhi came to the deluded conclusion that she could win an election. I suspect she couldn't stand being haunted by her great father's ghost any longer.

The people of India had taken the entire despotic episode in their stride. But who was to say it wouldn't happen again? This time in the form of my father-in-law, a charismatic military dictator who promised to save India from the seeming inertia of democracy?

We had ignored our history and become arrogant about our democracy, throwing it in the face of other democratically-challenged nations to show them how superior we were.

Now, I couldn't help feeling, an appropriate comeuppance awaited us.

Chapter 6

NEENA RETURNED TO India in triumph after charming Southeast Asia with her stylish saris and her in-depth understanding of their culture and art. General Bastard's media blitz made sure news of his tour drowned out anything of substance that the midget PM may have tried to trumpet during the week. The PMO was not pleased about seeing the vice presidential family on the front page of every newspaper for the umpteenth day in a row. The handsome Dayals were becoming superstars and there was nothing the PM or his aides could do about it.

I had my own problems with the idea of Neena's growing aura and it had to do with the paranoia that hit me every time I picked up a newspaper or magazine and was convinced that I would see a lead story that revealed all my secrets to the rest of the world. Time was running out. I was no nearer to resolving my predicament even after my talk with Dhillon Uncle. But I let that problem wait for the moment, since there was a certain young lady who had an amorous engagement to keep with me.

I called Neena the minute she got back, but all the woman wanted to talk about was the exotic capitals she had visited and the leaders she had met. I could not understand what she was hedging about for and let her know it. She got really mad with me for that and it took a lot of cajoling and all my powers of persuasion to gain forgiveness. I did manage it, though, and she finally consented to meet me the next evening – no parties, no media, no security, just the two of us.

To my great annoyance she changed the plan the very next morning and said we had to go to the Home Minister's residence as the neta was throwing himself one heck of a birthday bash. Her father wanted her to attend in his place, as he himself had been left indisposed; a little put out by his recent travels.

General Bastard really knew how to rain on my parade but I did not complain too much as there was nothing that could be done. Besides, these functions tended to end early, which still left the rest of the night for what I had planned.

AS COULD BE expected, the turnout was impressive with everyone of consequence present at the Home Minister's party. The PM with family in tow (sans first-born, luckily for me) was in good nick, playing to the media when we arrived. He could not hide his displeasure though when his audience was distracted by Neena's arrival. I didn't see why he had to give me a dirty look, but such is the caprice of the powerful. The Home Minister, a friendly soul who represented Orissa's predominant regional party, was overjoyed at seeing Neena and he introduced her to everyone within reach, till they were both soon surrounded by an admiring throng. I, fully aware of my relative unimportance, retreated to a safe distance.

The monsoons were over and autumn's moderate weather had started to make an appearance. It was just the right time for a lawn party. This was reflected in the convivial atmosphere. Since it was the Home Minister's private function, alcohol was being served, but it was being imbibed surreptitiously – no one wanted to make a show of their vices, I suppose. Not having to worry about my reputation, I knocked back a couple of stiff Scotches as I avoided the main throng of the get-together and observed the others, Neena in particular, from the outer reaches.

Watching Neena dazzle the people who swamped her, as I quietly sipped my drink under the fairy lights, got me in the mood for thinking – about Neena, my father, her father and myself.

'Once you start a job make sure you finish it, or it'll finish you,' my father had always said to my brother and me when we'd displayed signs of surrender in any sphere of endeavour. I had never doubted the veracity of his statement but sooner or later a man has to make his own rules. And standing there watching Neena I realized my priorities had never been the same as his – as much as I wanted to deny it, my father and I were very different people. I had wanted to emulate him all my life and had been following the path laid out by him. But having Neena by my side was making me realize the price I would have to pay if I stuck in this business.

I felt a weight fall from my shoulders at this sudden flash of insight. I was strangely relieved that at my core I was nothing like my father. Just as Neena, though she played her role of Vice President's dutiful daughter and hostess like a natural, was nothing like her dad.

With this new understanding of myself, I allowed my mind to open up options that I had blocked myself from because of a false sense of loyalty to my sire. But as Dhillon Uncle had said, Father was dead and it was I who had to find a way to survive.

'When you go into a fight with a stronger opponent, make sure the combat is brief and on your terms. That rule of thumb is as relevant to politics as it is to military tactics,' said a familiar voice from behind me, as if on cue, and I turned around.

Karan Nehru was talking on the phone and waving his drink for emphasis with his free hand, the weaker left one. Our eyes met and he gestured for me not to go anywhere. I guessed we were finally going to have that promised chat. He finished up his phone conversation in due course.

'Jasjit, just the man I was looking for,' he said, walking over and putting his overly developed right arm around me, directed my gaze towards where Neena stood, at the party's centre of gravity. 'You're lucky to have hooked that one before her stock hit the roof.'

'Won't argue with you on that.' It was best not to argue with Karan Nehru as a general policy. He said and did as he pleased, not tolerating dissent of any kind from underlings like me.

'I'm jealous of you, you know. And I don't just mean about your wife, I mean your current positioning in the web of power,' Karan revealed.

'Current positioning?'

'There is a big fight about to break out between the two ends of Raisina Hill, and you, my friend, will be able to play both sides against middle. Do you get what I'm saying?'

'I think so.'

'Of course, you do. Hang in there, Sikhu, I'll be in touch,' he said and was gone with another enigmatic wave of his drink, marching into where the thickest mass of white-clothed politicians had congregated, merging into them; and leaving me wanting to know just what a 'Sikhu' was.

I dismissed Karan from my mind and advanced to where Neena stood, encircled by a throng of admiring men. I knew I would have to just step in and claim what was mine; I did so with a touch of ill-humour.

'Is somebody jealous?' Neena teased when we got away from the admiring crowd.

'If I remember right you used to like being rescued.'

'Rescued? I was actually enjoying their attention.'

'I'm sure you were,' I said as I steered her firmly towards the dining area. Now that everyone who wanted to, had met Neena, we were left alone and reached the buffet unmolested.

We served ourselves and found a quiet corner to watch the proceedings and eat in peace.

'Quite a crowd,' I commented.

'Everybody's here,' Neena agreed.

'Each one probably has a closet full of skeletons.'

'I'm sure you know a few of them.'

'A few,' I said, trying to sound suitably self-important.

'Tell some, na. I don't get to hear much gossip anymore.'

I only needed to be asked – gossip was something I thrived on. It probably came from being a private banker working in India where you only had rumours to guide you to the dollar millionaires. I directed Neena's attention towards two men standing at opposite ends of the party, one a powerful PR man and the other an equally powerful and charismatic politician.

'What about them?' Neena asked eagerly. I pointed to a buxom woman spilling out of her sari blouse, who stood in a crowd of male admirers midway between the two men. 'Horrid woman! What *is* she wearing?'

'That woman is responsible for breaking those two men's decades-old friendship, because they are both obsessed with her.'

'I don't understand what they see in her. She isn't even very good looking.'

'With some women looks don't matter,' I said sagely. 'Because they've mastered the art of seduction, by moving, talking and smiling with sex oozing from their pores. Men go for that.'

'What nonsense. Who's that man she's with?'

'Her poor husband, which is a surprise because she's already grown tired of our two Delhi friends and is presently bedding one of those nerdy IT multimillionaires from Bangalore.'

'Where in God's name are all their wives?'

'At home, minding their own business. Don't blame these poor sods, my dear, they come from lower middle-class families and were married off early, never getting a chance to sow their wild oats. Now that they've made it in life, they have the resources to indulge in a late adolescence.'

'At least I can be sure *you* don't have that problem. You've sown enough oats for half the men here.'

'Talking about oats, I hope you're not planning to go home after this?'

'We'll see. Tell me some more stories about these people.'

The bloody woman was messing with me, but I wasn't going to score an own goal this late in the game. So I humoured her: 'You see that tall man with a moustache talking to the Home Minister?'

'I know him. He's Rohit Sareen, the big time lawyer.'

'That gentleman has made his name as a lawyer not from having a superior understanding of the law or being an ace in the courtroom but by corrupting a string of judges across the country to issue verdicts of his choice in exchange for money. Only the Supreme Court, so far as I know, is still immune to his enticements. When a client goes to him he doesn't ask about the merits of the case but asks how much money the client is willing to ante up to win the case. He names a price and the preferred verdict appears like magic – even whose wording some prize judges actually leave to Sareen.' I didn't add that what I hated about him was not his corrupt ways (how could I?) but that he was an amoral opportunist who had, for personal political ambition, used his special brand of law to successfully quash criminal cases against political leaders of all stripes. Whatever you might say about his character, he was certainly effective.

'So the judiciary is corrupt. Big deal,' Neena said, not impressed with my material.

'What exactly is it that you want to hear?' I was getting tired of this game.

'Something kinky and depraved, like the stuff I used to hear *you* were up to,' she grinned cheekily.

'Darling, I can demonstrate my depravity to you first hand.'

'I told you, later. Now come on pick out someone else from the crowd.'

'Very well…the Civil Aviation Minister over there has an arrangement with all the private airlines that in addition to his regular monthly remuneration, they have to take turns providing an air hostess to tend to his libido.'

'Everyone knows that. Tell me something *really* juicy.' Neena as gossip-monger was not something I had experienced before. If nothing else that was one thing we had in common. I looked around for a face that evoked a gossipy memory but most of the interesting crowd had already departed for their next party stop of the evening. So where memory failed, imagination always made for a good substitute:

'Well they say – and you have to understand I have no first-hand knowledge of this – that the Vice President's daughter of our fair land hasn't had sex in so long that she's become a virgin once again, just like Elizabeth the First.'

I got a nice rap at the back of my head with a purse from such an angle that no one else could have noticed the heinous attack on my cranium. 'You're lucky I'm a gentleman or I would give you a good spanking right in front of this lot,' I grabbed Neena's hand.

'You really are a horny toad, aren't you?'

'Your personal horny toad, madam. Shall we go now?'

'Hold on, I want some dessert.'

I tried to talk her out of it but Neena insisted on satiating her other senses first, so we got ourselves a plateful of assorted desserts. My serving was imposed on me despite her knowing I hated anything sweet, because she didn't want to eat alone. And they wonder why married men get fat.

'What were you talking about so seriously with Karan

Nehru?' she asked after sampling every dessert on her plate with visible delight.

'You don't miss anything, do you?'

'He's like you: a hard dog to keep on the porch. You both seemed quite engrossed in conversation.'

'He was predicting that World War Three will soon be launched between your Papa and our PM.'

'Well, Karan Nehru has been visiting our house fairly often this past week.'

'Mischief is afoot for sure.'

We both looked up from our plates at Karan Nehru who stood a short distance away, deep in conversation with a tall lean man whose face was obscured by the crowd. I craned my neck to identify him.

'Oh, that's Azim Khan,' said Neena helpfully. 'Nice guy. I really like his wife, Radha.'

Azim Khan? I felt an inadvertent thrill run down my spine. In the last elections, his party, the India Vikas Party, had won a dozen seats and, though Paresh Yadav was his rival, had supported the current government. Azim's MPs had been allotted important portfolios in the government but Azim himself had stayed out of it, not wanting to be personally tainted by an association with Yadav. Even a rat like me, couldn't help feeling a grudging admiration for him.

Azim Khan was the son of a bureaucrat who had inherited a medium-sized brokerage house from his maternal uncle and had turned it into India's largest private bank. And then the Babri Masjid had been demolished, followed by riots and the Bombay bombings. Shocked and disheartened by these events, he had introspected about what he was doing with his life and had decided to enter politics, with a new party, the India Vikas Party. He had chosen his ancestral home of Aligarh to start his political journey and had used his well-funded foundation as a vehicle to set up educational and medical facilities. He had won the Aligarh Parliamentary seat the same year that his schoolmate and best friend, Karan Nehru, had entered Parliament from Jawaharlal Nehru's old seat of Phulpur. Azim's IVP had grown in strength in the ensuing years and he had managed to wrest the Muslim vote of UP for himself, dominating swathes of political territory in western UP on that basis, though he had tried his best to rise above the tag of being just a Muslim leader.

Azim Khan wasn't charming in the conventional backslapping sense that Karan Nehru was; to most people he seemed cold and aloof, but when he spoke people stopped to listen. He was perhaps the only politician I really admired. Perhaps it was our shared background in banking that subconsciously attracted me to him. It was truly tragic that he would never become Prime Minister because of his last name. 'I want you to introduce me,' I said to Neena, like the giddy fan of a teen idol. I had never met him and I suspected he would not approve of my occupation but I didn't care.

'Why?' She eyed me suspiciously.

'Well, you know…' I could not quite put my enthusiasm into words.

'Fine, but if that lecherous creep Karan starts drooling over me, I'm going to blame you, not him.'

Karan Nehru's blatant womanizing was part of the legend of the man, but that was another story. I dragged Neena towards Khan and Nehru. They were both in their early forties, Khan considerably the taller of the two, but Nehru the stockier. The iceberg and the volcano.

'Neena, you look simply radiant,' Karan Nehru, true to type, began the verbal intercourse when we were still more than ten feet away. Neena introduced me to Azim Khan and then found herself pinned to the wall by Karan's agenda. I was a bit tongue-tied in Azim's presence; Khan's imperial demeanour did not invite familiarity. He peered down at me, his hooded eyes sizing me up. His eyes were as dark as his hair.

I let the silence linger.

'Jasjit, I have to confess I'm not an admirer of yours,' he finally said.

'That's too bad, because I admire you greatly.'

I was rewarded by just the barest wisp of a smile, 'Well, I suppose some would call that common ground,' Azim began – when Neena abruptly ended my brief encounter with Mr Khan by grabbing my hand and pulling me away with a hastily muttered excuse.

'*Now* let's get some of that dessert you have been clamouring for all evening,' she said, grinning wickedly at me as we walked off. It took me a second to understand to what she was cryptically referring, but enlightenment did come, and it was divine.

When I woke up the next morning, after a wonderful night whose details were much too personal to share, Neena had already left. She'd slipped out early because her Nazi of a father demanded her presence at the breakfast table every morning. By now we had become brazen enough about our relationship not to feel the need to hide our actions from him, so her official car and security had followed us to Jor Bagh, and she had zoomed back home in style. I lay in bed thinking about her and the party and then of Azim Khan's demeanour, his natural authority, the respect I could not help feel for him, and his disapproval of my craft.

A COUPLE OF nights after the Home Minister's lawn party, I was summoned to the midget PM's nephew's farmhouse. Ganesh Yadav's house was located in one of the many border villages of South Delhi, where the stakeholders of power live like modern-day nobility, in sprawling houses that have nothing whatsoever to do with farming. Perhaps this is also the reason why many of these farmhouses are illegal constructions – and built like mini-palaces.

Ganesh Yadav's recently-purchased house (that everyone knew had been paid for by his uncle the PM) was a monstrous Gothic entity with the architect having paid too much attention to size and scale and too little to aesthetics. As far as I could tell, the house had at least twenty rooms.

No reason for being summoned there was given to me, other than a warning that I should not tell anyone where I was headed. When I arrived, I was ushered into a gigantic room that reeked of sweat and betel leaf. It was past nine in the evening but the room was filled with men, some of whom I recognized as the Prime Minister's key political deputies. Shitij sat beside his father on an ornate sofa as the PM addressed the gathering. The room, it turned out, served as the midget PM's durbar. My eyes were smarting from the fumes of paan and body odour but I was rescued from terminal discomfiture by Sanjay Kumar, the only sensible fellow in the fawning political coterie that surrounded Yadav Senior.

'How are you, Jasjitji? Can you follow me outside? The PM has asked me to give you some instructions.'

I happily did as he said – anything to get out of the malodorous environment of the political durbar.

Kumar had been a big help in the run-up to the BCCI election, conveying the PM's wishes to the right quarters, and we got along reasonably well but he had always kept me at a professional distance. At first sight there was nothing particularly remarkable about the man. He was in his late forties and looked like any average working man on the street, attire to match. But everything changed when he turned his gaze on you. He set upon you with an acuity and intensity that felt like he was reading your thoughts. Sanjay did not give the impression of a man who forgot or forgave very easily. He had risen in the ranks the hard way – making use of his organization skills and loyalty to Paresh Yadav. Definitely a doer.

The two of us exited the house and made our way across the lawns to one end of the property where a two-storeyed structure stood. 'The garage,' Kumar announced.

I looked around. It might have *once* functioned as a garage but there was no evidence that this was still the case. I didn't see any cars. What I did see was a lot of security, in the form of men in safari suits holding walkie-talkies.

Kumar smiled, guessing my thoughts. 'But, as you must have surmised by now, we are using this building for another, far more important purpose.'

Even my vivid imagination could not prepare me for what I saw in the basement of this converted garage. We took a very posh lift down into what seemed like a long corridor. Walking wordlessly through to the end we came to a door manned by security personnel who buzzed us through. Once inside we were confronted by another door made of reinforced steel with an intimidating locking mechanism that I couldn't make head or tail of. I noticed the security chaps had not followed us into the area between the two doors.

'Can I ask you to turn your back? This is a standard security procedure we follow. You'll understand why soon enough.'

I turned away. Clicking sounds preceded the sound of a heavy door clanging open. Kumar gave me a little nudge and I turned around – and gasped! It was a vault the size of a largeish apartment with an extremely high ceiling, and it was stacked from top to bottom with bundles of money! Veritable skyscrapers of notes of all possible denominations! A shrine for the devotees of capitalism! I stood dumbstruck, in awed stupor.

'This, my friend, is our party's treasury, amassed over many years. Of course, it has scaled new heights in the last few months of government. Quite a sight, hain?' Sanjay searched my face for a reaction.

'I'm totally speechless,' I admitted, reaching out to touch the money to assure myself I wasn't dreaming.

I wasn't.

There was no way I could begin to ascertain how much money the room held, and that was good because a number would have ruined the effect of endless, incalculable wealth that the vault exuded. There was enough moolah here to swim in. Even a diehard Marxist would forget his idealism at the sight of all that money. And then I stopped short, acutely aware that another Yadav secret had been disclosed to me, and of the dangers that were inherent with this knowledge – the more I was privy to their dirty secrets, the tighter was the Yadavs' grip on me.

'The PM thought it would be a good idea to show you how the system worked, in case you needed to stand in for your father at some point. Also, we need money for Shitij's upcoming by-election campaign tour,' Sanjay said reading my thoughts once again. 'Push those trunks over here, will you.'

Three large trunks lay ready for us to fill and I was more than happy to assist. The feel of fistfuls of cash made me forget my worries for a little while. The vault smelt of money – its familiar, musty yet exhilarating smell pervading the entire space. We stacked the trunks with wads of cash and then dragged them out, one by one, through the outer door.

Once we'd lugged the trunks out, the security men took over the grunt work. We took the lift back up and were soon out under the night sky again. We returned to the main house with me in a very distracted state. *Had it only been a half hour ago that I had walked past here oblivious of the obscene wealth that lay below my feet?* The durbar was still in session so Kumar took me to a nearby den with a bar. Without asking, he poured me a stiff drink.

'Do those men guarding the vault know what is in it?' I managed to ask after a couple of sips.

'No, but I'm sure they have suspicions. Good salaries and fear keeps them from being too curious. They have been specially chosen for this job from the army and police so we've done a thorough check on their backgrounds.'

'I don't think I'll ever be the same again after seeing this place. Money to a banker is like sugar to a diabetic, I'm lucky I didn't drop dead of an OD right there.'

'Thank God you didn't because that would have been hard to explain,' Kumar laughed in a sinister sort of way.

'Did you put in that vault area after purchasing the property?'

'The previous owner, a former Cabinet Minister who shall stay nameless, had built the basement area for his loot but we added the vault and security arrangements.'

There was precious little risk as long as Yadav Senior was PM. What government agency in its right mind would dare raid it? Once he left office I suspected the vault would be put out of commission in a very rapid manner. Only power bought silence.

And that was the end of my evening excursion.

I had now been shown things that officially made me a part of Paresh Yadav's inner circle. They had pulled me into a clinch. There was no escaping now. Not, at least, till the equations of power had been reset.

A FORTNIGHT AFTER my monetary excursion, the marauding Australian cricket team began its tour of India with a test match in dear old Delhi. I promptly took advantage of my recent ascension into the ranks of cricket bosses to get myself a comfortable seat in the President's box at Delhi's Ferozshah Kotla cricket stadium. Thankfully, Shitij was missing from the scene as the PM had barred him from all cricket-related activities, not wanting to reignite the Slapgate controversy that had followed the BCCI election and then been smothered with great effort. Besides, Dhillon Uncle was de facto President of the cricket board now; having taken full tactical advantage of a situation he had helped create. I looked around but he wasn't to be found in the box either. The old rogue had probably started early on a liquid lunch. Sitting in my vantage position I was thoroughly engrossed in the game. The crowd around me was going wild. The reason for the screams of the twenty-thousand-strong crowd was the arrival on the pitch of the man who was referred to as the Little Master.

The Australians had succeeded in dismissing the two opening batsmen for a measly score. Any sorrow or sympathy that the partisan crowd, or I, had for the departing batsmen was quickly forgotten at the sight of our beloved hero.

He probably heard none of the noise; he seemed already deep in his cocoon of concentration. He walked to the pitch flexing and stretching his arms and chest, and shooting his customary upward glances at the sun to accustom his eyes to the light. Everyone seemed to be getting their money's worth (or at least, those poor souls who, unlike me, had paid to watch the game) as the maestro looked in especially good nick. The first ball he received was short of a length; he rocked onto his back foot and short-arm pulled it to the square-leg boundary. The crowd roared.

I could never find the words to adequately convey to a non-believer how much joy the little man had provided not just to me, but to millions of cricket-lovers across the world. The most exclusive club of sporting giants contained individuals who had a super-human will that did not allow for failure or quitting. The non-believers – those simpletons – just could not grasp this triumph of the human spirit, and I pitied them for it.

I could track most of my adult life by our hero's most famous innings. The man was a living God and I was more than willing to pay obeisance at his altar. I remembered the first time I had heard of him, two decades ago, when Father and I had laughed upon reading about the selection of the baby-faced, sixteen-year-old for the tour to Pakistan in the newspaper; the common opinion was that the precocious tyke would be cannon fodder for the best bowling attack in the world. That was the first and last time either of us doubted the *wunderkind*.

The reminiscing was literally flogged out of my mind when an over-pitched delivery was punch-driven straight down the ground. It was my favourite shot to watch, and the Little Master too seemed to enjoy it, holding his restricted follow through till the ball finished its quick trip to the boundary. It was a shot that exemplified the ease of execution that only great athletes seemed blessed with; an animalistic instinct that allowed them the all-important split-second of anticipation.

I was watching the match from the second row of the President's box and so I didn't immediately notice an unmistakable presence at the other end of the enclosure. Azim Khan was sitting nervously in a far corner, completely absorbed in watching every move made on the cricket field. I stopped a passing flunky and learned from him that Azim had asked the board officials not to announce his presence on their PA system and to keep TV cameras trained as far away from him as possible. No one had dared disturb him since his arrival because he had adopted his most frigid demeanour – a most effective deterrent I noticed – towards intruders. He was obviously here, like me, to see greatness at work and did not wish to socialize with any of those idle, chit-chatting, cocktail-circuit bubbleheads who sidled up hoping to exchange some trivial banter. I could sympathize. How could anyone be anything but completely engrossed in the game, when the Little Master was batting? Did they simply not understand?

I decided to leave him be and returned to my vigil. Like everyone else in the crowd I was enraptured. I felt as if the tremendous batting display was being put on for my sole benefit. And so it was a moment or two before I noticed that everyone in the box was staring at me. Mr Khan had seen me and was waving me over, inviting me to sit with him in his sequestered spot. I was thrilled by his invitation, and joined him readily.

'Since you're the only other person in this glorified cubicle who is actually watching the match I thought I'd send for you,' explained Azim Khan. I voiced my appreciation and, as in our previous meeting, let him control the pace of the conversation. I expected him to return to his former silence but he began to speak, of his love for cricket and, in particular, his obsession with the Little Master. An obsession that left mine in the dust. Cricket was perhaps the only thing this modern prince had in common with me or his voters.

Azim began telling me about this nagging superstition he had – his only one – that held him back from floating up into a cloud of unrestrained pleasure when watching the Indian cricket team in action. It seems a dastardly jinx hovered over Mr Khan at cricket stadiums, and had reached a mythical status among his family and friends. His wife Radha believed that if Azim were ever convinced to set aside his reservations about meeting an astrologer, he would not enquire about his political future, but instead would ask for a way of ridding himself of this sporting pox. The jinx was simple: in all the cricket matches that Azim had watched in person at various stadiums across the country and the world over the years, the Little Master had failed to score more than twenty runs. Or at least Azim remembered it that way.

I had to admit those were pretty lousy results from a man whose prodigious hunger for runs meant that he scored at least a fifty every second or third innings.

This time, Azim said, he did not dare wish for a hundred, fearing that the Gods might punish his greed.

We were jarred out of our cricket-induced trance when Azim received an unwelcome thump on the back. The identity of the culprit did not require much speculation on Azim's part; there was only one man alive, who would dare be so familiar with him in a public setting.

'Sorry, did that hurt?' asked Karan innocently, not because he was truly apologetic but because the noise that had emanated from his salutation had got the attention of everyone in the box. Azim assured him, quite civilly (for the consumption of the bemused onlookers), that no permanent damage had been done, though I had no doubt that he would curse him later, when they were alone.

'I see the champ is still batting. Has he made twenty yet?'

'No, he's five short.'

'Don't worry, dost, I'm sure today is the day that you overcome your curse,' said Karan, as if confident that his own influence stretched that far. 'In fact, I'm willing to bet on it. How about it, Jasjit?' Karan settled himself in the seat next to me.

'Not a betting man, I'm afraid,' I replied.

'Why would you be?' Karan said sarcastically and giggled to himself.

'What are you so jolly about?' Azim gave Karan a curious glance, before reverting to his locked-in visual fix of the cricket.

'Pooja's forgiven me,' pronounced Nehru, referring to his long-suffering spouse.

'I didn't know you were in the doghouse again,' replied Azim. I noticed that Mr Khan was more chatty and gossipy with his friend around.

Karan looked around to make sure that nobody was close enough to overhear them. Unfortunately, he caught the eye of an Indian cricket board grandee. That was all the encouragement the man needed to approach Karan and it was a few minutes before Karan returned, after fending off an insistent invitation for lunch. He found the coast clear as the box had emptied, with everybody headed towards the lunch buffet. Personally, I have trouble understanding how food can be more important than watching cricket, even if it now consisted only of defensive prods and pushes, as the batsmen did not want to make a mistake in the couple of overs left till the lunch break.

'She hasn't been talking to me since – ' Karan resumed talking then suddenly noticed I was still present, trying my best to give the cricket my fullest attention but unable to do so. 'Jasjit, you repeat this anywhere and there will be trouble. You get it?'

I assured him that I understood the dangers of gossiping about him, though I'm not sure why he did not tell me to beat it and be gone. I suppose it never occurred to him that I would disobey his directions to keep shut.

'My ass of a brother-in-law, Rajat, keeps telling her about my extra-curricular activities,' complained Karan. Everyone knew that Karan the politician was the creation of his late father-in-law Pankaj Mishra who had seen a Kargil war hero with the surname of Nehru and realized he had struck political gold. Unfortunately, this had caused dissension in his family, and his son Rajat Mishra, a Congress MP himself, vented his frustration by constantly trying to make Karan's life miserable within the homestead. Not that Karan helped his cause by philandering without limit. I had seen enough of it with my own eyes to know the brazen risks he took. Karan would have liked nothing better than to squash his brother-in-law but Pooja Nehru had forbidden any retaliation and so Mr Nehru had to grin and bear it.

Azim and my curiosity of Karan Nehru's marital travails had got the better of our interest in the cricket; where, truth be told, the players seemed to be now paying more attention to their lunch menu than the game. The Little Master's total had inched past the twenty mark and Azim found himself able to communicate civilly to one and all again.

'How did you make Pooja come around this time?' Azim's concentration shifted completely to Karan's tale of woe.

'Well, it wasn't easy, especially after her suspicious feminine mind went to work – goaded by insinuations from your dear wife, I might add. Ridiculous! It took some time but she finally came to her senses after I made her see reason.' Karan laughed triumphantly, stretching his feet on the seat in front and folding his arms behind his head. He looked to me like a man completely free of any worries or an oppressive guilty conscience. Which was why, I suppose, Azim could not control his wicked streak; the target was too tempting: 'What you mean to say is Pooja found out the truth and, as usual, you lied your way out of jail,' he said.

Azim's moment of one-upmanship only lasted a second as his smile froze on hearing a loud gasp of agony from the crowd. On the last ball of the last over before lunch, a part-time bowler had been put on and he had bowled a juicy half-volley to the Little Master; his carnivorous instincts had taken over and, unable to resist, he had tried to thump the bowler out of the ground. The ball had, unfortunately, hit a rough patch on the pitch and turned more than expected, hitting the inside edge of his bat and then crashing into the wickets.

Azim was inconsolable, much to Karan's delight who was relieved from the pressure of finding a worthy comeback to his friend's barb. 'Serves you right. If you can take anything away from this incident, Jasjit, it is that fate favours only the superior of the species,' Karan said gleefully.

'Oh, shut up, you ass!' muttered Azim and left the President's box with Karan's mirth-filled comments ringing in his ears. The loud-speaker announced with suitable gloom, '... clean bowled for a score of twenty-two.'

But, minutes later, Azim returned, phone in hand. Not looking peeved any more – but aghast. I could tell from the grim expression on his face that the change had nothing to do with cricket.

His news stunned us all:

'I've just heard that the President has resigned. Vice President Dayal has taken charge in his place,' said Azim and looked at me.

Karan let out a whoop of triumph.

My head began to swirl with all kinds of emotions that I could not identify because I was in utter shock.

General Bastard was now not only our first citizen but also the Supreme Commander of the Indian Armed Forces!

God save us all.

PRESIDENT'S RULE

Chapter 7

A JOLT OF electricity surged through the body politic of India. All calculations and assumptions valid a day before were now worthless. To put it simply, we were in a new world with new rules. Never before had an Indian General – particularly a former army chief – ascended to the country's highest constitutional post. Even Sam Manekshaw – the army chief who had orchestrated India's famous victory in the 1971 war and whose popularity had outshone even the mighty Indira Gandhi's – had had to satisfy himself with the toothless glory of a field marshal's baton and ceremonial five-stars. Daddy Dayal had trumped all his predecessors in one fell swoop. The thought of now referring to the villain as *President* Dayal, even temporarily, turned my stomach.

The entire civilian establishment – Karan Nehru apart – was in full-scale panic mode, the spectre of a strongman haunting their sleep. The Armed Forces were conspicuously restrained, not wanting to lend credence to the conspiracy theories already doing the rounds, but the officer corps must have obviously felt triumphant and vindicated, after enduring years of unwarranted and oppressive suspicion at the hands of civilians whom they considered, perhaps rightfully, beneath contempt.

The question remained as to how Dayal had swung such a political stratagem. I had little doubt in my mind that the sudden resignation of the President was no coincidence. The customary equanimity of the PM was shattered; he was not the best of company in the days following my father-in-law's taking possession of the entirety of Rashtrapati Bhavan, having already made himself serenely comfortable on the sprawling grounds of the estate many months in advance, almost as if he knew what fate had lined up for him. The newly renovated Vice President's house on Maulana Azad Road would sit forlorn and unoccupied for the near future. A nincompoop friend of mine actually thought it would be a marvellous idea if I made use of the vacant premises in the interregnum for parties and other such revelry.

Yeah, like *that* would ever happen.

It was not entirely clear that Dayal needed to be sworn in, since he would only be officiating as President until an election was held. But General Bastard being who he was insisted on a full-fledged swearing-in ceremony and that is what he got. Even Paresh Yadav held his nose and attended the event because he feared his absence would make his rift with the President public.

The media lapped up the spectacle and the Dayals dished out a performance that British royalty would have been proud of. Neena had never looked more beautiful and more gracious; General Dayal never more aristocratic. Even my mother-in-law, the frail Mrs Dayal, who came down from the hills to see her husband take the oath of office, bore herself with tragic elegance. It was my task to shepherd the poor dear around. You could not help but notice the sadness that loomed upon her visage, as if life had dealt her more than she had been able to cope with, particularly in the form of her marriage. I had always liked her and got along with her well enough. They said she had looked like Neena in her younger days, though without my wife's vivacity. Neena, evidently, got that from the other side of the family.

Mrs Dayal and I – the ignored members of the first family – exchanged polite conversation during the oath-taking ceremony. She seemed somewhere far away to me, not quite aware of what she was observing, almost as if she were in a trance. Maybe she had it right; maybe it was all a figment of our combined imaginations because recent events were too bizarre to resemble any reality that one had known till this point. Once the ceremony was over, the first lady was shunted back to the Dehradun estate, leaving Neena to take up the duties of presidential hostess.

The resignation of our President, a wily native of the great state of Kerala, was particularly curious because he only had six months left to serve of his term. There had been no warning to his act and he gave no real reason for it other than to say – in his only public statement – that he felt his age and failing health made him incapable of carrying on with the onerous responsibilities that accompanied the Presidency. In so doing, he became the only Indian politician to ever retire from elected office without actually being wheeled out in a hearse, Pandit Nehru onwards. Nor did the act fit in with the Malayali politician's previous, morally-chequered career.

My name returned to the shores of media interest as son-in-law to a President who, even I had to admit, walked and talked in a way that seemed appropriate to the grandeur of his office. Though I did not appreciate being compared to Pandit Nehru's forgotten son-in-law, Feroze, who was muscled out of his marriage to Indira Gandhi by a possessive father-in-law. It hurt because I knew there was much truth in the comparison.

THE MIDGET PM started damage control exercises once he had made peace with the thought of a President Dayal, by pressuring the Election Commission to announce an immediate presidential election. The three wise men of the Election Commission, each appointed by a different political entity, came to three different conclusions and became deadlocked. All they managed to agree on was to cut the time to elections somewhat and to hold presidential elections in four months' time. Basically, nobody got their way.

The Prime Minister would have liked having the election there and then because he did not want to risk Dayal gaining such a critical mass of public goodwill that no party would then be able to oppose him without risking public anger. The President would have liked to gain stature in a leisurely six months, instead of the more rushed schedule that had now been laid out. Unlike the vice presidential election, where the electorate comprised just the members of Parliament, the electorate of the presidential election would also include every member of every state legislature in the country, making it one right royal mess. The value of each member's vote was calculated through a system that involved proportional representation and a lot of number-crunching that was beyond me to understand or explain. Suffice it to say, even more so than the vice presidential election, no one party or alliance had anywhere near the majority needed to have its personal favourite candidate elected.

The circumstances were perfectly suited for strife and corruption, and, more precisely, for General Bastard.

A MONTH AFTER the swearing-in ceremony, I received a call from a character who had not been in my thoughts for a very long time. Mohan Patel, the reigning emperor of the Empire Oil conglomerate, wanted to have lunch with me. I had met him several times in the company of my father. Since he was normally interesting, if not always edifying, company I went over to Taj Mansingh Hotel at the agreed-upon time. The venue was the top-floor Chambers club, the Taj's exclusive and super-efficient entertainment area, where you could also survey Delhi on either side of the building for as far as the eye could see. The Taj was one of the very few high-rise buildings in the heart of Lutyens' Delhi. It allowed an unobstructed view of the capital to the high and mighty, like Patel. From that height Delhi was expectedly dense and vast but surprisingly green as well.

I was shown to where Patel had set up base in the drinks lounge. Chambers was having a slow day but I still saw a few familiar faces and waved to them. Luckily, the hall was large enough to ensure a reasonably private conversation.

Mohan Patel was chomping on the mixed nuts with such ferocity that the bowl in which they were contained looked like it too was in danger of being ingested. If the oily, overweight proprietor of a neighbourhood ration or sweetmeat shop were pulled out of his environment and dressed in the best that Savile Row could provide, without the accompanying gentile breeding, I think the result would be as close a likeness of my father's favourite interlocutor as I can conjure. His cunning and his business ingenuity, however, were one of a kind and bore no comparison.

No man had prospered more in conjunction with Father's services than Mohan Patel, who had taken a shady inheritance, involving smuggling and illicit liquor production at its heart, and from it constructed Empire Oil, the company best known for having the largest privately-owned retail chain for petroleum products, particularly petrol pumps, in the country. It was his dream to add a series of refineries to his kingdom, but he had not as yet succeeded there. Father's death must have been a setback to fulfilling those ambitions. He seemed genuine in his condolences, or at least, I suppose, as genuine as he could be. I assumed he wanted to discuss his expansion plans with me, but I was in for a giant surprise.

'So, the other day I went for a walk and on the way home I decided to buy myself a President.' Mohan Patel made this innocuous little announcement cramming nut after nut into his mouth and staring calmly out into the horizon of South Delhi. I looked around quickly and was reassured to find that we continued to have a buffer of privacy. I didn't want prying ears to catch my companion's scandalous revelations.

'Tell me you're joking,' I responded.

'You didn't *really* think this political earthquake took place without someone oiling the machinery with rupee-notes, did you?' Patel belched and then signalled to the waiter as he got unsteadily to his feet. We made our way half a floor down and across to the other end where the dining area was situated. The side-on view that now awaited us was that of Raj Path from India Gate to Raisina Hill, in all its regal glory. A more fitting backdrop could not have been provided for Patel's tale, I thought.

Patel and I sat down at a comfortably secluded table and quickly placed our order. I never care to over order. I eat little and what is familiar, and the fish was good enough. I believe that like one's food, power should be savoured; gluttony is for the seemingly wealthy but power-deficient. Patel was the exception to that rule, since he ordered enough food for a small army and had enough of the establishment in his pocket to get most of his interests taken care of – at least for now.

'It all started with your father's helicopter accident. We had made plans, plans that had been paid for, and Sidhu sahib as usual was executing each phase to perfection. But when he died, all hell broke loose. More money was demanded. I gave them the benefit of the doubt once. Even when the promises were replaced with excuses I did not react. I am a businessman, after all, and the Prime Minister is the Prime Minister. But to threaten to start using the machinery of State against my interests unless I paid up, that was really too much. We businessmen understand how this country works, the politicians need funds and we are happy to be providers as long as our interests are taken care of in a relatively systematic manner. We understand when a genuine problem or delay takes place, that is life, but what we have going on now is complete chaos.'

Patel bit into his breadstick with vigour. I did not interrupt him. I had heard similar frustration with the Yadav Government being aired by many industrialists since my return to India, and from the poor wretch Dinesh Parmar on my working visit to Dubai. However, I had not realized how far the frustration had forced Patel and his colleagues to go. The waiter returned with the soup; onion I think it was, and not bad. Patel continued:

'There have been two elections in close succession, both of which we were expected to bankroll at a steep cost with the capital resources of our industrial houses. And then we get this government of thieves and scoundrels, with the BJP and Congress so punch-drunk that they sit dazed in the Opposition while each minister is king of his domain, opening up an auction stall and letting his moneymen pick the highest bidder. Just go downstairs, you can tell the cabinet portfolio of the moneymen according to which restaurant or bar they sit in, and the same goes for every nook and cranny of the Oberoi and Maurya. They're all over the place, like vultures, tearing at our carcass. Other small countries may be run like this and may even prosper, but this cannot happen in India. It is too much. Jasjit, you know, I'm no saint, but I cannot do business in this kind of atmosphere where you don't know who is going to hold up and at what price. Not to mention that their incompetence has brought the economy to a screeching halt. Industry is being squeezed from both ends.' A buttered bread roll disappeared whole into the Patel gullet.

'Let me guess. So this is when my father-in-law appeared on the scene, a saviour providing the path to paradise?'

'He didn't make the initial approach, but you get the *general* idea,' he laughed, his mouth full of bread, at his own pun; a hideous sight. 'I called up the double-crossing Malayali President of ours and we reached a deal on how much it was worth for him to sacrifice six months in office. The Mallu shitbag asked for the sky and we paid it to him without bargaining, all in cash. God knows where he's going to hide it. He did ask for some of the money to be transferred abroad to his grandson in Dubai. Whatever the amount, it was cheaper than getting the Congress and BJP to bring this government down before bankrolling another election. India's captains of industry need order now and we are willing to give Dayal a free hand to fulfil our wishes. What do we have to lose?'

His question was rhetorical but I doubt he could possibly comprehend the repercussions of what he and his fellow billionaires had inadvertently done. They had opened the door to a problem so big that they would reminisce about the days of the Paresh Yadav premiership.

'So you bunch of rich fuckers basically bought and sold India's democracy without a moment's thought for anything but your own bottomline? Bravo, bahut accha.' I did not mean to sound that livid, but after hearing what I had it was impossible to keep my emotions bottled in.

'Come off it, Jasjit, the way you talk somebody might very well mistake you for an idealist or a paragon of moral purity. You are no one to judge me or anybody else. You're down in the gutter with me and everyone else, where we do what it takes to survive. You do know I hope, or have you forgotten what Sidhu sahib was up to all these years? His life's work, my boy, a beautiful thing,' Patel smirked.

Patel was correct to a certain extent, at least in terms of Father bending and using the system to enrich himself and his clientele, but his activities had always been within the system, never a threat to it. What was taking place now was a whole -scale remaking of the structure and traditions of how modern

India governed itself. I was not so far gone that I did not realize that prospect.

The waiter brought my fish in white sauce. It smelt delightful. I had, however, lost my appetite. Patel had ordered some greasy lamb chops, a selection repugnantly unsubtle like himself, and he attacked it rapaciously. Patel never made a move without the chance of it benefiting him in the end. Watching him stuff his face I said, 'I'm pretty sure you want something of me, because otherwise you wouldn't have confessed your dirty deeds to me today, when you know very well I can't stand the sight of the President and vice-versa.'

'I want you to talk to the PM. We have our dog, Dayal, by the collar. If the PM sees reason and accommodates us we will be willing to step back from the brink and roll it all back. Tell Yadav what I told you, I think you'll find he's receptive.'

I would have loved to see my father-in-law's face if he had heard Patel comparing him to a canine. But the rules of nature meant that men like Patel were not capable of looking into the eyes of men like Dayal. I may have hated Dayal, but a fact was a fact.

'You're absolutely right, the PM will be very reasonable now. But there's no point in his dealing with you about the President's future actions.' I rose from my chair, leaving my fish untouched.

'I'd like to hear why you believe that, young man?' Patel looked up from his plate.

'You see, Mr Patel, you are correct in saying that you hold a dog's collar in your hands, but unfortunately the dog, a heck of a beast, has bolted and is long gone. You idiots have opened Pandora's Box and there are no heroes on hand to slam it shut again. Congratulations and enjoy the rest of the afternoon stuffing your face, you repulsive ass!' I threw my napkin on the table for dramatic effect and left in a huff, without stopping to catch Patel's reaction.

My last words were said loud enough for the other tables to catch them, as I had intended.

You look for self-respect wherever you can find it – especially in times when it is in short supply.

Chapter 8

A FEW WEEKS after the new President took charge, the PMO received word that President Dayal had refused to sign off on the PM's choice for our ambassadors to Washington, DC and Riyadh as he believed them both unsuitable. The worthies proposed for these prestigious posts were political appointees from the PM's party, disagreeable choices to be sure, but well within Yadav's right to choose. Crass political patronage was at work in the times we lived in; it was to be expected that a PM would think about his personal interest before that of the nation's.

The truth was that I was not sure I disagreed with the President's opinion. The PM's choice, for the American assignment in particular, was what we call a history-sheeter, the star protagonist in a series of ongoing criminal cases that included charges of murder, rape and armed robbery. I had met the man on a couple of occasions and though he was far more civilized than the cow belt goon type of personality I had expected to encounter, I still shuddered to think what people would think of India in Washington, DC if he ever reached there. Had anyone else been President, I would have publicly lauded Rashtrapati Bhavan's stand on the appointment. However, I knew the President had only rejected the ambassadorial choices out of spite and as the opening salvo in a battle of wills that had not become public so far.

The Law Ministry argued that the issue was whether or not the President had the right to decline the head of government's choice for ambassador, which they believed he did not. They said the President had to honour the Constitution that had accorded him only the status of a nominal head of state. This was all good and very lawyerly of them but what was correct, constitutionally speaking, did not necessarily make it politically enforceable.

The PM knew he was on a sticky wicket when it came to the issue of his ambassadorial pick and he decided not to make a big deal of it. That was easy for him to do when the presidential veto was hidden within the boundary of Raisina Hill but it soon became a public slap to his face. The presidential press office began gleefully leaking the news, and saying that the President would enforce his authority regardless of how short his tenure ended up being.

The media, as is their wont, lapped it up – after all it had been a long while since there had been such direct friction between South Block and Rashtrapati Bhavan, and it was a first during the age of the twenty-four hour news cycle. The PM barrelled through it with an outward show of great restraint, but the action plan to retaliate, already in place from before, was put into high gear with my role in it growing by the hour.

OVER THE NEXT week, all anyone in the country could talk about was how General Bastard had done the right thing by teaching the PM a lesson. This obviously only agitated the PM further. In private, he began to demand vengeance in more harsh language. I never got around to telling Yadav Senior or anyone else about my eventful lunch with Mohan Patel and his role in the making of President Dayal; it seemed pointless to discuss the reasons why a natural disaster had happened when we were still trying to survive its after-effects.

Retaliation did begin finally, and, as is the case with all memorable ego tussles, pettiness abounded. The Government informed the Rashtrapati Bhavan that a heightened terror threat posed to the President meant that he could not travel outside of Delhi, not even domestically. The high-flying President was brought down to earth. Neena told me that some more crockery had met its end when her father was informed of his newly grounded status.

Rashtrapati Bhavan rejoindered by going to battle stations.

The President had acted very swiftly to acquire the suitable manpower for his office, indeed it was almost as if he had acted *before* his predecessor's resignation. Dayal had called up the army chief and asked that Major General Madan Januha, the number two man at the Defence Intelligence Agency, be appointed to fill the vacant post of Military Secretary to the President.

The Defence Ministry had cleared the request, as at that early point any knowledge of the differences between the PM and President had been restricted to those few of us in the know. Later, when hostilities of a more public nature began, this move met with considerable interest from the media as well as the PMO because, though the position of presidential Military Secretary was a cushy one, it was normally assigned to major generals with plateaued careers and not to officers like Madan Januha on the fast track to senior command positions.

Januha was barely a month away from gaining the rank of lieutenant-general. Everyone expected him to be appointed to head a major field assignment, a corps command in all probability. Later, it transpired that the army chief, taking into account Januha's seniority and command prospects, had given him the option of refusing the presidential posting but Januha had insisted on serving under the President. Januha was a warrior and warriors weren't known to give up a chance to command a corps of fighting men for the tedious ceremony and protocol of a Rashtrapati Bhavan assignment. Something was definitely afoot.

It was clear from the start that Januha was not going to be a regular Military Secretary. He received the office and powers of the Secretary to the President, thereby sidelining the senior bureaucrat at Rashtrapati Bhavan, who proceeded on leave and was not missed. Januha had an impressive track record as a commander in the field and was known for his no-nonsense approach and intimidating demeanour – behind his back his subordinates had nicknamed him 'the bulldog'. It was said that when Januha had been in command of a Special Forces battalion, years ago, he had personally led raiding parties across the Line of Control in Kashmir to neutralize terrorists trying to infiltrate and had, with his own hands, executed more than a few of them. As a soldier he was the exact opposite of General Bastard and that is perhaps why they got along so well, nicely complementing one another.

Dayal had saved Januha from enduring a premature end to his army career after almost beating a soldier to death for molesting a local girl in Assam. The bulldog had never forgotten the favour that Dayal had done him and he had proclaimed his undying loyalty to his benefactor. General Bastard certainly knew how to accumulate a team of fanatical followers or maybe the price you paid for making him get off his high horse to help you was your soul.

More recently, Januha, as the Deputy Director-General of the tri-services Defence Intelligence Agency, was said to have used military resources to accumulate files on some leading politicians and bureaucrats at the President's behest. If those files existed you could be sure that they had accompanied Januha to his new post. The ball was in the President's court and everyone was speculating on what his next move would be, especially now that he had brought Rashtrapati Bhavan under military rule.

A phoney war was initiated between the warring parties. This stretched on till the end of September. Both sides remained officially silent but allowed their opinions to be known through the subterfuge of media leaks. Not a day went by without either the PMO or the Rashtrapati Bhavan trying to don the role of the aggrieved party in an attempt to win public sympathy for their cause. The Opposition parties, when anybody paid them any heed, blamed Yadav of criminal nepotism and the President of overreaching. The parties in the governing alliance kept their own counsel and prayed for the entire mess to resolve itself and go away.

Despite the PMO's best efforts, the President was being perceived to be in the right by both the media as well as by the common man.

For the great man of the people, Yadav Senior, this was simply too much to stomach. Every trusted official in the PMO was ordered to drop all other business and go through the President's tenure as army chief with a microscope.

The PMO started asking for files from the Defence Ministry relating to General Bastard's army career. The news, unsurprisingly, made its way to the Supreme Commander. A presidential press conference was called and the media stampeded Rashtrapati Bhavan. Everybody loved a good fight.

I spent the rest of September working behind the scenes, keeping a lower profile compared to what I had since my return. I did not see much of my wife either, her duties as official hostess kept her busy from morning to night. I had wanted Neena to slip off with me for a weekend to Goa to attend the wedding of a close friend of mine. When money is no object and you have the right company any place is paradise.

Goa would have been an especially wondrous sanctuary for the two of us, far away from the cacophonous soundings of the political conflict that threatened to spike our renewed passion.

However Neena had received a lot of grief from her father, and ultimately, a little tired by her being unable to make up her mind, I had left for Goa alone.

I RETURNED THE night before the press conference and went to the Prime Minister's residence the following day to watch the press conference with the midget PM, Azim Khan, Shitij and Sanjay Kumar, the latter three having recently returned to Delhi after the by-elections in UP. Shitij's homecoming had been less than triumphant – with mixed election results. Azim and Karan Nehru had won significant victories in constituencies that signalled that they were gaining support outside their traditional bastions, at the expense of the main caste-based parties and the BJP. The scent of a new order was discernible. Nevertheless, I congratulated Yadav Junior and Sanjay before Azim showed up for the meeting.

Though he was a member of the coalition government I was surprised to see Azim present, particularly since it was known to all that he and the PM were political rivals, if not enemies, and that theirs was only a marriage of convenience. Azim would later brief me that Karan Nehru, who was the only national politician who had a stated position of wanting the Lok Sabha dissolved for another election, had made his intentions clear and was now the President's chief political adviser, his aim being to make the PM's life as difficult as possible, baiting him till he was left a political wreck, thus enabling the subsequent rise of the Congress in the Hindi heartland. Karan, though, had failed to share his strategy with the Congress party's patrician President, who was fretting about what his unpredictable cousin was up to. To neutralize Nehru the PM had beseeched Azim to help, and Mr Khan had agreed to see what he could do without making any commitments. From what I had seen of him, Azim was a calculating man who was in the business of accumulating political power and would only act when it suited his interests. As a man perceived to be the leader of Muslim India I think it made him extra careful with his emotions and actions, not wanting to startle anyone, particularly the majority community, whose trust he was trying to assiduously earn. Nevertheless, his presence heartened me – at least one person among us could be counted on to display competence.

The five of us arranged our chairs in a semi-circle around the prime ministerial television and waited for the presidential press conference to commence.

'What do you think he's going to say?' Shitij could always be relied on to ask the obvious.

'He's going to attack me,' Yadav Senior answered as obviously.

'Dayal hasn't moved into Rashtrapati Bhavan, has he?' Sanjay was out of the loop on the latest goings-on in the presidential household. The question was naturally directed at me.

'He booted his predecessor out within a week of his stepping down, and has been nicely ensconced in the residential wing since then. Our President likes the good life,' I informed Sanjay.

'From what I hear Rashtrapati Bhavan is being run like a military headquarters already. There's a uniformed chain of command with that Januha fellow ruling the roost,' Azim said, clinically highlighting the structure of the new presidential secretariat.

'Not to mention getting political advice from a former military man,' the PM could not resist adding.

'Yes, Karan feels quite at home there,' Azim agreed. But he refrained from filling us in on the details of what his friend was up to. It was impossible that he did not know. Karan Nehru had a pathological need to boast.

'The press conference has started,' the PM announced and brought an end to any further discussion as General Bastard appeared on the screen right on time. Shitij raised the volume on the fancy entertainment unit's speaker system. It sounded like we were almost in Ashoka Hall, which was the site the pompous President had selected to address the country from. It was where Prime Ministers were sworn in and it was from where President Dayal would launch his attack on the latest member of that select set.

The TV cameras showed Dayal striding into Ashoka Hall looking like an actor perfectly cast to play the part of President. Nature rarely allowed such perfect physical casting in real life. General Dayal wore an impeccably cut, black sherwani, an attire that was well identified with the office of President, indeed many previous occupants had taken to wearing it in an attempt to ape the Nehruvian sartorial style, but none had worn it as well as the present head of state. A podium adorned with the presidential seal awaited him, and he walked up to it like the general he had once been, erect and purposeful. He took his place behind it; he would stand, not sit, using his considerable height to loom over the media.

Then President Bastard came straight to the point:

'Ladies and gentleman of the press, my countrymen, I have taken the unusual liberty of calling this press conference today due to my great alarm at activities that the Central Government has been involved in during its short term in office. I held my tongue for months, much before I was handed this great honour to serve as your President. I had hoped they would see the error of their ways but now it appears they will not abide by reason and so I must act.

'This Government's decision to send men of such disrepute and low standing as our representatives to the world's only superpower and to the home of Islam convinced me that if I did not take a stand now, with the powers that fate has decreed in me, I would be complicit in their ongoing debasement of our system of government. I simply could not live with that on my conscience...'

General Dayal was speaking from a teleprompter but he was doing it with such expertise that most people would believe he was speaking extempore. And the real surprise was that he spoke in Hindi, of a basic variety to be sure, but with great fluency and emotion. He made use of simple words, understandable to even the most Anglophile of Indians, but strung together, they forged a persuasive argument.

'...the man who leads the present government has surrounded himself with despicable individuals who have only one task, which is to plunder the Treasury of this country and hide it abroad. Some of you know of whom I speak and I ask you, the press, to rid them of their veil of anonymity, so that the people of this country can see for themselves that they are being governed by charlatans.

'I have served this country since my youth and would have in the course of my service readily given my life for my country had that been asked of me. Therefore, if the price I pay for speaking out today is that I lose the high position you have so honoured me with, it will be but a small sacrifice for saving the country that I so dearly love from further abuse. Thank you very much. That is all I have to say. You may ask questions. My Press Secretary will direct the proceedings and I must insist that there be decorum. Remember you are standing on hallowed ground. Any misbehaviour will not be tolerated here.'

His voice commanded authority and even the usually unruly media brigade understood he meant business and marginally toned down their act – from rabid to boisterous.

'Reny John, *Times of India*. Sir, are you demanding Prime Minister Yadav's resignation?'

'That would be a futile act on my part. I am asking for self-correction from within the Parliament. I ask the sane members of Government to decide what is right for the country and act on their conscience.'

'Sushil Simte, *Aaj Tak*. What will you do if your pleas fall on deaf ears? Are you willing to dismiss this government?'

'I do not know what the coming days will bring but I do know that as long as I am able, the vital interests of this country will be safeguarded.'

'Rohini Bhagat, *NDTV*. Do you think an alternative government formation is possible without the PM's crucial chunk of MPs from Bihar and UP?'

'If our present system of government can no longer throw up a proper representation to govern then I feel that other options should be explored. The presidential form of government has remedies to the problems that our Parliamentary system has thrown up. The lowest common denominator cannot be allowed to lay claim to positions of responsibility where only the most talented must serve.'

'Shakil Ahmad, *Hindustan Times*. Mr President, when you say "the lowest common denominator" do you mean that the poor and backward of this country cannot be allowed to have a stake in deciding its future?'

Immediately, the President lost his composure: 'Don't twist my words, young man. The corrupt and immoral are who I want out of our hair. That's enough, I've said what I had to. It's up to you now to ensure accountability where it is due. Good evening.' And he departed in a huff, probably struggling very hard to dissuade himself from having that last reporter taken out and shot.

SHITIJ TURNED OFF the television as the media pundits came on immediately afterward to dissect the President's words as if they were religious text. I looked at the midget. The PM had not said a word throughout the broadcast. Yadav Junior had let fly with a few expletives at one stage but had buttoned it up after he got a dirty look from his father.

'Fine then. If he wants to play politics we will play politics,' said the PM after a long silence.

'I think we can take advantage of his dig about the lowest common denominator,' said Sanjay Kumar.

'We can make it about his upper-caste denigration of all backward castes everywhere,' agreed the PM. 'And you, Jasjit, better be prepared for some pretty serious media attention,' the PM looked squarely me. 'He targeted you pretty clearly and I'm positive his press office will be giving your name in background briefs, probably even as we speak. Your father's name is going to be invoked too. Arrange some security for your residence.'

He was right. I had been fingered. The papers were bound to take my name, tentatively but categorically. And that would change everything. I was about to be removed permanently from the shadows and the searchlights trained on me. Also, Dayal would look painfully honest and above reproach if he was seen to take on his own son-in-law; I would become the first example of corruption to be caught and denounced as part of his righteous crusade to rid the country of all that ailed it. It sounded like a brilliant plan to me.

'We're missing something,' said Azim, speaking finally. 'From what I've learnt of Dayal in recent days, this kind of frontal assault does not fit his personality or the way he's conducted himself so far. He's not a lion but a fox, a tactician, a commando to be more precise, who tries to defeat his enemy with cunning rather than overwhelming force. This kind of move by him smells of an urgent attempt to knock the PM out with one punch.' Azim's political instincts were coming into play. He was, albeit gingerly, taking sides as well.

'You're right, Azim. I think it can't be a complete coincidence that it comes in the wake of our initiating an investigation into his years in the army – particularly of his tenure as chief of staff.' Yadav Senior took Azim's point a step further.

'Oh, so he's hoping to topple you before you find something,' Shitij said, as usual coming late to the party.

'Then, we better find whatever it is the General is trying to conceal. I suggest, Sanjay, that you take over the search committee at the PMO. I trust my staff, but babus have a way of taking their time even when one has a fire raging under one's backside.' The PM stood up, and immediately we all followed suit. 'Remember, we are in this together, there may be a rough storm ahead but we'll get through it – and hit *him* back where it hurts,' he said.

I could tell that the midget PM was already thinking ahead to the next step, for further attacks. I watched as the PM put his arm around Azim's shoulder and took him aside, no doubt to work on him, to get his whole-hearted support. I had a feeling it would not be as difficult to win Azim over after the press conference. I had observed him, and as inscrutable as Mr Khan was, I got the sense that he was disturbed by what he had seen.

For now though I was worried about myself. Open warfare had begun and I was to be part of the leading charge. Despite Yadav Senior's assurance, I wasn't convinced I would survive the altercation.

Neena called as we dispersed. She was worried and wanted to talk but the last thing I wanted to think about was how the crisis would affect us. I told her I could not talk, too many prying ears, and would call her first thing in the morning. Neena did not sound too pleased, but she would have to understand. I was fighting for my life and her feelings would have to play second fiddle to the prospect of my survival.

I decided to go along with Kumar and assist him in his search for any hint of scandal in the President's army tenure that we could use against him. I had not been at South Block long when Mother called and distracted my efforts. The television vans and journos had arrived at our house en masse. I had been forewarned by the PM of my name being leaked to the press and thought I was prepared for this eventuality, but when you become the story – the epicentre of such a major scandal – you can never be prepared for it, whoever you might be. I was reluctant to draw further attention with the unwarranted – from a security perspective – use of government security and so I called the security firm that I had given a ton of business during the cricket elections. They immediately sent over a team of their best men.

Then my phone started to ring. The media had started barraging me with phone calls to hear my side of the story and I decided, after a little discussion, that the worst thing I could do at this juncture was to hide out. Instead, I decided, I would talk to the most influential and reliable news organizations and deny all of General Bastard's indirect allegations. By so doing, I would appear like a man who has been spitefully maligned in public without a shred of evidence.

Unfortunately, my engagement with the media did not work out as I had hoped. I had thought I would get away with a couple of targeted interviews to the most influential media outlets, but then every media organization demanded equal access, failing which they threatened harsh retaliation in their coverage; so I capitulated. I would have liked to avoid coming on television myself, but avoiding them was no longer an option. It was going to be a very long and tiring night.

I decided I did not want to hold a press conference where I would be the focal point of their combined attention. I would deal with them individually, one media entity at a time, to impress on them that I had all the time in the world and nothing better to do, quite unlike someone who was busy hoarding the PM's ill-gotten wealth.

Print journalists are wilier than their counterparts on TV, but the television lights were disconcertingly new to me and I struggled to perform at first, hoping to convey my martyrdom. Still I had a story to tell and after repeating it a few dozen times

I made up the initial lack of authority on my part. The PMO had some trusted allies amongst the fourth estate and they were brought in at this critical juncture. These were editors who wanted to continue getting special access to the PM and accompanying him, at government expense, on his foreign travels. It was pathetic how easy it was to seduce some of these so-called paragons of virtue. Then there were others who made no bones about being independent and would do your bidding for a monthly fee or for a helping hand from the State in a deal they had in the fire.

Since Dayal had not mentioned me by name I only had the most loving things to say about my wife's father, trying to impress on the media that the Prez and I were on the best of terms and they had it all wrong about his accusing me; that their sources were taking them for a ride. I actually told them that I thought General Bastard would make an excellent President, should he get elected in a few months. The art of being economical with the truth and not batting an eyelid while doing it was the only part of the entire act that came naturally to me. I was met with incredulity by the reporters but they only had hearsay to go on so they *had* to take my word for it.

It took several days of being hounded, before the media got off my back. By the end of the blistering and repeated cross-examination I was completely exhausted. The nonstop TV coverage was a blur; I may well have been talking gibberish because I was on autopilot and had no recollection of what I said. Though it may not have been pretty to watch, I fought for my life and did everything in my power to hold off an immediate execution by firing squad – our new President had always darkly joked, perverse sense of humour that he had, about dispatching me by that method.

Despite taking advantage of all the media's weaknesses great damage was done over the days to come. I could only hope to contain it to some extent. The name of the Sidhu family had been besmirched and was being raked through the muck. Father would have been horrified at the situation. Because he had understood better than anyone that if I became the story then I would become useless, even a liability, to my clients. He had called that his arch-principle.

Well, so much for it.

WHILE I DEALT with the media firestorm, Sanjay Kumar stepped up his efforts to unearth some damning documents on Daddy-in-law. Unfortunately, he was unable to find anything significant. His team could not locate any document that even came close to implicating the President.

Meanwhile the noose of public outrage kept getting tighter about our necks as we desperately tried to bat away the accusations that had surfaced against us in the days that followed. Conversely, it was a coup for General Bastard, pardon the pun, with everyone from the Opposition to the press to most Indians, outside of the PM's strongholds, seeing him as a saviour and protector of the nation's supreme interest.

The Sidhu family became the villains of the piece and the target of pent-up rage for all the nation's ills. I could not leave my house without the risk of being followed by some intrepid reporter trying to make a big name for himself by linking me to some future scam, real or imagined. I froze all contact with my financial friends and stopped all activities that had to do with any of the foreign accounts I still controlled for the Yadavs and their tribe.

For public consumption, Yadav Senior announced that though he knew me as the son of his late aide, what we shared was far from the close association of the sort that was being hinted at by presidential sources.

The feeling of isolation from the world grew. Mother was so distressed by the continual negative coverage that I feared she would suffer a nervous breakdown. I took the beating with as much stoicism as I could dredge up. Though, I have to admit that the anger smouldering within me was the driving emotion that spurred me through the tough times. I couldn't get used to seeing my face on the front page of newspapers and that too under scandalous banner headlines. I had the dubious distinction of having made the jump from Page Three, as Neena's spouse, to Page One, as the President's son-in-law and chief whipping boy. Valiantly, I continued answering all queries that were thrown at us, regardless of their venom, but decided that whatever else I did, I would never hold a press conference or go on television ever again to defend myself. I was clearly not suited for that sort of thing.

Despite my being relatively open with the media, it was amazing how much they got wrong about me. If one newspaper reported that I had flunked out from college, then a TV news channel stated, with absolute certainty, that I owned palatial homes in Goa and Bangalore. I didn't mind too much being put on the mat for something I had actually done, but some of the baseless reporting made me quiver with indignation. Since the deals Father had swung were, fortunately, so well hidden from view, the media had to resort to fabrication. They were not too interested in Father, being beyond even their long reach, and left him alone with a passing reference to his prior jobs and his reputation as a power-broker. So that left poor little me in the spotlight, as the young wheeler-dealer and playboy with an ultra-glam lifestyle that included being the consort of the officiating first lady, but who was now in mortal combat with none other than his fair lady's father, the realm's tallest, most noble leader and crusading saviour, who had loudly accused the young man and his associates, the ruling clique, of treason.

The screenplays of far-fetched Bollywood movies didn't get juicier than this. Everybody wanted to know who I was, exactly, and spent way too much energy trying to find out.

I had become nationally infamous; in some young and impressionable circles I was also deemed something of a 'cat'.

Father had always believed that the mistake those of our profession often made on being caught in the act was to forget their core competence and to set out to defend their conduct in public – an arena with which they were not familiar – and as a result they only managed to make more trouble for themselves. I had partly broken that rule, but then Father had never envisaged a scenario where I would be picked up by the President of India, who also happened, by some ghastly coincidence, to be the father of my bride. It was too bizarre for words.

But it was also my life and if I had to make new rules to survive, then that was exactly what I was going to do.

I WAS EDGY and troubled whenever Neena and I met. Though she and I continued to see each other it was not quite the honeymoon that it had been prior to her father's televized assault on me. The progress we had made in our relationship was most certainly stopped in its tracks. We had to grapple with our being together having become the source of scandal that I had feared it would. The worst had happened and there was nothing to do but fight it out like the midget PM had advised.

Neena and I met rarely now, out of sight of the public, in the houses of trusted friends or at isolated spots in Rashtrapati Bhavan. She could not come over to my house because there were still, even two weeks after the President's press conference, television crews hanging around outside the gate. In a country where famines, floods and all manner of other natural and man-made disasters take place with regularity, nothing newsworthy took place during this period of time to distract from the battle of wills between the Head of State and the Head of Government.

General Bastard, as I had predicted, even managed to squeeze credit out of our relationship as many a fawning editorial was written marvelling at how the great President had held the nation's interest above the happiness of his own daughter. He could do no wrong.

When everything, true and false, had been dug up about me by the political reporters, the Page Three rumours began their bombing run. They were the most damaging of the lot. They announced to the world that Neena had left me for reasons as varied as she had given in to pressure from General Bastard, to I had cheated on her, to she had found someone else because she was disgusted by my corrupt ways. Admittedly, all of these were realistic scenarios.

Each news report drove Mother to tears and Neena into a successively darker mood, during which she would do a rather good impression of an ice princess with whom I found it impossible to communicate. How would she have reacted if I had been a real rogue and philanderer, whose many conquests had gone to the press in unison to confess their dalliances with me? For once in my life I thanked my stars that I lacked a facility for luring women into my bed.

I could not begin to imagine what General Bastard was putting Neena through every day in terms of mental pressure. She never complained, but she did not talk freely about it, either. I decided that this intolerable state of affairs could not be allowed to go on and I had to pro-actively handle the situation so that no further damage would be done to the person most traumatized by this feud.

The storm was slowly subsiding; there were others handling the larger strategy to counter Rashtrapati Bhavan. I realized that on the personal side I had left Neena dangling in the wind, without any protection. That would have to change. So I asked her to come over to Jor Bagh; if a wife visiting her husband was all it took to fuel more rumours then there was nothing I could do about it. Luckily, there was a police shooting somewhere in the city that day and the press hyenas were busy covering it; no OB van was available to spy on the Sidhus.

Mother, uncharacteristically considerate, retired to her room when Neena arrived looking pale and tense. I could tell she hadn't been sleeping well. I made her a drink, a vodka lime, her weakness. Neena drained the glass with a thirst that was simultaneously extraordinary and worrisome.

'How are you holding up?' I asked tentatively.

'A little part of me is dying every day. Especially when all the TV news people seem to care about showing is the dueling sound-bites of the two most important people in my life. Over and over and over…' She sank onto the sofa and buried her head in her hands.

I never felt so driven by the need to protect someone as I did then. I put my arm around Neena: 'I want you to immediately release a press statement disassociating yourself from me. You should not have to suffer so greatly for the acts of the men in your life. This is exactly what I wanted to avoid but now that we are here, I must bite the bullet and free you from the obligation you feel towards me.'

She wrenched herself away. 'Bastard, all you men think about is yourselves. Do you think I can live without you now?' Far from crying as I had feared, she sat up proudly, her eyes radiating determination. I was amazed at her transformation. 'There is no need to play the martyr again. You are the love of my life; all other factors are immaterial to me. You continue to do what you think best, I will be by your side through anything that the future holds. You don't need to worry about me; I'm a General's daughter.' That much, was certainly true.

I had imagined this scene playing out many different ways, but this display of courage and inspiration completely overwhelmed me. She was on my side, supporting me! I began to feel irrationally euphoric and optimistic. I had come to help her and instead she had lifted my spirits! I must have appeared as dumbstruck and awed as I felt because she asked, 'What? Surprised I'm not running for the woods?'

'I certainly would have,' I added honestly, but idiotically.

'I'll be sure to remember that.'

'You know what I mean, Neena. You shouldn't have to face the kind of stress and scrutiny that being with me is causing you to be put through.'

She held out her glass. 'Make it just vodka and ice this time.'

'Is that really the wisest choice? How about something lighter?' I was concerned she might be overdoing it.

'I'm the adult in this relationship, so just do what I say, Jasjit.'

'You won't get an argument out of me on that.' I had done my job and warned her, if she wanted to go home smashed that was up to her.

'I want you to have the same attitude towards something I want you to do for my sake…'

'Why do I get the feeling this has got to do with General Bastard –' the nickname slipped out inadvertently and I knew there would be trouble.

'Is that how you refer to my father behind my back?'

'No, only in my head. This is the only time I've said it out loud and I promise it won't happen again.' I was mortified by the verbal slip.

'It better not. I don't let him curse you in front of me either,' she said, to make clear to me that the rules were equal for both warring parties.

'What did you want to ask me before I distracted you?' I wanted to move on from the General Bastard screw-up as speedily as possible; I was prepared to have a discussion on tampons with her if need be.

'If you love me you will abide by what I request of you now.'

There it was, the love test that all males know is a no-escape ultimatum.

'You will under no circumstances speak ill of my father in public. I know you haven't so far, even after my father slandered you, and I thank you for that with all my heart. You have to be the bigger man in this; I *expect* you to be the bigger man.'

He was the President of the Republic and *I* was supposed to be the bigger man? She had some nerve to ask that of me when it was her rotten father who had unleashed the ire of the entire country upon me and mine. I was supposed to permanently give up the right to defend myself in public, which was my weapon of last resort? 'Is there any logic behind this bizarre demand of yours?'

'It will keep the situation from deteriorating further and me from slitting my wrists. Is that enough logic for you?' said Neena, as she roughly grabbed the bottle for another refill.

The suicide card, played ever so effortlessly, left me with minimal room for manoeuvre. 'There's no need to be so dramatic, Neena. What I do or don't do is of no consequence. The PM has decided to pay your father back in spades and he is prepared to do whatever is necessary. You must prepare yourself for the worst.'

'I told you, I only care about what *you* do. I understand the PM is playing a bigger game, a game that my father initiated for reasons beyond my understanding. But you must make me this vow of silence. I will ask nothing else of you for the remaining duration of this crisis.'

AFTER NEENA'S VISIT I felt newly determined to find a way out of my troubles and sat down to systematically analyse the situation.

As a private banker you are trained to make an investment profile of your clients before deciding what kind of investment to recommend them. The idea is to judge their ability to tolerate risk by putting down on paper everything you know about them, from their personal particulars, like their age and number of dependants, to your impression of their personality. It helps to gauge which client will be able to hold himself together and not sue you when the stock markets go through a bad patch. In reality, of course, no bank will ever tell a big client who wants to invest a serious amount of money in the stock market that they won't allow him to do so because they believe his risk profile indicates he should invest in fixed income. The client is king and his wishes are paramount, but management still lectured us financial consultants about knowing our clients inside out, and we kept filling out stacks of forms to prove to the compliance people that we did. It was an annoyance, but I found the exercise occasionally threw up hidden nuggets about the client that even sustained personal contact would not have unearthed. Believe it or not, I had put together a profile for the Yadavs as well, which had been extremely helpful, and I don't mean just from the point of view of investing their funds.

I decided to do the same with General Bastard, but for the purposes of a purely non-financial analysis. I wrote out everything I knew about him and tried to see what it all added up to. My main sources of information other than my own interaction with him were Neena and Captain Chavan, the latter being more useful for attempting to understand how the President operated on his turf. I stayed awake half the night trying to find an answer to what General Bastard's secret was. I was sure it was concealed in there somewhere, in the handwritten sheaves of paper on my desk.

Brajesh Dayal came from a rich family, which was how he could claim with a straight face that his estate in Uttarakhand was inherited property. This background had not stopped him from making money on arms deals, particularly the Israeli deal, when he was army chief, but he was way too smart to leave any tracks behind, of that I was sure. The money he had received from the Israelis had been made to an account I had not dealt with, and I had no way of ascertaining its details. He was very careful about these things. If it was not corruption I could trip him on, then it could be his administration of the army. There, too, his record seemed blameless. None of the retired officers we had talked to had described his tenure as army chief in anything less than glowing terms.

I was about to doze off when my mind latched upon a certain Mrs Das – the serving army chief's wife – and how it was rumoured she had been responsible for getting her husband promoted to lieutenant-general. I pondered the possibility of there being other army wives out there who had set the precedent for Mrs Das. Wives of husbands who were *not* grateful for the payoffs; who took exception to their wives' dalliances with the chief. All it took was a single stubborn man who had not been a willing participant in the affair and had dared to complain against his chief. I concede that it was a bit of a stretch, but I thought it merited further inquiry.

I AWOKE EARLY the next morning and headed straight for South Block. I found a bleary-eyed Sanjay Kumar holed up in Father's former room with stacks of dusty files piled high around him. They gave off that that musty official smell that shrouds all government offices and never leaves your nasal passages if you have smelt it, as I had, throughout your childhood: a smell not so much of power but the hopeless, musty pungency of bureaucratic inefficiency and decay. Sanjay had barely left the building since getting his orders from Yadav Senior to search for the proverbial needle in a haystack. After I told him of my hunch, he produced the President's personnel file from the mess that was Father's former desk.

I recounted to Sanjay the conversation I had had with Captain Chavan during my golf game with General Bastard and what I had learned from it, including the President's constant communication with the service chiefs and how he had won the allegiance of the present army chief. I then explained how I thought that the Mrs Das anecdote could be pertinent to our problem.

'Why didn't you tell me about the army chief earlier?' Sanjay asked, not hiding his annoyance; understandable since he had been slaving for days trying to unearth something against the President.

'It didn't seem important till now,' I lied.

'In the future, let us politicians be the judge of that. I doubt very much you will find complaints against the President in any of these documents.'

'Whitewash?'

'The army chief is all powerful within his service in matters of discipline. Even if there is a complaint made of the sort you are talking about, I doubt very much that the complaint or the complainant's career would survive.'

'I'm sure there must be a record of it somewhere.'

'The army can be very discreet and effective when they need to be,' Sanjay said; the voice of experience.

'If that's the case, then the President shouldn't have panicked as he did when you started snooping around in his affairs,' I surmised, pushing a stack of dusty files off a chair and plonking myself down.

'Or he fears something else.'

'*Or* there is a record of his indiscretion but we haven't been allowed access to it due to his having subverted the army chief into working for him,' I countered.

Sanjay mulled over my hypothetical comment for a moment or two and then said, 'It might be worth our while to let the PM know about your theory and have him direct his temper at the Defence Ministry. After he rattles some cages down there, you never know what may fall into our laps.'

As envisaged, the midget PM did blow his top after talking to us. He saw me as the leading candidate to blame for keeping crucial information to myself. After he cooled down and was convinced of my innocence, he picked up the phone and gave the Defence Minister a real roasting. He followed it up with similar phone conversations with his new Defence Secretary – (his physically abused predecessor, who had been assaulted by his fat son, had since retired. I never did find out why the blackmailers never revealed his secrets to the world) – and last but not least the army chief whom he threatened with court-martial proceedings if he did not play ball.

Within a day we were handed two files of complaints that had been registered against General Bastard during the course of his career. The first was a case where he, then serving as a corps commander, had been accused by a junior officer of physical assault; but after investigation the file had been closed with no witness having come forward to corroborate the junior officer's story. Most mafia dons would have been impressed with the Omerta-like silence. The second case belonged to the period when the President had served as army chief and, as I had suspected, was related to matters of a sexual nature.

A colonel serving at army headquarters had accused his chief of having an affair with his wife – who judging from the picture attached, was quite a bombshell – and had demanded that a board of inquiry be installed. The file was missing a report by the investigating authority and the only other document in the file was a letter from the colonel, dated a month after the original complaint, explaining that he had been under a lot of stress recently and that he had been in that state when a misunderstanding had taken place regarding his wife's relationship with General Dayal. He apologized for his conduct, and to his chief. You did not have to be a great detective to figure out that General Bastard had successfully brought all the powers of his office to bear on his accuser.

The name of the victimized colonel was DB Shetty. After pulling out his service record we found that he had sought retirement soon after the incident and had taken up a job in Bangalore. Surprisingly, he was still married to the same woman, whose name was Usha.

I booked myself on the first flight to Bangalore, knowing every minute counted because Rashtrapati Bhavan would have certainly been made aware of the file having come into our possession. I was met at the airport by an IB officer who briefed me on whatever they were able to dig up at such short notice about the colonel's present existence.

I WENT STRAIGHT from the airport to Colonel Shetty's office, having earlier fixed an appointment with him under an alias, with the stated purpose of discussing business. I was ushered into the colonel's office without being made to wait. He did not look like an army officer. Not, at any rate, one who might have led his men with any great distinction in battle. He was bald and wore the kind of thick glasses that you would expect a scientist to wear. I thought he resembled a schoolteacher. He recognized me on sight, notorious as I had become by now, and I got right to the heart of the matter, telling him what I wanted to talk to him about.

His shoulders slumped at the mention of the President and the opening up of an affair I'm sure he had believed consigned forever to the past. I would have ordinarily felt sorry for him but my interests were much too dependent on getting him to talk.

'I cannot assist you on this subject.'

'Why?'

'My wife and I have moved on from those dark days. No good can be served by re-visiting them.'

'It is your duty as an officer and a citizen to show the country the true character of this man who claims himself to be purer than driven snow. Can you allow him to grow stronger every day, knowing that he is a menace?'

'He is not a man I wish to take on again. One go was enough, it is somebody else's turn.'

'All right, at least tell me exactly what went on between you, your wife and the President. The official file only gives us the beginning and the end of the affair, nothing in the middle.'

Shetty asked his secretary to hold his calls and then got up to lock his office door. I expected him to pull out a bottle of Scotch next and place it on the table with two glasses but he didn't. I had seen way too many movies for my own good. He paced the medium-sized room as he spoke:

'We had just moved to Delhi after I had been posted to the Operations Directorate at Headquarters, a prestigious assignment. It was an Army Day function, all the officers and their spouses attended. General Dayal saw her there, and that's where it began. He hunted my wife down like a predator and viciously took advantage of the problems Usha and I had been having in our marriage for a while – my long postings to non-family stations being the main reason,' Shetty laughed dryly. 'Dayal is a charismatic and powerful man, there aren't too many women who are capable of resisting him. Usha definitely couldn't. I became the laughing-stock of the service. My colleagues were right. If I couldn't control my woman how was I going to lead men in the field? I tried my best to ignore what was going on, rationalizing that she was having a one-off fling, that it would end soon. I only blew my top when she informed me one fine day that she was in love with Dayal and wanted a divorce. I could not allow him to get away with that.' Shetty stopped for a drink of water and to calm himself down. It was apparent he still felt violated, which meant the need for vengeance could not be too far behind. I made a mental note to use that.

'So you filed the complaint?' I prompted him.

'The very same day.'

'Then what happened?'

'All hell broke loose. To start with, he broke off all contact with my wife, which knocked some sense back into her. My Commanding Officer called me into his office and strongly reprimanded me for my actions. He almost ordered me to take back my accusation. I respectfully declined to comply. You see, I knew the very act of accusing the army chief of misconduct had finished off my career and the best thing I could do was to stick to my guns. A couple of other successively senior officers tried to make me back down but I was prepared for battle. Finally, I was produced before the vice-chief of army staff, General Sundaram, who had got his job mainly because he had made a career out of serving as General Dayal's attack dog and bag-carrier, the role General Januha is playing today.

'Sundaram kept me standing at attention as he threatened me of ominous but unnamed consequences if I didn't undo what I had done. I knew they would try and dig up dirt on me but I thought I was on strong ground since I had never done anything in my career that would show me to be anything other than an honourable man.'

I did not need to hear the rest of the story to know how the rest would unfold. The same sequence of events that had happened all through history to decent men like Colonel Shetty when they demanded their rights from despots like General Bastard; they got run over.

'I went on leave and waited for my day in court, but, as you know, that never happened. They stalled for three weeks with one bureaucratic excuse after another and then I was again called to South Block. I didn't know whom I was to meet on this occasion until I was escorted into the Chief's office. To my surprise he greeted me like a long-lost friend, shaking my hand jovially and asking if I wanted anything to drink – '

I interrupted. 'Seeing his behaviour you must have anticipated trouble?'

'I'm afraid I wasn't quite that discerning. I took his friendliness to mean I was in the driver's seat and that he wanted to bring an amicable end to the dispute. I, of course, couldn't have been more wrong. They had spent the intervening three weeks finding a way to trap me. Sundaram was present as well, and they sat me down, handed me my drink, and then began to delineate what trumped-up charges of misconduct and corruption I would face. He thundered that the top brass was united against me and there was no chance of my being able to defend myself. He reminded me that I had two children who needed me and I should think about them. I did think about them, and my resolve began to waiver. I became aware of the futility of my position. This is when General Dayal started to speak and assured me that if I went along with their wishes I would be given the opportunity to retire honourably and swiftly. I'm ashamed to say so but for one of the few times in my life I took the easy, cowardly way out. I wrote out the letter taking back the charges against General Dayal and it was over, along with my army career.'

He returned to his seat.

'You and your wife didn't divorce?'

'We separated for a while, but ultimately reconciled. Forgive and forget, that's the mantra I live by now.'

'You don't mean it applies to our President, do you?' I began to make my pitch.

'I know what you're trying to do, Mr Sidhu, and it won't work. This is not my fight.'

'Colonel sahib, I can't believe that the sight of President Dayal smiling smugly from the newspapers doesn't bother you every time you see your wife sitting by your side. I look at you and see a proud man, a man who yearns for revenge. Nobody should have to go through what you went through without gaining his pound of flesh. Sir, I am offering you the opportunity to gain some peace of mind. Take the step you couldn't take years ago; this time you have powerful allies at your side.'

'You are very persuasive…If I were alone it would be an easier decision but there are others who are dependent on me.'

'Your family will be well taken care of. All you have to do is name a price for your participation.'

'Money?'

'You are taking a risk by stepping into the firing line and we would not dream of putting you into harm's way without suitably compensating you.' I took a sheet of paper from his desk and wrote a figure I thought would leave no doubt of our seriousness. He looked at the number on the paper and was left seriously dumbstruck. He could work for a hundred years and not save that much.

'Your son can do the MBA in America that he wants to do and you can marry your daughter off in the style she deserves.' These bits I got thanks to the good services of the Intelligence Bureau. 'And you can rid yourself of the daily grind of a civilian job you don't enjoy and retire in comfort. What do you think?'

'I cannot imagine…'

'Just think of it as a service you are providing that we need and are ready to pay the market price for.'

He put the piece of paper aside and gazed out of his office window. He was mulling my offer, which meant I had made a breakthrough past the outer shields. 'I'm not sure if my wife will find it appetizing to have everyone talking about her adulterous past. I will have to talk this over with her first.' His level of resistance was rapidly declining.

'She owes you your chance at reclaiming your honour.' I veered the decision away from money. I had introduced the money as a vital factor but a man like Colonel Shetty would ultimately be seduced by talk of what he had lost to General Bastard and how I was providing him a way to restore it.

'They might bring up those trumped-up charges again.'

'I doubt any record of them exists. In any case you have nothing to worry about, we control the Defence Ministry, not the President.' Which was theoretically true.

Without any further indecision, Colonel Shetty stood to attention and offered me his hand. 'Very well then, I'm your man.'

I shook his hand, bemused by how quickly he had covered the final stretch to such an important decision. I spent some more minutes with him discussing how we would orchestrate an attack on the President and also how he would prefer the cash, which I promised to get to him in any form he wished. I advised opening an account somewhere abroad, set up personally by me, and he agreed.

I left his office humming happily to myself. We were in business. General Bastard was shortly going to have his backside singed.

SANJAY KUMAR CALLED me to get the details of my trip soon after I landed. I had already texted him a message heralding a successful outcome before getting on the flight.

'Colonel Shetty is a good man, I fear he may not survive what we will put him through,' I said after recounting my meeting.

'He'll be fine. Rashtrapati Bhavan will try to go after him but we'll be one step ahead of them all the way,' said Sanjay, suddenly confident.

'If *you're* confident then I have no choice but to *be* confident, right?' I extrapolated.

'Miles to go yet, and many worries to face down. To begin with, there is Neena.'

'What about Neena?' I asked, intentionally playing dumb.

'Whose side is your wife on?' he asked bluntly.

'That's a complicated question,' I hedged.

'Okay, tell me this, if she has to choose between her father and you, which way will she go?'

'I have no way of knowing for sure.' I really did not and that was the honest truth.

'You have my sympathies. Marriage is tough enough without having to play out all your differences in a national drama.' Sanjay's voice had a hint of real concern. Bonds of camaraderie were forged between the unlikeliest of pairs in the trenches. I doubted he and I had anything in common other than what we were doing and for whom we were doing it.

'I offered her an out after Dayal's press conference but she wouldn't hear of it, saying she was with me till the end,' I revealed, needing to talk about it with someone, anyone, even him.

'Strong woman,' he remarked, a little discomfited by my having shared too much, crossing the boundaries of what was nothing more than a professional friendship, if that.

'But this is real life and happy endings are for fairy tales,' I concluded.

'Sad but true. You need to be prepared for an eventuality where events may make it impossible for either of you to continue this relationship. We are about to call her father a wife-stealer and a power-crazed bully. How do you think she's going to react to that?' He veered back to realpolitik.

Neena loved her father. That was a variable that had not, and would not change. That was a given. 'Not well,' I grimly conceded.

'You are innocent civilians and don't deserve to be caught in our crossfire.' Sanjay was trying to make me feel better.

'I appreciate the sentiment but I don't think you can call me an innocent in what's going on.'

'Since making a run for it is out of the question, I guess we'll have to get you out of this jam in the old-fashioned way – fists flying and no surrender.' There was keen anticipation in his voice. I suppose I too would have been excited to stand by and watch the drama of my life unfold, perhaps even participate as one of the minor warriors, but to be completely enmeshed in the proceedings was too much excitement and worry, even for me.

After our talk I needed a drink, and more. I got shit-faced drunk after a long time and compounded my sins by phoning Neena at an unearthly hour and getting overly emotional with her. I think I may have actually wept.

Believe it or not, that was actually a step forward for us.

Chapter 9

COLONEL SHETTY'S STORY hit the political scene like a tsunami, unexpectedly, and with violent consequences. The media had already set its impression of the President in stone. He was the noble crusader. There was no room in that image for an episode involving him as a sexual predator who had abused the powers of his office to keep his doings quiet. Overnight, it wasn't so easy any more to take sides against the midget PM with the self-righteous certainty that the President's distinguished and blameless career spoke for his integrity.

The media had an ego, and when it found that it had been taken for a ride by a false prophet, hurt pride turned to anger and the inevitable backlash. General Bastard was taken apart piece by piece. The scales of public opinion returned to a semblance of balance. From a formerly binary state, opinion on the subject was fractured into three factions. Respective diehard supporters of the PM and President Dayal formed the first two groups while a majority of the people placed themselves in a third group of undecideds and sat on the sidelines waiting like spectators to see who would land the next blow before they decided on their allegiances.

Sanjay handled the media strategy masterfully. My initial apprehensions about him proved absolutely unfounded. He saw the moderate success I had enjoyed with my micro press strategy and took it further. Sanjay and I did not want Colonel Shetty to have to enter an uncontrolled environment where he was liable to get startled and veer from the script. Separate interviews were granted to carefully chosen media personalities, each of whom was asked to present questions in advance. The interviews were held in Bangalore in the relative comfort of the colonel's home. We wanted him to feel as relaxed as possible, far from the madness of Delhi.

The PMO, turning a deaf ear to accusations of unfair access, saw it fit to blatantly ignore media houses that had, shall we say, a more independent nature. The print press was selectively brought in later, once television had generated the required initial frenzy. For two weeks there was nothing on TV or in the papers except for Colonel Shetty's story of woe. He was portrayed as an honest and brave soldier who had been victimized by a vile four-star general for no fault of his other than being married to a beautiful woman.

Rashtrapati Bhavan made a half-hearted attempt to talk about the trumped-up charges that had been brought against Shetty so many years ago, but there was not a shred of evidence on record to prove their veracity. Even the army chief, General Das, was forced to admit as much on record.

When it looked like the story was about to finally lose steam, Azim Khan, having apparently been cajoled into it by the wily Yadav Senior, began giving interviews and taking part in panel discussions on TV, and raised questions about Dayal's suitability as President considering he had brought disrepute to the uniform he had once worn. Azim portrayed this as a pattern of despicable behaviour that the President had always been guilty of and the PM as just his most recent victim. He said it was clear the man felt that no code of conduct applied to him. He insisted that the President was a danger to Indian democracy who had to be removed before he engaged in further 'constitutional atrocities' – I loved that last formulation.

Rashtrapati Bhavan countered by sending out the hapless presidential Press Secretary to defend his liege, but the match-up was uneven and Azim demolished him with ease.

This was when Karan Nehru entered the fray as a representative for President Dayal, and things got *really* interesting.

General Bastard and the midget PM, not satisfied with the dissension that they had already created, also managed to get these best friends and political soulmates to publicly face off against each other in verbal combat for the first time. Karan and Azim were the most talented debaters of their generation and they did not disappoint in their skilful altercations, which were always intense, each forcefully making their case, but never getting personal. Karan Nehru did come close to losing his head on occasion; a congenital failing with him.

THE DATE FOR notifying the presidential elections and the start of the election process was still well beyond the horizon, yet the pressure on both sides increased with each passing day. By disseminating Colonel Shetty's allegations we had put an impediment on what was initially promising to be a General Bastard coronation. But the President, in turn, had succeeded in weakening the PM's authority within Government and Parliament. The clock was ticking and the stakes were the highest imaginable. Both sides searched desperately for that elusive knockout punch that would end the stand-off in their favour. Until then, there would be a series of tactical skirmishes, Dayal and Yadav in a battle of attrition while Government came to a standstill.

All told, a somewhat unhappy situation.

We, in the PM's camp, had made an amazing comeback, but victory was far from guaranteed. You could say we had pulled even. At least, from a personal perspective, the pressure built up on the Sidhu family was greatly reduced. President Dayal's doings were understandably of greater interest to the press and the wider public. Thank heaven for that.

Neena continued to avoid going to non-official events with me as the Shetty revelations had only made her life more difficult and she was in a bit of a funk about my having overdone the attack on her father. She had snapped at me a couple of times for no good reason, so I decided to leave her alone for a bit and diverted myself by making a partial return to society.

I COULD NEVER fully understood why the fortnight prior to the festival of lights had come to be regarded as a period when even the most conservative of middle-class Indians, assured of society's whole-hearted sanction, lowered their guard and put their luck to the test – if I remember correctly it had partly to do with an obscure legend about the Goddess Parvati playing dice with her husband Lord Shiva on the day.

The season of Diwali parties had commenced and I naturally had entrée to the best of them. Every year my lawyer, a most social creature, threw a party for all his hotshot clients and friends, with what passed as the cream of Delhi society in attendance. It was expected that breakfast would be served at these lavish Diwali parties; the distinction between weekdays and weekends was temporarily erased, and as a result not much work was done during the desi Christmas season, economic downturn or not. I was never one to decline an invitation when it involved a really good party in flashy company, so I went along.

The drawing room of my lawyer's posh house in Maharani Bagh had been converted into a gambling den with card tables – the stakes greatly varying on each – snaking their way across to the dining room and making their way on to the large veranda. The rich, famous and corrupt all sat at gambling tables with cards in their hands and bundles of rupees stacked by their elbows. You could not tell them apart. It was like that silliest of American festivals, Halloween, where everyone was given free rein to hide themselves behind a mask and behave as wantonly as they could get away with. No chips were used in this den; it was the visceral feel of cash in their palms that drove the lives of those present at the party; the dullness of plastic could not replace that effect.

I had never cared for the sedentary and fleeting excitement that card playing provided so I kept out of the way. Or it could be, as Neena liked to tease me, that small vices did not attract me. While Karan Nehru, who much preferred hearing his own voice to gambling, worked his magic and kept the other non-gamblers occupied with his animated views, I stood with Azim Khan and talked about everything under the sun except politics, of which both of us had quite had our fill recently. The initial wariness between us was long gone and Azim Khan was now officially my friend, a rare honour. I was as surprised that this had happened, as he must have been.

Mohan Patel had called the band I had associated myself with 'vultures' – the facilitators of ministerial venality – and they were a hard-to-ignore presence at this party as well. They stood out like stars studding the night sky; a resemblance attributable primarily to the soft glow emitted by their unsubtle choice in wristwatches. I could not really call myself a member of their fraternity, having never swung a deal on my own steam, but they believed me to be the leader of the pack as I was the PMO man, he whom, they felt, wielded the ultimate, visible power. Like most other outside observers they failed to differentiate between Father's position and mine. Nevertheless, I did not mind their attention too much since they were always an interesting lot – after all they had to be the best of courtiers to maintain their position in Delhi's durbar.

These 'bag-carriers' had formed a trade union of sorts and liked to congregate on Saturday evenings at the newest nightspot. The stories I had heard about their antics normally involved the use of VIP areas; an endless flow of Dom Perignon; influential guests looking to spend other people's money for a good time forgetting nothing was ever truly free; and models. These 'Dom attack' evenings, as they were brashly christened for the belief that champagne made everything possible, were now mostly centred around the sprawling and exotic-sounding Siamese Lounge. Fear of Neena, losing all self-control, and public exposure, in that order, had stopped me from accepting the open invitation I was repeatedly proffered by this lot. I will admit I was tempted and often wondered if one unforgettably sleazy night would not be worth all the consequences that would inevitably follow. This was when I recalled my absinthe-soaked adventures and snapped out of it. There was hope for me yet.

Anyway, the vultures were keeping their distance from me this particular evening as the formidable Azim Khan had no use for them. In Azim's company I believed myself free of the danger of being waylaid by them, and by all bores in general, but that turned out to be too much to expect. Ah, the notoriety of television!

I saw him approach from the corner of my eye. He was a stray who had managed to evade Azim's intimidatory aura. I refused to acknowledge his presence even though he was standing a foot away from me. Azim and I continued our discussion on some inconsequential topic, trying our best to give him the cold shoulder. We soon discovered that we were dealing with an extremely thick-skinned specimen who refused to budge. I gave up and turned around. He was thrilled to have finally got my attention.

'Beg your pardon, sir, my name is Harbir Sahni. I am a big admirer of your father's,' said the excited Sikh gentleman whose appearance automatically telegraphed to me his particular clan within the faith even before it was confirmed by his name. It was a response that came instinctively to every Indian – the barometer for gauging caste and creed was inbuilt. Right or wrong, it was a fact and you just dealt with it.

Azim, meanwhile, assessing the situation as hopeless, silently glided away.

Mr Sahni's beard went all the way up to the bottom of his eye sockets and his pointy turban was of the kind you stuck on your head like a hat after hardening it into shape. I had before me what we Jat Sikhs considered to be a stereotypical Bhapa, a caste distinction in a religion supposed to be free from the maladies of Hinduism. Even Islam, a faith that demanded complete obedience of its adherents, had not been able to totally break the back of the caste system in South Asia, so it was not particularly surprising that the Sikhs had brought their deeply ingrained caste identities with them to their new religion.

If the Jats saw themselves as farmer-warriors, they saw the Bhapas as archetypal money-grubbing traders and merchants who lived soft urban lives and did not toil or make use of their hands to earn their living. They were disparagingly grouped under this term and were thought of as being merely a step away from reverting to Hinduism, with whom – unlike the Jats – they even shared common surnames. The prejudice felt by Jats towards all non-Jats was just another example of men making judgements about fellow religionists based on the purity of birth rather than that of character. Sunni vs. Shia, Catholic vs. Protestant – they were all arguments arising from the same human urge to segregate. The Khatris – the caste name of the so-called Bhapas – in turn, thought of the Jats as uncivilized hooligans who were never happy unless they were at war or on a bender. I must say that the allegation was not without merit and I make this admission as a top-tier Jat, being a Sidhu, which made me a kinsman of the most aristocratic Sikh family in contemporary Punjab, the royals of Patiala

– a position, I must confess, they dubiously earned by siding with the English against Maharaja Ranjit Singh, Punjab's only unifying monarch, and arguably the greatest Jat Sikh of all. For this they earned over a century of colonial patronage and pampering. You could say deal-making was in my blood.

Jats deeply revered and admired the tenth and last Sikh Guru – who incidentally in a stark historical irony had been like his nine predecessors a Khatri himself – for founding the Khalsa in his war against the Mughals and forever after ingraining a rebellious, martial streak in the members of his flock. The streak was very deeply ingrained in the self-image of the Jat Sikhs and led to their acting like an unruly band within which everyone wanted to be the leader and no one a follower. During peace this made for relative chaos but when war came knocking there were not many, in my admittedly prejudiced opinion, who could out-fight a sardar in full battle mode. That probably explained why Sikhs made up a disproportionately large part of the Indian Armed Forces in comparison to our two per cent share of the population.

Dhillon Uncle often said that those who engineered the 1984 anti-Sikh riots in Delhi had had no idea what monster they were arousing. They had targeted the peaceable urban Sikhs, code for Khatris, not realizing there were thousands of crazy Jats in the rural interior of Punjab who were always spoiling for a good fight. The fight that ensued had lasted a decade and cost way too many innocent lives.

I personally had no problem with those that met the definition of Bhapas and actually got on better with them than with my fellow Jats, whom I found a bit too volatile. Especially since, with my cut hair, I myself was not considered a pure Sikh. This did not concern me too much, but did put me at the back of the line to Sikh heaven; an unlikely destination for me anyway.

Returning to my encounter with Mr Harbir Sahni – after

introducing himself he recalled at length how my father had saved his then fledgling business from the income tax authorities who had been out to get him for some 'small oversight' on his part in filing his company's income tax.

'What business are you in, sir?' I asked, wanting to divert him from the subject of my father and avert, as was likely, his disclosure of how much Father had charged for the service of calling off the bloodsuckers in the income tax department.

'I am a consultant,' he said, with pride.

You would think they would have come up with a better euphemism for bogus business activity by now. 'What service do you provide?' I was almost afraid to ask.

'Anything that will make a profit and put food on the table. I'm a man who is flexible.' His fuzzy answers got my banker's antenna beeping. Despite myself, I began to be intrigued by the shady sardar. Sahni insisted on speaking in Punjabi, a language I could understand but spoke like a non-native, so I replied in my best Hindi, a patchy endeavour that involved a lot of holes being plugged by English words. He did not seem to mind, and acted as if we were conversing conspiratorially in a common tongue, our mother tongue, in fact.

'Flexible services, you say? Then, I'm sure the economic slowdown hasn't touched your business in the least.' Experience told me that people who made a livelihood illegitimately were normally dying to show off about it and only required an opening.

'Actually, in hard times demand for my services improves a touch. There is a premium to be had for efficient execution.'

'Which is?'

'I have already imposed my presence on your good self for too long. Let me present you my business card. If you ever need any help in any matter please call me. I owe your father a lot, and since he isn't with us to collect anymore, I thought it only fitting that you should do so in his place. If we sardars don't stick together then who else will?' He valiantly tried to bridge the caste divide and handed me his card. When I looked up after glancing at it, he was gone. Very much the mysterious character. The business card was generic and did not enlighten me any further on what services Sahni provided.

I located my host and pulled him aside with great difficulty.

'Who the heck is Harbir Sahni?' I demanded.

'An important associate of mine. He doesn't look like much but he's a one-man cruise missile. Why are you so interested?' My trusty lawyer waved at guests who were entering the party and was ready to run off. I grabbed his arm to make sure he stayed put.

'He came over to me and told me that since my father had helped him out once he owed my family a favour. What is his real story?' If he wanted to do me a good deed I needed to know what service he provided.

'Did he tell you what he did for a living?'

'He said he was a consultant of some sort. How exactly is he an associate of yours?'

'He runs a security firm that has a reputation for never saying no to any client request. The firm also specializes in the protection of computer networks for corporations, which is why I know him. He has put together a team of the best hackers in the country to work for his network security division. Their services come at a high price and I get a juicy cut for referring him to some of my clients.'

'I can't believe it. Why didn't he just say that's what he did in the first place?'

'Once a spy always a spy.'

'What?'

My legal counsel was losing patience with my questioning but he gamely persevered, 'He was directly recruited into RAW and made a name for himself as an unobtrusive and effective operator.'

I always found it interesting that the acronym used for India's external intelligence agency spelt WAR in reverse.

'Around ten years ago he was posted as the chief spook of our embassy in Mauritius. Our High Commissioner there is literally like a viceroy and to maintain our position of influence in the island we pay off many of the leading politicians. The discretionary funds are disbursed from RAW's secret account. There was very little supervision of this transaction. Taking advantage of this, the High Commissioner and Sahni got together and started merrily skimming from the funds, believing for some reason that their bosses and the locals would never compare notes. Unfortunately, they did and both officers were shipped home. The senior diplomat's career was sidelined but he avoided facing a vigilance case because the foreign office could never publicly admit to the existence and purpose of the embezzled money. Sahni was not as fortunate and he was removed from service. Luckily for him he had an innate entrepreneurial flair.'

The back story did not match the individual I had met. 'Come on, I'm not sure he can even speak English.'

'You've seen too many James Bond movies, yaar,' said my lawyer friend. 'Most of our spying is done in the seedier parts of our neighbourhood, where speaking English fluently is a liability and could even get you killed. Sahni was one of the best at melting into the background.'

'With his turban?'

'He has short hair underneath. And don't ask me about the beard next. You can use your very fertile imagination on that score.' My incredulity was starting to get on my host's nerves. He was understandably keen to re-join his party.

'I would have never guessed. Being an ordinary businessman now must be boring for him.'

'He gets his share of thrills. I've noticed that once he signs on a new client, the main competitor of the said client suffers some kind of industrial espionage incident shortly thereafter – and I'm not just talking about an invasion of their online systems.'

'Physical raids as well?'

'For select clients and a special fee he is said to provide plumbing services.'

'Does he restrict himself to the business world?'

'I don't know for sure, but I've heard rumours that he has clients in the political world.'

'Interesting,' I murmured. 'My first impression of him couldn't have been more off target.'

'You know what they say – never judge a book by its cover, now go get drunk. See you later!' He resumed his hosting duties.

I had mistakenly convinced myself, after my recent experiences and before meeting Sahni, that I had lost my capacity to be shocked. It goes to show you that the only certainty in life is its uncertainty. I could not figure out how this seemingly unremarkable man could ever be the lethal character that had just been described to me. All the same, I suspected his offer of a favour would come in handy one day. I shook my head a couple of times, put Sahni's card carefully in my wallet, and re-joined the party.

AFTER WEEKS OF action-packed days, the face-off between the PM and the President settled down to a more sedate pace. Rashtrapati Bhavan was still reeling from the PMO's body blows. All the President's men were probably laying low studying the changed ground situation to chart out their next offensive. I was relieved that the public pressure had eased and some sanity had returned to my life. The PM's coalition allies gave him some much needed breathing space and conditional support to take on the President in his way. Yadav Senior had not made any direct criticism of President Dayal in public as yet. I imagined he was waiting for the most opportune moment to speak out, when his words would make the maximum impact.

I sat on the sidelines quietly and kept my nose clean, waiting for what would happen next.

In mid-November Sanjay Kumar came to meet me in my house in Jor Bagh bearing a most bizarre proposition. It was late in the morning. We sat in my father's office at the back, the only room in the house where he could smoke, as per Mother's dictum.

'You are causing a problem for us,' he stated in his customary direct way.

'How so?' was my startled response. I expected him to pull out a revolver and finish me off right there.

'It is pretty clear now to everyone, whatever we might say to the contrary, that you work for the PM. The subterfuge of your being an independent financial adviser working out of your mother's house is not credible anymore. We don't have an answer when the Opposition asks us what your role in our operations is. Your father was the Prime Minister's Senior Domestic Adviser, but who are you? First you were seen handling the cricket elections with Shitij and now the whole country recognizes you by sight.'

'What am I supposed to do about that?' I felt helpless.

'Follow my instructions. I have talked to the PM and he agrees that you need to be co-opted into our campaign against Rashtrapati Bhavan.'

'Politics?'

'You have been appointed our new attack dog for the English news media, particularly television, effective immediately.'

An instant was all it took for me to transform from a behind-the-scenes adviser to a fully-out-there political operative. And what if I was only a pseudo one? Weren't they all fake in one way or another? But I was crap on TV: 'Did you not see the sorry performance I put up trying to defend myself against Dayal?' I asked Sanjay incredulously. 'Right. Of course, you didn't see me, you were buried under all those files from the National Archives. Let me tell you, I was horrendous and nobody I know said otherwise. Azim's been doing a splendid job as it is.' I pleaded for a reprieve.

'Azim Khan has opposed the President expertly, true, but that's different from staunchly and unconditionally making the PM's case. Whether we like it or not, the English media is where the editorial line of the nation is set; all the vernaculars follow its lead. You're the man for the job, Jasjit.' He looked at my stricken face. 'We'll only make use of you sporadically,' he reassured me.

'I can't stand the sight of the press. The PM is asking for too much,' I exclaimed, the irritation welling up inside me.

Sanjay looked around urgently for an ash-tray in a house that as far I knew probably did not possess one. I shoved a dustbin at him, and he stubbed his cigarette out in it. 'What nobody is going to stand for is you as a free agent, with seemingly extra-constitutional authority, going around without having a defined role of any sort. Besides, you speak English better than all of us put together and the PM thought you performed wonderfully on TV considering how much pressure you were under. I'd advise you to trust his political judgement on this.'

The exit was slammed shut. Sanjay was a skilled debater and I was not going to win this round; not with his argument being reinforced by the wishes of Yadav Senior. 'If I do that, it's going to spell the end of my marriage,' I stated in despair.

Sanjay was here to do the PM's bidding; not provide a shoulder to cry on. 'You have no choice. It is time to take sides and hope for the best.'

'Is this is how you plan to recruit a fresh crop of leaders, then? Using blackmail and pressure tactics?' I asked, thinking that there was no avoiding a confrontation with Neena now; she had asked for too much when she'd demanded I not take on her father.

'Not at all,' Sanjay laughed dryly. 'Those are coming fast and furious, spawned from the loins of present leaders. Nepotism has taken over politics like it has Bollywood. For a smart boy to shimmy up the political grease-pole in this day and age without family connections requires an amazing amount of political talent and luck. To get a ticket to run for any office you have to queue up behind wives, daughters, sons, nieces, nephews, and lovers of both sexes.'

'Somebody like me wouldn't stand a chance.'

'You, my dear boy, have every chance in the world. Just say the word and I'll get an MP to resign. His seat will be yours with a minimal amount of campaigning.'

I was touched that he considered me worthy of such an effort, even if the offer wasn't entirely serious in nature. 'Thank you but no, I'll pass. I've found politics too high-risk for my liking.'

'Good. I admire a man who knows his limitations. Let's go and announce your new role to the press.'

We drove over to the party headquarters to unveil Jasjit Sidhu, the Political Spokesman. My conversion to the dark side was complete. I had now become a card-carrying member of the Yadav army. My marriage to Neena was in severe jeopardy. Why was I tossing aside the one person I genuinely cared about? I think the tide of events was just too strong for me to take on by myself.

TWO HOURS LATER, appropriately dressed in a kurta from Fabindia, I was produced in the press enclosure. I was happy to see that the news of my new appointment had not been leaked. Only the milder beat reporters hung listlessly around. Seeing me must have made their week. Kumar briefed the reporters on this latest development and asked me to say a few words. I obliged with the fewest words possible and withdrew. The PMO could answer the avalanche of questions that was sure to follow.

After the press conference, I hot-footed it back to the safety of Jor Bagh and began mentally rehearsing an explanation to give to Neena and my mother, both of whom were completely unaware of my news. When I told Mother she was encouraging and said she was confident that I would do fine – I suppose she felt there was no harm in granting a doomed man an iota of false hope. But it was Neena's reaction I was really worried about.

I closeted myself in Father's office, forwarded all incoming calls on my mobile phone to my voice mail, readjusted the settings of the phone to only pass through calls from a select few, and began watching the news on the small television set in his room. I found I had the honour of featuring on a breaking-news banner on almost all the news channels.

Then came the call of the only person I truly feared, and it was not General Bastard: 'So you've become a wretched neta now. What's next, Prime Minister Sidhu?'

'Good afternoon to you too, my love,' I greeted Neena as sweetly as I could.

'Don't good afternoon me. Should I have found out about this from the television? What the hell are you playing at?'

'Actually, it wasn't my decision to make. It was more like a firman from the high command. I was told about it only two hours ago. I can't say more on the phone. Where are you?'

Neena was out of town with her father. President Dayal had defied the PMO's security alert and gone on a visit of three southern states. The President could not be blocked from travelling domestically; as much as Yadav Senior would have liked to, he was unable to stop him.

'I'm in Cochin today.'

'The IB will probably be eavesdropping on us.'

But Neena couldn't care less. Her voice went up an octave. 'Will you please explain your actions?'

'There is no need for you to get all hostile, I've been pushed into the political sphere against my will. This is a job partly given to me so that the PM can answer his partners and opponents as to why I am so visible in and around the PMO. Is that a good enough explanation?' I wasn't pleased at having given so much information over the telephone with God knows how many people definitely listening in but Neena had been in a better mood since the temporary cessation of hostilities, and I wanted to keep it that way.

'That's what they want you to think. But you're more in their grip than ever.'

She was right but I wasn't going to discuss the point on the phone or tell her that I would have to break the promise I had made to her about never criticizing her father in public. 'When are you coming back?'

'Tonight.'

'Is there any chance of my getting any loving on your return?'

'It depends on whether you're planning to surprise me with more stupidity in what remains of the day.'

Was that a yes or a no? I figured mixing power-politics and sex was a bad idea. I was finding this out the hard way. To be at the mercy of a woman's whims was not easy for me to handle and I decided to go hit some balls at the Delhi Golf Club. Pointlessly smashing shot after shot was a good way of relieving pent-up frustration.

Neena did ultimately take pity on me and I paid a secretive, highly risky visit to her quarters in the Rashtrapati Bhavan, on her return. I am sure General Bastard was informed of my presence but I was careful to make sure I did not run into him, and he didn't dare invade his daughter's privacy. He couldn't have been very happy, but I was with my wife and he was not about to make me feel guilty about that.

GENERAL BASTARD TOOK his revenge a week later, when Mother and I found on returning home from a wedding in Gurgaon – quite an excruciating experience in itself – that intruders had broken into it in our absence. Mother went into a panic but I was not overly concerned. The house contained no incriminating evidence of my international banking activities. There was not a shred of paper relating to any accounts within the territorial limits of India. The intruders had mainly targeted my bedroom and Father's office. The rest of the house had been superficially manhandled to make it appear like a simple robbery.

I looked over the ransacked office and discovered that only my laptop had been stolen. They would not find anything on the computer because I did not use it for any of my dealings either – mainly porn, actually, and they were welcome to it. I had given strict instructions to all my private bankers, not an Indian among them, that under no circumstances were they to directly contact me, either by phone or electronically. I contacted them myself every few days on a mobile phone whose SIM card I changed each time. The amount of money I played with was so vast that I had employed an investment strategy of capital preservation that meant very little investment in the stock market and required minimal day-to-day monitoring of the portfolio. If there was an emergency they were to call a Dubai number I kept and leave a message on the voice mail, of which I would be intimated by e-mail.

General Bastard's henchmen had executed a clandestine operation with great proficiency. The security personnel, who were on guard, never even knew there had been an intrusion. Our house was a corner one with a narrow, poorly lit service lane running behind it, and the intrusion took place from there. The operation was extremely professional. Not an inch of either my room or the office had been left untouched by the search. It had taken place in the dead of night and there had been no witnesses. They had good intelligence, knowing we had gone to Gurgaon for a marriage and would not return till late. They also knew that our domestic help had been given the night off and would not be in the house to get in their way. I did not need further proof to conclude who was behind the incident. They should have been smart and made a couple of deliberate amateurish mistakes to leave some doubt about their identity, but the efficient military mind could not be expected to think that way. I informed all those who needed to know about what had happened and assured them that no secrets had been compromised in any way.

For me the really worrying part was that this incident clearly showed there were now elements in the army that had gone rogue and were acting on the orders of Rashtrapati Bhavan. The possibility of a coup suddenly became much more ominous. Men like General Bastard did not care to lose; if he lost the battle for public opinion he would not hesitate from putting other tactics into play to win the war.

Despite the darkening forecast for the country's political future, there was a spring in my step after the break-in. I was in agreement with Sanjay's analysis of the event, which was that Rashtrapati Bhavan was running out of ideas and unless they were prepared to throw out more than sixty years of democracy we had nothing to fear from them as long as we did not make any silly mistakes.

This new development was only known by a few people as we had kept it from the media, who reported on the break-in but did not have the foggiest idea who was behind it. We did not want to leak what we suspected because there was no clinching evidence and it would have escalated the crisis in a direction we were not prepared to go yet.

There is a special kick you get in possessing the knowledge that the end of the world – or in this case Indian democracy– is nigh, as everybody else complacently goes about their business. The gossip in me was itching to scream out everything I knew.

A COUPLE OF days later, as I sat contemplating an India under military rule in the back seat of my car, I was treated to an even more horrific sample of the possible future under military rule.

It was around midnight. I was returning from the airport after a two-day business trip to Bangkok where I had gone to meet an associate from Singapore. I'd made it out of the airport unusually quickly that night. Karnail Singh was waiting for me outside the VIP parking lot – one perk of being a PMO stooge. It had become like an old drill for us and we did not even exchange a greeting when I emerged from the arrivals gate. He took my overnight bag and we walked wordlessly towards the car. Within a minute we were speeding away on the airport road towards the national highway. Traffic was thin so I was immensely bewildered when a vehicle came and rammed us from behind. I was jolted out of my seat with my neck and back bearing the brunt of the assault.

Karnail pulled the car over on the side of the road. After making sure that my injuries were not life-threatening he got out of the car to holler at the guilty party, who it seemed had stopped right behind us. That they had not made a run for it was surprising and to their credit I thought, as I made a check of my various body parts. Then I heard sounds of a scuffle but a truck roared by just then and obscured my view. The next thing I knew five masked men, completely clad in black, were making their way towards the car. Karnail Singh was nowhere to be seen. I tried to jump out of the car and make a run for it but my back made an escape impossible. Not a single car passed by as the men grabbed me and pushed me into the back of their SUV. I was blindfolded, gagged and tied in a manner that made the pain in my back excruciating. They pushed me out of sight, with my face pressed against the floor of the vehicle.

After they threw me in the back I heard one of them, probably the man in charge, order another to drive my car and follow close behind. No word was said about what had become of Karnail Singh. I feared the worst. The ride to wherever they were taking me was short, which was predictable, since the army cantonment occupied a major part of south-west Delhi. I was dragged out and carried for some distance. Then I felt my carriers descend some steps. I was thrown upon the floor and my bound limbs freed. I was commanded to stand up by the same voice of authority that I had heard earlier and I obeyed despite my back, which was in a bad state. I was still blindfolded and could not find the courage to remove it. The voice then ordered me to take off every piece of clothing I had on except my underwear. I baulked and got slammed in the back of my head, which was all the encouragement I needed. I removed my clothes at record pace. Within moments of my stripping I was pushed down into a chair, to which I was bound again. I must have been in this position for about an hour with no idea where I was, but pretty sure who was responsible for abducting me.

I was a fool not to have predicted what the next move of the linear-thinking President would be: if there are no incriminating documents then get to the man who holds the required secrets in his head, i.e. yours truly. I should have had the foresight to step up my security; at least it would have made it more difficult for these army thugs to nab me.

My blindfold was ripped off and my eyes adjusted to the bright room I was in. I was not in a dungeon like I had feared. The room resembled a hospital room and was bathed in fluorescent white light. The men in black had been replaced by two men in army uniform who were glaring at me with barely controlled violence. In the movies, this is the point when the hero spits out a taunt. But I was not about to give them another reason to whack me. Then the door to the room opened and General Madan 'mad dog' Januha himself, walked in.

Januha was all upper body, with legs forming a very small proportion of his physique. He had arms that would have given Popeye a complex. His face was jowly, his skin loosely draped on his face, and his features drooped downward. He walked up to me and put his staff under my chin. 'Do you know who I am?' he growled self-importantly.

'My worst nightmare.'

He laughed. 'That I may well be, but I go by the name of Lieutenant-General Januha.'

'Congratulations on your third star, General. Too bad it's going to be ripped off very soon.' I wasn't about to give up without some kind of a fight, false bravado though it might have been.

'Very feisty. Now shut up and listen to what I have to say.' He put his face inches away from mine. I smelt the booze on his breath. 'You have caused enough trouble for us, but you have the chance to make up for all your wrongdoing. Tell me about Yadav's bank accounts and I will allow you to leave here on your own two feet.' He straightened to his full height and turned his back to me.

'That is not going to happen,' I stated, trying to control the tremor in my voice.

'Then we'll just have to extricate it from you, won't we?' He seemed pleased that I hadn't broken down straight away and that wasn't good news.

'What are you going to do, beat me till I break?'

'Not even close, Mr Sidhu. When I was serving in Assam we came up with a particularly effective way to make ULFA militants talk. It wasn't bloody and there was no danger of the prisoner passing out or dying too quickly. Nor did it leave any obvious marks for human rights monkeys to holler about. Would you like to know what it involved?'

It was a rhetorical question. He didn't wait for my reply. He went over to a table in the back of the room and returned with a plastic box filled with some shiny metallic material. He reached in the box, carefully pulled a specimen out and then displayed it for my benefit. It was a needle, a large one to be specific. I visibly cringed.

'Yes, Mr Sidhu, it is a needle. I can't wait to see your expression when I tell you what I plan to do with it,' he sniggered, and taking their cue from their leader, so did the other two men in the room. 'You see, in Assam we would strip the militants naked and then go to work, plunging one needle at a time into their *testicles*.'

I grimaced in the singular way that all men do when they hear or see a fellow male get hit in the nuts; only this was much, much worse.

'I know, it hurts just to think about it. Imagine what you will go through when we start puncturing your balls. Most of our prisoners didn't make it past the single digits, but there was this one mad bugger who set the record with thiry-two needles before he gave in. A sturdy sardar like yourself should have no trouble beating that record.'

'You bastard, you wouldn't dare. You're bluffing. They must already be out looking for me and you are running out of time. When Neena finds out about this, your boss is going to have a lot of explaining to do.'

'It's one in the morning, my dear sardarji. Of course for you it's always twelve o'clock. Everybody you know is fast asleep. Nobody is going to miss you till sun up and by then you will have spilt the beans. And then you can tell Ms Dayal whatever you want, because after we are through with you there won't be much you will remember.'

'So what are you waiting for? Get to it if you're so sure of your methods.' I was praying that he was bluffing and he would admit it to be so.

'Patience, patience, now. Anticipation is half the fun. I'm a man who doesn't believe in resorting to violent solutions unless absolutely unnecessary. In that spirit, I will give you twenty minutes to think about what you really want to do without my distracting presence. Hope you see reason.'

He marched out of the room with the two guards at his heels. I was alone. There were two possibilities, that Januha was bluffing and my balls were safe, or he wasn't and my balls were in for some serious puncturing in the very near term. I wouldn't know what game Januha was playing till he actually stuck one of those ghastly needles where he was threatening to. It came down to me asking myself how far my fiduciary responsibility to the Yadavs extended. The crystal clear answer I came up with, understandably, was that it did not extend to sacrificing my balls. So, I came to the decision that I would continue to play the loyal banker till the first needle broke skin, then all bets were off.

I was not a brave man nor did I pretend be. I would start by revealing account numbers of old clients of mine from when I worked in Dubai. That ruse would succeed for a while, then I would have to reveal some genuine account information but as little as possible and at as slow a pace as I could manage. I had to somehow stretch it till morning without causing too much damage. Even if they knew where the accounts were, and the account numbers, it would not help them much since they could not get to them or prove the Yadavs had anything to do with the accounts. They needed documentation and a money trail, neither of which I could supply sitting in Delhi even if I wanted to.

Januha returned much sooner than the twenty minutes he had given me, which told me that he was running on a deadline. I had a clear strategy now and my wits were more together than during our last chat when he'd had a clear mental advantage over me.

'Have you come to your senses?'

'Sardars never do.'

'Very well, have it your way.' He knocked on the door and was joined by a lanky figure with emotionless eyes, in surgical scrubs and gloves. 'I will not introduce you, he's the lucky fellow who will be doing the needlework tonight. Feel free to scream all you want, this room is soundproof. I'm amazed every time at how easily the needle slides into the scrotum, like it were a thin leather pouch. There's plenty of space down there for the needles.'

The masked man opened the briefcase he was carrying and began preparing his syringes meticulously. I looked away from him with a shudder and initiated negotiations with Januha. 'Any account details I could provide would be of no use to you.'

'The prospect of pain appears to have got you thinking straight. Good. You'll have to give us the names of the bankers handling the accounts as well. Then you will call them from here and ask them to fax you the latest account statements.'

'I have given them strict orders that even if I ask for it, not one document is to be transmitted to India. I follow strict protocol when dealing with them. They'll know something is wrong if I phone them and make that request.' Which was true but if I did demand a fax none of my bankers was going to argue. The size of the accounts made sure of that.

'You may be lying but I will go along with your story. Ask them to fax it to the Defence Attaché in one of our embassies, who will then forward it to us. Any objections?' Januha could really play the game. No wonder General Bastard had brought him in to serve as his chief aide.

'There is no way you can connect the Yadavs with the accounts, even if you get your hands on the statements.'

He brought his face close, his nose millimetres from mine. 'Why don't you let me figure that out for myself after I see the statements?'

'All the offices must have shut by now,' I tried again.

'I'm positive you can get what you want whenever you wish.'

He wasn't going to be fooled and I was running out of excuses. 'I doubt you will ever let me out of here.'

'Actually, it's entirely in your hands. Co-operate and your freedom will be restored to you. Frankly, I don't see why you are being so loyal to Yadav, the rat would drop you without a thought if it were in his interest to do so.'

'You want me to believe that if I tell you what I know I will walk away without any problems? If the Yadavs go down they will come looking for me. I'm protecting them as much as I am safeguarding my own interests.'

'You must have made yourself a very rich man, doing what you do.' He turned his back to me, arms on his hips.

'Would you like to join the ranks of the extremely rich?' Bribery was worth a try.

'Are you trying to buy me off?' I had caught him off guard; he turned around to face me, wearing a quizzical look on his baggy face.

'My cheque book is in my hand baggage,' I offered.

'You really are something else! I have you by your balls, literally, and all you can think of is money.'

'Everyone has a price and my balls definitely do to me. How much to let me out of here, unscathed?'

'You disgust me, Sidhu. I am an officer of the Indian army and my loyalty to our commander-in-chief is absolute. Integrity is obviously a phenomenon alien to you.'

'I'm sure all your torture victims will vouch for your

integrity.' I was snide and got smacked as a consequence. Maybe I imagined it, but I think I tasted blood. I was too shaken to gather my senses and confirm this.

'Keep talking. In a few minutes all your cockiness is going to evaporate. I am really looking forward to see you grovel.' If he was bluffing he was doing a darn good job of it.

'I am ready,' the man in the scrubs announced. Januha ordered the two bodyguards to get me to my feet. Then with scalpel in hand the gloved torturer came towards me and sliced my underwear off me in two neat strokes. I was standing naked in front of these four dangerous men and I debated whether it was time to give up the tough guy act. I can report that my member was shrivelled with fright and did me no honour. The fading voice of courage inside me insisted I hold out a while longer. I gritted my teeth and resisted the urge to scream. My eyes were brimming with tears. I would have done absolutely anything right then to get out this mess, anything at all. I was no martyr.

'Strap him down on the examination table,' said Januha. I tried to resist but the apes were well trained and handled me expertly. I was forced to lie down on the examination table and all four of my limbs were put in braces. My legs were spread-eagled to make room for the masked man to gain entry to my nether regions. He cleaned me with a cotton swab soaked in disinfectant. How very considerate.

'Last chance,' said Januha as the masked man picked up the first needle. It was a normal sized needle but from where I lay it looked bigger than any needle I remembered seeing before. I had reached my limit – I decided to throw in the towel.

The words of surrender were on the tip of my tongue, a fraction of second away from being uttered, when somebody knocked on the door. One of the guards unlatched it and a man dressed in a black uniform, similar to those worn by the goons who had nabbed me, walked in.

'Sir, you have a phone call,' said the new arrival. I was able to recognize the voice as that of the leader of the abduction squad. He didn't glance at me once; a major feat of discipline considering the unusual situation I was in.

'I told you not to disturb me under any circumstances. What part of that order did you not understand?' Januha did not care to hide his annoyance.

'Sir, I was ordered to get you to the phone.'

'By whom?'

The man in black hesitated and then whispered something in Januha's ear. He immediately stood up and left the room. It was apparent who was waiting on the line. Januha returned a minute or so later cursing like a mean drunk. He threw a chair across the room and then said something to the masked man in a low voice that I was unable to catch.

The last memory I had of my visit to that ghastly room was that of the masked man giving me an injection in my arm. Everything went black after that.

I WOKE IN my own bed with the comprehension that I had had the worst nightmare in the history of nightmares. Only latterly did it dawn on me how real the events had been. Neena came into my room and hugged me in tears. My back did not appreciate the roughness of her affection and it let me know so in a violent way. The doctor came and checked me over. No permanent damage, he reported. After Neena left to personally procure the prescribed painkillers for my back I checked my crown jewels and was overjoyed to find no damage at all. It was a close race now between Januha and General Bastard, regarding whom I hated more. You cannot make animosity more personal than by going after someone's manhood. I mean, that was just not done. It was going to be no-holds-barred from my side as well.

Neena returned with the medicine and my mother – who

insisted on physically enveloping me in maternal affection and wailing about how close she had come to losing me. She was not wrong about that. I had many questions, as did they, so we spent an hour exchanging notes. I left out the unpleasant part about the proposed acupuncture of my nether regions. The ladies did not need to hear that and I definitely did not want to relive it.

The hero of their tale was the man who had gone missing from mine – Karnail Singh. From what they told me, and from what I further confirmed after getting more details from Karnail later, I would have been done for if the abductors had not made one mistake.

When Karnail got out of the car to confront the assailants he instantly realized something was wrong by the way the men in the SUV that hit us were dressed. The sight of their weapons left little doubt of their intentions. He told me that there wasn't anything he could have done had they not got distracted by a truck that zoomed by in the lane close to where we had come to a stop. Karnail used the kidnappers' momentary lost of focus to dive into the darkness of the foliage on the side of the road. They fired three of four shots in his wake but they weren't interested in wasting time chasing a secondary target with every chance that somebody passing by could catch them in the act. Speed was of the essence, so they concentrated on their primary task of grabbing me. I hadn't heard the shots because Karnail Singh said the weapons had been quietened with silencers. From what he saw he was certain the men must have been from the Special Forces. It made sense that Januha would have only entrusted the operation to his comrades of old.

Lying low in the bushes and shrubbery, Karnail emerged after he heard both vehicles being driven away. His phone having been left in the car, he sprinted the short distance to the conglomeration of shops along the national highway where he found a telephone and informed my mother of what had happened. She did not need to be told who was responsible and what would be the most effective way of finding me. Mother immediately called Neena, who in turn confronted her father.

General Bastard had vehemently denied having any hand in my disappearance. All the same, within an hour of his denial I was found unconscious outside my house in the passenger seat of my car. The security guards had not got a good look at the men who had left me there but did see them drive off in a vehicle similar to the one that had been driven by my abductors.

By the time I had regained consciousness, the PMO was functioning in full crisis mode. The army's loyalties were seriously in question. This would have to be taken into account in deciding our next move. How we could have allowed the confrontation to sink to such a state I will never know. But the midget PM was not about to take the high road in response to Januha's treatment of me. He could and would go lower. With vengeance burning in my heart, I for one, was all for it.

It took me one week to get back on my feet and recover from the shock of almost having become a human voodoo doll. During my recuperation I told everybody who asked to meet me that I was resting in bed because of a severe cold and cough. Winter was making its presence felt with a dip in the mercury and my excuse was very believable. The back specialist said my spine would heal, but slowly, and I should not overexert myself until then. So much for sex. I was having a grand old time of it.

Stuck in my room I had nothing to do but watch television all day. I would have preferred to read, but my mind was whirring at such a pace that I could not find the concentration. Television did not require that much mental effort, and I searched for programming that would divert me. I could not remember the last occasion on which I had lazed around like a couch potato. But instead of relaxing me everything on TV aggravated me. Having become a news-junkie, largely out of necessity, I could not stay away from the news channels. Anyhow these days, every second or third channel was one, and most of them seemed to be largely manned, barring the odd veteran or talented exception here and there, by perky youngsters who had probably never entertained a single political thought in their heads before they were hired. They had to bring in so-called experts to explain every single situation to the viewers. The trouble was that these experts were commonly print journalists or academicians or retired bureaucrats who were incapable of adapting to the visual medium that required a pleasant face and succinct commentary.

American and British television news divisions, the pioneers, in their early days, had poached much of their talent from radio news, getting people who were already accustomed to the art of instant news dissemination. I suppose our news people would learn and improve with experience. In the meantime, the viewers would have to wait for Indian television news to sufficiently mature, for the first batch of authentic anchors and reporters who understood that when asking questions less is more and parroting the government line or conventional wisdom was not reporting. For the sake of my blood pressure I restricted my television viewing to movie channels and, my favourite, the History channel.

Neena kept me company as and when her schedule would allow. I was sure General Bastard had given instructions to keep her as busy as possible. What I could not understand was why Neena felt she had to fulfil these commitments for a man who had plainly ordered my physical degradation, if not death. I almost asked a couple of times but I bit my tongue. There were too many fronts open right now and I did not need to open another one with her. She was trying her best to play the good wife and I decided to be thankful for that.

I jumped out of bed one week after my midnight rendezvous with General Januha and felt ready to take on the world; sore back notwithstanding. I was fully dressed and about to proceed to the PMO when Neena arrived. I had begun to get used to the constant presence of her security detail so I did not at first notice that she was accompanied by two important personages.

'Where do you think you're headed off to?' asked Neena

'I am a fully grown man, madam,' I bristled. 'I cannot be expected to stay under house arrest because of some minor injuries.' I was feeling hemmed in and needed to leave the house. This may have led me to sound a bit churlish.

'Well, before you head off to rule the world, we'd like to have a chat. Why don't you grab a seat?' I turned to glower at the men who had walked in with Neena. Azim Khan and Karan Nehru had followed her into the house! Azim was smiling. I'm glad he intervened, because from the look on Neena's face, she was about to explode.

'Let's sit out in the veranda and take advantage of the weather,' Karan suggested and everybody agreed.

Karan Nehru appeared unusually grim and did not greet me with his usual good humour. We sat outside on my mother's garden chairs and tea was brought out to us. It was one of those crisp Delhi winter mornings when a seasonally weakened and caressing sun lulls you into a false sense of well-being. The sun's balm was not working on me, however. This was because my better half ominously refused to meet my eye.

Before my visitors could bring up the topic they wanted to discuss, my phone rang and I wandered back into the house to take the call. I recognized the number as Sanjay's but Neena had followed me in and wrested the phone angrily from my hand, disconnecting it.

I had no defence so I did what I knew how to do best, beg forgiveness. 'I'm sorry for snapping at you. After all that you've done for me it was unforgivable.'

'And in front of those two. What must they think?'

'They've probably already forgotten about it.'

'Is this how it's always going to be between us? Turbulence with small pockets of clear weather?'

'It'll definitely never be dull, darling, but you knew that from the beginning. We both did.'

'I am not going to stand for any more of your little temper tantrums. I don't have the energy to deal with an overgrown baby along with all that's going on. Understand?'

I took my punishment and we returned to our guests.

'Neena, how is the atmosphere in the Rashtrapati Bhavan?' Azim came to the point immediately once we were seated.

'Tense and panicky,' Neena admitted. 'The staff thinks it is fighting some sort of war. Januha has turned the place into a military camp.'

Karan nodded in agreement; he seemed somewhat chastened from those early days of open support for the President. 'Your father? He took the Shetty revelation very badly, didn't he?'

'Do you think he was aware of Januha's abduction of our poor Mr Sidhu here?' asked Azim and gently patted me on the shoulder, signalling he was glad I was okay. With that small gesture he had assured me of his support. That was all I needed from him. The man had a way about him; that of a leader.

'He says he wasn't.' Neena's body language was getting stiff. I wanted to warn Azim but he persisted with his questions. She clutched at her cup of tea, her hands taut with tension.

Azim Khan was not insensitive to Neena's feelings. 'You know him better than anybody, Neena. How did you judge his response that night? And if you don't wish to tell me, that's fine too. I only want to know because if a compromise is to be reached, as Karan and I hope it still can be, his mindset will be an important input,' he said gently.

Neena returned her teacup to the tray. 'He told me he didn't have a part in the abduction and I believe him. I have to believe him because I mean the world to him and the father I know will not lie to me. Having said that, he has changed in the past weeks and his aides, Januha in particular, are taking advantage of his insecurities and fears. I have never raised my voice to my father, ever, but yesterday I did and I told him that if any member of his staff tried to hurt anyone I care about again I will pack up and leave the Rashtrapati Bhavan. He was almost in tears when he pledged to me that the episode would not be repeated. He even said that he would have removed Januha from his post immediately but he couldn't because he would be weakened in his fight with the Prime Minister. I shudder to think what would happen if I were not around to make him remember his humanity.'

Neena was eloquent in her grief. Her words laid bare the conflict within her soul. I felt for her and reached my hand out to her; she took it gratefully.

'No, you are right, Neena. It's important that he continue to receive your rational counsel. I want you to sit him down and ask him if he can see a way out of this dispute that he can live with,' said Azim, taking charge.

'You want her to play peacemaker?' I questioned.

'Not just her. You have to go with her,' Karan interjected.

'I am not entering the same building as Januha for the rest of my life.'

'Don't be scared, I'll be there as your protector,' said Neena, gaining a measure of revenge for my earlier harshness.

'I really like this girl,' said Karan with a chuckle.

'Does the PM know about this peace mission?' I asked.

'He doesn't so far. And if it fails he doesn't need to know. One step at a time,' answered Azim.

'The IB will inform him about my going to see the President.' I tried to find a way to wriggle out of my new responsibility.

'They cannot get past the gate and they've seen you go in before. They'll take it for a social call,' Karan assured me, though he was more than capable of fibbing.

Neena told me that it was best to visit her father during the cocktail hour, when General Bastard was his most approachable, and then stood up to take her leave, saying she had another engagement.

After Neena had left, I turned to Karan and Azim. 'How did you learn of my experience at the hands of Januha?' I asked.

'The PM told me, he was quite shaken,' said Azim. 'After hearing how the military was being used by the President to settle personal vendettas I realized how desperate the situation had become. I got a hold of Karan and knocked some sense into him.'

'Yeah, politics is one thing, but this was more than combat, it was terror,' Karan agreed. 'I can't imagine what you went through. Januha has been crazed for a long time; he should be in a mental asylum not the Rashtrapati Bhavan. I was siding with the Prez only to make Paresh Yadav's life difficult – not to have anarchy rule the streets.'

I was impressed by his contrition; normally Karan Nehru would have made several bawdy jokes about my experience even before entering the house.

'We agreed that our next step was to speak with Neena and you. I called her, and here we are,' concluded Azim.

'This situation is about to get completely out of control and this is the last chance for us to avoid total chaos,' explained Karan, leaning towards me for emphasis.

'Jasjit, you have a foot in both camps, so if anyone can pull this off it has to be you. Or else India could be headed for turbulence,' stated Azim.

If I was India's last chance then we were really screwed. 'But what exactly am I supposed to negotiate with him?'

'An immediate ceasefire, followed by terms for a peace treaty,' Azim answered precisely.

AFTER SEEING OFF Karan and Azim I remembered the call that Neena had forcibly disconnected. I called Sanjay. 'The twins are back in town and they're already making a nuisance of themselves,' he announced.

Thoughts of meeting General Bastard were instantly swept from my mind by this news. The Naik brothers aka 'the twins' had been my father's greatest rivals. It was they whom he had unseated from the highest reaches of influence in Delhi. Father had been no angel but there was a code of conduct he abided by; the Naik twins, however, would do anything in their quest for loot. While Father had always worked, phantom-like, from within the government, Vijay and Pramod did not follow the rules of discretion that my father had based his career on. They had never hidden their involvement in government deals and were currently the most high-profile among the fraternity's wheelers and dealers. Father had had an artist's appreciation of the subtleties of a well-structured deal, the Naiks came at a deal like a herd of elephants. Father had used his mastery of the levers of power to get work done but the Naiks were businessmen who only knew how to bribe and use other vulgar enticements to subvert bureaucrats and politicians. Ironically, the twins themselves were vegetarians and teetotallers and, apparently, completely faithful to their wives. They had used their loot to construct so many temples around the world that I was sure they believed it was possible to bribe God into pardoning their sins.

Vijay and Pramod Naik were identical twins and were therefore equally grotesque in appearance. Short, fat and ugly was the accepted description. Vijay wore spectacles and that was only the clue that allowed you to tell them apart. They were among the few people who looked as sinister as they were. The book matched the cover, so to speak.

I had heard a true story about them, confirmed from multiple sources, that gave me a fair idea of how they operated. A decade or two ago, they had accompanied the Defence Minister of the time to Moscow for the signing of a big defence deal worth hundreds of millions of dollars, which they had brokered. After the deal was signed, and the Naiks had assured themselves of a big pay-day, the rustic Defence Minister, on returning to his hotel, hinted that he would be interested in some female companionship. The Naiks promised to send him the best that Moscow had to offer and took their leave. They went downstairs to the street in front of the hotel and sent up to the minister the first two-bit hooker they could find. The hill-billy minister, of course, could not tell the difference. A Russian gori was a white goddess to him. The story exemplified to me how the twins operated. They were cheapies; and not men of their word. It was this main weakness in their operation that Father had taken advantage of.

A few badly handled deals had come back to haunt the Naiks and they had been laid low by political scandals and legal troubles – another weakness that Father had fully exploited. But the Naiks had always bounced back after each misstep and had managed to keep a hand in the pie for all these years. That is, until Father had joined the PMO.

Within a few weeks of taking over he had sent a message to the twins – who were based in Geneva – informing them that he had unearthed enough evidence against them to send them to jail for extended sentences, and that if they were smart they would not return to India. They had taken his advice and the establishment had written them off as a vanquished and spent force. We had stupidly taken our eyes off them and would have to pay the price for this error of judgement.

Father's helicopter crash had given them a reprieve, but I had found copies of the incriminating documents in my father's South Block office while cleaning it out. I had kept them in a safe place for just such an occasion.

I made some more inquiries about the presence of the twins in Delhi and found out that the reason they had felt confident enough to show their faces in the country at all was because they had tracked Shitij Yadav down in London – holidaying there on a recent government junket – and had won him over. The greasy Naiks and Yadav Junior had proven to be a perfect match. Shitij had arranged a meeting for them with the midget PM back home and the twins had flown in. They had already met Yadav Senior for dinner the previous night and, after conversing with them, the Prime Minister had subsequently asked for a meeting with me.

Alarmed, I rang up Sanjay. He decided to come with me to the meeting to get a sense of the damage the twins had caused. He knew them too and knew them well: something to do with a bad experience he had had with them that he was not very specific about, but I could well imagine.

When we went to see him the PM did not mince his words: 'I am not happy that all our secrets were almost spilt to Rashtrapati Bhavan. Only sheer luck saved us from disaster that day when you were nabbed by Dayal's goons,' he said as soon as we entered.

'Even if I had broken down, I couldn't have told them anything that would have been very useful to them.' I played with the truth.

'I don't care. What we need is… is… what was that phrase you used, Shitij?'

'Risk diversification,' prompted the fat ass of a son.

The Naiks were after my accounts. This was not good news.

'Exactly. There is so much at stake that I think more than one person should handle our accounts abroad and they should not be based in the country.' The midget PM was not fooling anyone in the room.

'And by that are you referring to the Naik twins?' I inquired ever so sweetly.

Paresh Yadav grinned guiltily, like a child who had been caught with his hand in the cookie jar. 'Jasjit, I don't know why

I even try keeping secrets from you. You heard of my meeting with the twins yesterday?'

'Prime Minister, I am no one to tell you whom you should or should not consort with, but let me advise you to stay away from those two. They have destroyed many political careers in the past and will no doubt do so again. That is my advice.' I tried to sound as professional as possible.

'I am well aware of their track record –'

'We can handle them,' Shitij butted in, cutting off his father.

'Bewakoof, did anyone ask for your idiotic opinion? How many times do I have to tell you to keep your trap shut and listen? Jasjit, is what I propose so unreasonable?'

'No, sir, you are the client and you have the right to do what you want with the funds. But I would then ask you transfer *all* your accounts into the control of whomever you pick. As I have told you before, I have put in place for you a financial network that grants you as close to full protection as you can get. If you insist on bringing in an outsider then you are threatening the security of the funds.'

'You will not share the job of managing the funds?' asked Yadav Senior, taken aback.

'Not only that, I will not be able to share the details of the financial network I have set up. Anybody you choose to replace me with will have to open other accounts for you. I will transfer the money out and then make sure that none of your old accounts can ever be proven to have existed. If my successor makes a mistake and the authorities get to your money they will never be able to trace it back to me. We will cut all financial links from then onwards.'

I was not about to allow the Yadavs to tell me how to go about my business.

'You could then lead the authorities to me, if you wanted,' suggested the midget PM suspiciously.

'I almost had my manhood punctured for your sake, Prime Minister, I think I have earned the right to be trusted by now.' The Naiks must have given him a good working-over the previous night. The PM, like any client, was now only trying to explore his options. I decided to cut him some slack. All he needed was to be reassured of my competence.

He thought this through for a couple of minutes. Then the midget said, 'You're absolutely correct and I apologize for doubting your character. I think the twins have put me under a spell of some kind. I am not about to trust them with my money but they may have other uses.'

'But…' Shitij tried to voice his dissent.

Unfortunately for Yadav Junior his dad was even more impatient than usual with him on this occasion. 'Enough, Shitij. Please leave us and go do whatever you do. You are not to meet the Naiks again.'

Shitij left the room, the epitome of dejection, not even bothering to send one of his customary scowls my way. Life's knocks had broken the boy, it appeared.

'Sanjay, could you tell the head of his security to keep him away from the twins?'

Sanjay nodded and assured him he would do the needful.

'What is to be done with the twins?' I asked, thinking how happy I would make Father's soul if the Naik piglets were locked up for a stretch.

'I know what you have in mind, but let's hold off on that for the moment. In addition to consulting on my finances they had made an intriguing proposition regarding our troubles with General Dayal.'

'Do they claim to know him?' asked Sanjay, entering the conversation.

'They say that they've been bosom buddies with him since the days he was a lowly colonel.'

'What did they propose?' I asked.

'They wanted to broker a Shimla agreement between Rashtrapati Bhavan and us.'

'Do they have access to the President?' Sanjay was unconvinced.

'They say they do, but then they always say that.'

I got to the core issue. 'What do they want in return?'

'To get back into the game, without the threat of imprisonment hanging over their heads.'

'They expect a lot for men who are cornered,' said Sanjay. 'Do you want me to have a talk with them?' he asked the PM.

'Okay, talk to them and see if they are just gassing, or have an actual connection,' decided Yadav Senior.

'While you're doing that, may I suggest that I ask Neena to arrange a meeting for me with the President this evening to see if he can find any scope for an agreement?' I interjected nonchalantly.

The PM's ears stood to attention instantly. Yadav Senior had no way of knowing that the meeting had already been arranged, nor of Karan and Azim's joint appeal to me to somehow manage it, but I thought it made sense to cover my back in case the Intelligence Bureau was more competent than Karan had allowed for.

'Do you think that is wise? He may see it as a sign of weakness,' said an extremely agitated Sanjay.

'Dayal is a sharp operator, we need to be careful. Let's not be over-smart, it may backfire. Ask him simply if he will agree to a secret meeting with me. Man to man. He'll understand that language,' the PM said after mulling it over. The instinct of an experienced politician was a powerful tool and we supported his strategy. Personally, a more specific assignment was easier to handle for me than Azim's plan to get into a wide-ranging discussion on the dispute with a man who would very likely walk out of the room at the very sight of me.

The rest of the day crept slowly by with my dread of running into Januha again far overshadowing my apprehension at meeting General Bastard. It had only been a few days since my abduction and I think I was justified in feeling shaky.

I REACHED RASHTRAPATI Bhavan in the evening. It was a grand public building, a fusion of colonial and Mughal architecture, a masterpiece in sandstone and marble built to awe and intimidate, but I did not hang around to admire its architectural brilliance. I cut through the famous red-gravelled forecourt to the cobble-stoned North Court with a fountain at its heart, which always brought to my mind the setting of a Dumas novel, and then walked straight upstairs to the set of rooms that made up the presidential family quarters, a surprisingly modest-sized dwelling at the rear of the first and second floors.

I went up and hung around in Neena's room, waiting for her father to finish with his dastardly deeds for the day. As was my habit when scared shitless I drank more than I should have. Neena was in and out of the room, so she did not take much notice of my self-medication.

The hour of reckoning arrived. I was directed into a sort of study-cum-sitting room in the family wing. I strode into the room with purpose but General Bastard was not there yet. Neena went to fetch him. This was the first time that I had been shown into this room. I looked around. The Dayals had certainly unpacked all the way. I spotted Neena's paintings on the walls – their value had gone up exponentially since her elevation to acting first lady. There were a lot of family photos too. I inspected a snap of Neena as a tyke with her mother. They both seemed so happy back then. I wondered if Dayal had taken the photograph; I could not imagine him doing anything as familial as that, but I had to admit he did dote on his daughter. What really made the room though, was the spectacular view

– the Mughal gardens, laid out in perfect symmetry under a moonlit sky that flickered in the water channels of the famous garden. It just added to the surreal feeling that I was in some exotic medieval tale, awaiting the reigning despot to intimate me of my imminent end.

I moved on to inspect a shelf full of curios and artefacts. The first family caught me unsheathing an Omani dagger that lay invitingly on a side-table.

'Don't hurt yourself, Sidhu. Wouldn't want Neena to blame me for that as well.' My father-in-law was clearly in his element.

I'd expected my nocturnal experience with the army was going to be a point of conversation. 'No need to worry, Mr President, I've been recently made very aware of the dangers of sharp objects.' Take that, asshole.

'If you came here looking for an apology let me warn you that you've come to the wrong place.' Father-in-law was curtly unrepentant.

'Why would I possibly expect you to apologize? I was under the impression you had nothing to do with it.'

A bearer, wearing the traditional red and white uniform of Rashtrapati Bhavan, entered with a portable bar and brought a brief ceasefire to our verbal altercation. Neena had sat quietly so far, I doubted she would if tempers rose further. The bearer served our drinks of choice and departed.

'Jasjit has a message from the PM for you,' said Neena once the drinks were served.

'What does the runt want?'

'He wants to meet you in private,' I said.

'Why?'

'He didn't tell me, but it's reasonable to assume that he wants to make his peace with you.'

'I doubt it very much. He's trying to set me up for a fall.'

'You're being overly suspicious, Papa,' said Neena soothingly.

'That's the only way to handle Yadav and his gang. They think the Shetty episode has shattered my confidence and they want to intimidate me into a premature surrender.'

'You should spend less time listening to General Januha,' said Neena sharply.

'Neena, why don't you leave us so that we can speak alone for a few minutes?' the President asked his daughter nicely.

'No way! You say what you have to in front of me.' Neena was defiant. General Bastard knew there was no point in pursuing the matter.

'Sidhu, you go back and inform your ringleader that I would rather eat rubbish than have any dealings with him. The people of this country expect me to follow through on the promises I made to them and I will not fail them.' He was in full saviour mode.

I assessed that I had no choice but to hold my nose and massage his ego: 'Sir, you are without doubt the most popular public figure in the country and you have done more than any President to raise the prestige of your office. Even the Shetty revelations didn't damage your image that much. But if you take this fight any further you will lose. The PM is a master of political warfare and he will wear you down bit by bit. You had surprise on your side when you launched your initial assault but we survived it and you must face the reality of that failure on your part. Back down with your honour intact.' I tried to explain the situation to him in military terms that he was familiar with.

'You overestimate your precarious hold on power,' he insisted defiantly.

'He is the Prime Minister and history has shown that the power of the PM always triumphs in a contest of wills with the President.'

'And how many of those Presidents were former army chiefs?' The question was put to me conversationally, but the sinister implication was easily decipherable. I had finally heard it from the horse's mouth.

'Be very careful of what you say, sir. For the good of our country I am going to pretend that I didn't understand what you very clearly intimated. Nothing good can come from harbouring such thoughts.' It was going from bad to worse.

'Young man, our political leadership has become the problem and only a fresh start will get the country back on the right track. If all else fails I will not hesitate to use all the options I have at my disposal.'

'Papa, I'm shocked at you. What has happened to you?' Neena had come closer than ever before to seeing her father for what he really was.

'I have a vision for India and nobody will stop me from fulfilling my destiny. Tell that to your blasted Prime Minister.' Saying that, General Bastard stomped out of the room, slamming the door behind him for added effect.

If always having the last word was a criterion for dictatorship, I could vouch from personal experience that he was well qualified. 'You wouldn't be interested in taking the next available flight out of the country with me, would you?' I turned to Neena, with a desperate smile.

'This is hardly the moment for humour.'

'I do remember predicting that you would become a dictator's daughter one day.'

'You cannot relay the last part of what he said to the PM. Is that clear?'

'He has to be told.'

'At least give me a chance to see how serious he is.'

'Were you sitting in this room or not? Your father basically said he was going to take over the country. And I have no doubt he can.'

I didn't hang around very long after General Bastard's exit because my superiors expected me to brief them in person on the meeting. Neena did not mind because her father's behaviour had shaken her and she probably needed to be alone. I was glad she had gotten a dose of how he dealt with others; me in particular.

I WAS ON my way out of the Rashtrapati Bhavan when my pal Captain Chavan caught up with me. Januha had sent him to pat me down to ensure I had no recording devices on my person. I told him I didn't but he had to go through the motions because he told me every inch of the building was being monitored by closed circuit cameras and Januha was watching us as we spoke.

'Can we talk?' I asked Chavan after he had finished with his task.

'Yes, but keep walking. Our back is to the cameras. The Military Secretary has convinced the President to wire the place with listening devices, so those will also be in place soon.'

'How have you been?'

'I would describe myself as a harried soul but I am not about to complain about my life to you. I heard of what you went through,' said Captain Chavan. It was something all males could relate to.

'Not a very enjoyable experience.'

'These commando-types are the most arrogant and crazed group you'll ever meet; maybe they have to be, to do what is required of them. They wear maroon berets and call themselves the Red Devils. I'd say the name is appropriate.'

'I didn't see any maroon berets. The ones that came after me wore all black.' We had reached the exit.

Chavan turned to me: 'Look, you need to know that if the PM pushes Dayal too far there is going to be trouble. A dozen senior serving officers of the Indian army go through these halls every day. The army officers on staff have doubled, with new recruits comprising those who have taken leave to serve under the President. This is a military facility now. Januha is readying the ground for a takeover and is only waiting for the word from the Commander-in-Chief. The PM must not give the President an excuse to act. I'll try and get in touch with you if I find out anything else of importance. Now, for the cameras, laugh as if I told you a joke and then go to your car.'

I followed his instructions obediently; Chavan's words were chilling.

Rashtrapati Bhavan had suddenly become a very dangerous place.

Chapter 10

I WENT DIRECTLY from Rashtrapati Bhavan back to the Prime Minister's more modest residence. He was waiting for me with Sanjay and Shitij. Yadav Junior's banishment had been of an extremely short duration. It was all hands on deck, I suppose.

'Did he agree to a meeting?' asked the PM as soon as I arrived. I think he fully expected an affirmative reply from me.

'Not only did he reject the meeting but he openly hinted at a coup.'

With that one utterance I got everyone in the room to freeze in horror.

The threat of a coup is not something an Indian Prime Minister usually thinks he or she might have to confront in the course of their term. We Indians related authoritarian rule to countries like Pakistan, Nepal and Bangladesh; less than civilized places where true democracy had failed to take root. We believed we were much too evolved and complex a nation to fall prey to a despot; the Emergency was an aberration, we maintained, and we had learnt our lesson. Now another myth about our much vaunted democracy was on the brink.

Expectedly, a bunch of sceptical questions from Sanjay and Shitij was thrown my way. The PM shushed them both and asked me to describe my conversation with the President in detail. He wanted me to describe his adversary's mood and body language. I did my utmost to give them an unadulterated version of what had transpired and included what I had found out from Captain Chavan. The PM displayed an uncanny ability to immediately spot when I tried to soften some of the President's comments.

'The Armed Forces are not in our control,' pronounced Sanjay clinically at the end of my report.

'If they ever were,' said Shitij.

'Then the time has come to unveil our option of last resort,' decided Yadav Senior.

I had no idea what he was talking about. Nor did his son. 'What option?' he asked.

'If the army has displayed such disloyalty to its civilian masters, then we have every right to take our revenge. Anticipating this eventuality, I had asked the Law Minister a month ago to draw up legislation that would involve introducing a reserved quota for scheduled castes, scheduled tribes and other backward castes in the officer corps of our Armed Forces. This will mobilize the masses in opposition to the army, backing them off. In addition, it'll get Dayal where it hurts. When we served together in the Defence Ministry I remember there was nothing that irritated him more than when I asked about the caste-wise break-up of his officers. He would say there was no caste in the army. Well, we'll see about that, won't we, General sahib?'

The populist street fighter had come out in the open. General Bastard was about to get a kick in the solar plexus from the PM.

I was staggered. 'This has major political implications,' I said.

I looked at Sanjay. He was giving his fullest attention to cleaning his reading glasses. His supreme disinterest was a giveaway to me that he was the moving force behind the plan. Pooling political and administrative skills to obtain a desired result was his forté and this legislation had all those hallmarks. The military brass had been pinpointed as the source of the enemy's strength and they were being attacked using the midget PM's greatest political asset, his identity as a crusader for social justice. It was sheer genius, no political party would dare oppose it. National security, as always, would have to take a backseat.

'The upper castes and the Jats will desert us forever,' said Shitij in a rare display of intelligence.

'The Bihar and UP assembly elections are both coming up next year. Shitij is right, this will affect our poll prospects, for the good and bad. We may lose our paltry upper caste support, though we could also get a decent share of the Dalit vote,' Sanjay analysed.

'Gentlemen, I don't think you realize the gravity of our position. If we do not survive this tussle with Rashtrapati Bhavan, there will be no elections, Parliamentary or Assembly or Panchayati, for the foreseeable future.' Yadav Senior's brutal statement of fact awoke the rest of us to what the country was in store for if we failed.

'We will find some way to appease the upper castes later. At this moment I need to fall back on the core of my support base and leverage it against the army. We need to project the officer corps of the Armed Forces as an upper caste cabal that has to be broken; as the last barrier to social justice in India and the culmination of the Mandal movement.' The midget PM was trying out his new sales pitch and it was compelling stuff: 'The issue itself will automatically mobilize the backward castes not only in our strongholds but the rest of the country as well. We've been demanding reservation in the military for years.'

'What percentage is the reservation going to be set at?' I asked.

'We'll start with a demand for fifty per cent, like it is in the other central services, but that is unreasonable. I think we'll settle for around twenty per cent, divided proportionally between Dalits, STs and OBCs,' replied the PM.

'But it will just be applicable for the entrance exams for those applying to be officers with permanent commissions. The selected cadets will still have to pass out from the respective military academies on merit before they receive their commissions. That's no small test. The quota will naturally not apply to permanent commissions in the technical wings of the forces and for short service commissions,' Sanjay clarified, betraying a tremendous grasp of the minutiae of the proposed legislation that was supposedly the PM's brainwave.

'We are playing with fire here,' I said. The Jat Sikh in me, however dormant, was reminding me that some people, regardless of their caste, were born to fight and others just weren't cut out for it. The defence forces were held in high public esteem precisely because of the quality of officers they had produced over the years. That is why, of all the major central services, only the Armed Forces had been excluded from the reserved quota regime. It was universally understood, despite some political grumbling, that wearing the uniform was an honour that you had to earn through merit and your fitness to command. Our meddling and petty politicking was about to change all that forever.

'Jasjit, I am not entirely comfortable with this either, but we have to fight back or everything we believe in will be brushed aside by the broadsword of the military,' said Sanjay. He was right. There was no room for quibbling with the remedy when our entire way of life was at stake.

The army had brought this on itself, I tried to convince myself. 'You're right. Let's get to it,' I said.

'Okay, now that everyone's convinced, I want to talk about the strategy going forward,' said Yadav Senior.

'We need to get the Defence Ministry to report directly to the PM,' said Sanjay.

'What about the Defence Minister?' I asked.

'That's easy enough to arrange. I'll tell him to take to his bed,' said the PM confidently. Nobody doubted that the Defence Minister would do as he was told. His existence as a politician depended on the leader of his party, the PM.

'What difference will that make?' I questioned.

'You don't know what Sanjay is capable of. Let him spend one week in the Defence Minister's office and I can bet he'll be dividing and ruling. The Armed Forces are as faction-ridden as the rest of us, possibly more so,' said the PM looking proudly at his chief political aide. And, just like that, Sanjay Kumar became de facto Defence Minister.

'Is the legislation going to be in the form of a Constitutional Amendment?' I asked.

'Correct. We will have to pass it with a two-third majority,' answered Sanjay. 'Technically, we don't really need to, since the government has the constitutional powers to enforce quotas on the army through a simple executive order, but the Law Ministry says that the Armed Forces has always been treated apart on this issue, even in the Constitution, and a legal challenge can be made on that basis. So it's best to go the route of the Amendment.'

'Passing the legislation won't be a problem. No party's leadership is suicidal enough to ignore the size of the backward electorate. The hard part will come when the President has to sign the passed Bill into law. *That* will be the moment of truth,' predicted the PM. Shitij looked pretty much lost by now and was playing with his fancy new smartphone.

'We should arrange demonstrations of support for the legislation near army cantonments to fire up the people against the army. We have to vilify the officer corps of the Armed Forces for the public. If the President finds he doesn't have public support, I don't think he will dare do anything. It will kill any chance of his election if he doesn't sign it,' said Sanjay.

'A dictator does not need public support,' I pointed out to the politicians.

'Initially, when he is consolidating power, he will need it,' Sanjay replied.

'Hopefully we won't have to find out,' said the midget PM as he brought the meeting to an end.

Shitij had procured a set of high-end Bose speakers during his trip to London, with the Naiks' credit card no doubt, and he insisted on demonstrating their superior sound quality to Sanjay and me after the PM had left. He was trying to be friendly, I suppose, so we played along. But talk about having warped priorities at a time like this. We stuck around patiently while he figured out how to get the damn things to work.

'What did the twins have to say?' I whispered to Sanjay as we waited. He had met the Naiks while I was at Rashtrapati Bhavan.

'Same old stuff, one drop of truth in a bottle of lies. President Dayal hardly knows they exist, it is Januha they are trying to please.'

'How?'

'They offered money, girls, boys, and various other inducements but hit a stone wall. It seems General Januha's only weakness is his vanity. They are now egging him on against us and offering their support to make his delusions of grandeur a reality.'

'They told you all this just like that?'

'No, I convinced them that I was a free agent and would work to protect their interests in the PMO. The little beasts are petrified of what you might do to them with your documents but are possessed by a need to stick around and continue with their scheming as well.'

'How did you convince them?' I didn't see the twins revealing their plans to Sanjay on the basis of a vague pledge of protection.

'They like me… plus, I earned their trust by giving them the inside scoop on what Januha did to you and how Neena got you out of it. They are the biggest gossips and live for a gem like that, it made them feel like they were back in the loop. Januha had self-servingly not told them the whole story.'

I was mortified. 'Please tell me that you're pulling my leg.'

'Don't be so sensitive, we need them to help us stay in touch with what Januha is planning next. I don't want any more surprises. Giving your story was a very small price to pay,' Sanjay admonished me.

'Why don't we just bug them?'

'They have been doing business in this town since before you were born and probably take more security precautions than the President of the United States.' It was easy for him to be so nonchalant, after all it was not his most humiliating experience that was in danger of being leaked to the cocktail circuit.

Shitij's snazzy speakers came to life at full volume and made any further dialogue impossible. We had to suffer his music for a further half-hour. My ears rang all night.

I LAY AWAKE in bed for a long time deciding what to do. Then I remembered the mysterious Mr Sahni. I called him as soon as it was a decent hour to do so. He greeted me by name even before I uttered a word. I knew I hadn't given him my business card so he had to have already had my number stored on his phone. It normally would have worried me but this time I took it as a sign of his competence.

I outlined the situation to him and asked him if it was possible for his team to hack into the Rashtrapati Bhavan telephone lines and computer system. He said it would be a breeze. I warned him about the hi-tech equipment in use. He said that governments, even the Israelis, were always two steps behind actual technological breakthroughs that were taking place around the world. The babus in uniform didn't have a chance against his breed. They wouldn't even have to set foot inside the grounds of Rashtrapati Bhavan. He seemed almost disappointed that the excitement of the old days, when physical danger was always a given, had gone. If only he knew.

I told him to inform me if he found something of importance and I left it to his judgement to decide on what intelligence would fit that criterion. My delegation of authority got him pepped up and he promised me that the job would be given the highest priority as it was of national importance. The RAW agent was reporting for duty.

When I asked him about his fee, Sahni said he couldn't possible ask for money. I lied to him that it was not my money that was being spent and he should charge more than his regular fee because the job was as dangerous as it got. I described Januha and his functioning to him. Only then did he name his price

I had the cash delivered within the hour. Paying him made sure he would take the job seriously. I was not about to rely on the double-dealing Naik twins to keep us informed about Januha's activities. I had a bias towards a more proactive approach to solving problems and I hoped it would pay off again. The PMO did not have to learn of it till Sahni came up with something concrete.

Next I phoned Karan and Azim. They both agreed to meet me immediately. We sat out in the lawn in Jor Bagh as before and I filled them in on all that had transpired since our previous meeting. Karan said that there was no way Dayal currently had enough support in the Armed Forces for a coup, but he was convinced that once the news of the Constitutional Amendment was leaked there would be a stampede of support for the President and the coup would become a self-fulfilling prophecy.

Azim heard us both talk but stayed silent. He was unsettled

and saddened by the turn this mess had taken. The Amendment would complicate his politics as well, since he would have to take a position on the Bill and it would be important since he was a partner in Government. Karan knew his leader and party would take the easy way out and support the Amendment, as would the rest of the parties.

THERE WERE TWO weeks before the winter session of Parliament came to a close. The PM had insisted that we get the Amendment to the President's desk within the ongoing session itself. He did not want the issue to lose momentum.

Overnight, the set-up in the PMO was changed with the Defence Ministry being brought directly under its umbrella. Sanjay was busy in the ministry so he relied on me to tackle Parliament; nothing upfront – just some routine running around to lay the groundwork for the Constitutional Amendment. I took it as a great compliment that he thought me, a political naïf, capable of even playing such a role.

Three days later the PM announced the Constitutional Amendment on the floor of the House and took everyone, including his allies, by surprise. In a speech tailor-made for his constituents, he demanded that every able-bodied Indian be given an equal chance to wear a military officer's uniform and serve his country in the most noble way possible.

The media immediately trashed his decision to politicize the Armed Forces. If they only knew what Dayal and Januha were up to. Still, at the grassroots level – the only opinion that really mattered – the midget PM was lauded for his courage and leadership.

After the MPs had recovered from the PM's bombshell, the usual cry for an unhurried discussion on the Amendment between all the parties so that a 'consensus' could be reached on the issue, was made. Basically, this was a standard ploy to scuttle the Amendment through delay since Parliament was incapable of reaching a consensus on anything that mattered except fiscal profligacy. But the PM dug in his heels and said he would resign if the Amendment was not passed in the present session.

In a matter of days, minority groups of all shapes and sizes started to demand their pound of flesh. Not satisfied with what they had already got, some Dalit leaders insisted that quotas also apply to promotions, particularly for advancement to senior ranks. Sanjay got so incensed on hearing the demand that he had the ungrateful wretches scurrying for cover. The Muslims rightfully claimed that their representation in the officer cadre of the Armed Forces had been minuscule since Independence and they wanted to be included in the reserved quota. That was not on the cards – the introduction of reservations based on religion was a subject so communally charged that it was capable of single-handedly sinking our Amendment. Besides which, Azim had absented himself from the negotiating process.

The British-selected martial classes, comprising the Sikhs, Marathas, Rajputs, Gorkhas, Jats and others, wanted their traditional hold on the Armed Forces to be maintained and protested the Amendment in its entirety since they were, for the most part, not in the list of those considered backward. These ethnic groups protested forcefully in their respective states, but were fighting a losing battle. They were politically outgunned and outnumbered by the backward castes. The raucous claims of interest groups resounded in every part of the country. It was less of an issue in the south but a national debate was taking place and everyone's opinion was being heard, no matter how inconsequential the argument. Populism was the name of the game, and the line of claimants was endless. Parliament had become the target of all varieties of pressure groups.

Had my own interests not been so interlinked with the Constitutional Amendment I'm pretty sure I would have been extremely opposed not only to the legislation but also to the kind of politics it represented. This gnawed at me but I suppressed my stab of conscience and pressed ahead like the amoral professional I had worked so hard to become.

After the Amendment was passed, and if the President ultimately signed it into law, the judiciary would be the only state institution left free of enforced quotas. As it was, government services had seen a steady erosion in the quality of people looking to serve with other, more attractive, career opportunities becoming available and the calibre of officers had suffered. Reserving fifty per cent of all new recruitment for backward castes did not help matters. I cannot deny that prejudice existed among upper caste government servants in relation to those that got in through the quotas and treated them accordingly. I had noticed Father too was often guilty of this mindset – explaining the conduct of a certain officer with a specific derogatory caste slur, completely sure that the man's caste was the reason for his misdeeds. I would have thought he would have known better; he'd met heinously corrupt individuals covering just about every caste and ethnicity in the country. It was only a question of who had the opportunity.

Military officers were trained to lead their men into battle even if it meant certain death. This was a job for a special kind of individual, regardless of class and caste, and only merit, based on an aptitude for warfare, would be the determining factor. By a simple progression of logic, it could be argued that the sovereignty of a nation came before every other constitutional obligation simply because the nation could not exist without the sovereignty that the presence of the Armed Forces guaranteed. So you could argue that the vital role of the Armed Forces gave them immunity from the necessity for social justice, an important policy of state though it might be. That is why I believed quotas had no place in the armed services. Still, here I was, facilitating the passage of legislation that would make sure these quotas came into force.

On the phone, Neena recounted for me how General Bastard, on hearing of the Constitutional Amendment, had cursed me for being a traitor to my class; if I indeed was that, then he was to blame for it.

ABSOLUTELY NO MONEY exchanged hands in the legislation process that was undertaken for the Constitutional Amendment. This was a unique experience for me. The corruption involved was ideological, not monetary, in its form. The numerical majority of the backward classes made it impossible for even the most bigoted of upper caste members to be openly seen to criticize the Amendment. If anyone had been foolhardy enough to use national security as an argument against the Amendment they were likely to have been attacked by the rabid social crusaders as an oppressor of the backwards and then, in the next election, they could kiss all the invaluable backwards' votes goodbye. No leadership of any political party was going to be caught on the wrong side of this issue. The tyranny of the multitudes had made Indian democracy incapable of keeping the country safe from mindless populism and cynical voter appeasement. The culture of reasoned debate was dead. To each his own and let the country go to hell. Thousands of years of caste oppression had still to be made up for and the idea of a modern, progressive India was not a worthy enough goal to forgive the past and re-think this divisive agenda.

The politics of quick fixes was in fashion – buy the voter off with a caste quota for some crummy government job that kept him in your debt forever; reform and development were somebody else's problems. Unwieldy coalition governments caused uncertainty and uncertainty meant that you made sure your supporters were taken care of as quickly as possible.

Pandit Nehru and Indira Gandhi had comfortable majorities that gave them the luxury of thinking of five-year plans, which was why both had, fortunately or unfortunately, left such an indelible mark on the land. The small men and women who were the leaders now couldn't see past the coming weekend, if that. Politics in India had been reduced to a voting contest bereft of any vision for the country's future.

So the PM tied up the desired two-thirds majority in both houses of parliament and managed it with minimum effort. What was left of the liberal political class possessed no backbone and had crumpled upon hearing the government's predictions of electoral doom for them. There was going to be a Parliamentary debate but the result was known in advance: the Indian Armed Forces would have to become part of the great social re-engineering experiment. I dearly hoped we would not be fighting any more wars in the remainder of my lifetime.

The only way I was able to assuage my doubt was by never allowing myself to forget that the real objective for the Constitutional Amendment was to help us harness people power as a weapon to defeat the evil designs of Rashtrapati Bhavan. As the PM and Sanjay worked on smoothing the way for the passage of the Amendment, the PMO concentrated on portraying the officer cadre of the Armed Forces as a monopoly of an upper caste mafia who had worked relentlessly to keep the backwards out and undermined them when they did succeed in getting a foot in the door. The message was repeated in every form of press interaction that a member of government was present at.

THE MILITARY TOOK this pummelling stoically, and Rashtrapati Bhavan maintained a deathly silence. Former service chiefs and senior officers were united in their opposition to the Amendment. They beseeched the Government to reconsider its stand because in the field of battle there were no castes.

Creating artificial fissures would affect the very fabric of the military. They stated that the enlisted men had to believe in their Commanding Officer and if there was any doubt in their mind about the fitness of their officer it would affect their morale and fighting ability. The former officers argued that military-run schools spread across the country had quotas for the most backward castes, which provided them with ample opportunity to gain admission to the National Defence Academy. But their voices were drowned out by our propaganda. Nobody expected former generals, admirals and air marshals to be unbiased on the matter.

Gradually, the public began to give increasing credence to our spiel that the officers were part of a closed club and would do anything to control entry into it. I'm sure General Bastard and Januha followed our every move with daggers in their eyes.

Neena thought everybody had gone bananas. I could not prove with any confidence that she was mistaken. I was thankful that I had not been told to activate my role as spokesman and savage the Armed Forces; I would have been totally unconvincing. I think that is why the PM did not press the issue.

Among the castes and communities that would benefit from the Amendment the opinion was absolutely unanimous. There was general agreement that Yadav Senior was the greatest leader the country had ever seen, Gandhi and Nehru be damned. The midget PM had, in one master stroke, turned himself into a giant of the social justice movement.

The problem was that he had also empowered the President amongst his core supporters – the officer cadre.

Neither had a reason to back down now.

THE DEBATE ON the proposed Constitutional Amendment began as tamely as any other legislative piece of business. The Bill was brought up for debate and members started having their say. Speakers from both the Government and the Opposition outdid each other describing the Amendment in successively glowing terms. Their breathless attempts to curry favour with the backward castes would have been hilarious if the consequences hadn't been so far reaching.

I was illegally seated in the crowded visitors' gallery reserved for Rajya Sabha members and taking in the scene when Sanjay, who was really a member of the Upper House, appeared beside me, seemingly out of thin air. 'The twins have been hard at work,' he declared.

'Working on what?'

'Causing trouble for us.'

'That bit's obvious. I'm looking for details.'

'Januha has handed a number of incriminating files over to them, files that he had put together on the doings of politicians while he was posted in the Defence Intelligence Agency. With the information gleaned from these files, the twins have been using their blackmailing skills to get specific MPs to do Rashtrapati Bhavan's bidding.'

'Which is?'

'I'm sure we're about to find out. That's why I left everything and rushed here.'

'The twins couldn't have told you about this.'

'No, your pal, a certain Mr Sahni, did.'

'How the – ?'

'He was having trouble getting through to you here, so he got hold of me and introduced himself. I thought it was a crank call at first but he was very convincing.'

I had been in Parliament for more than an hour. Mobile jammers installed for reasons to do with security and decorum made mobile phones useless. I had left my phone in the car. The only way to get an urgent message to me would have been by calling the Prime Minister's parliament office, Sanjay's base of operations. Naturally Sahni, ever resourceful, had thought to call there.

I assumed Sahni had revealed to Sanjay what I had tasked him to do. 'He's broken into their systems?' I asked.

'Apparently. He was very well informed.'

I had more questions but the commotion on the floor of the House attracted our attention. The leaders of the Indian political firmament were making their views known on the subject. The PM made his case for the reservation policy purely on a social justice plank, not mentioning his disagreement with Rashtrapati Bhavan even in passing. He sat down to a barrage of desk-thumping and cheers. He was followed by two titans from the south: YK Naidu, the respected lion of Andhra who was also a Cabinet Minister, and V Srinivas Murthy, the wily leader of the BJP, the saffron party's first southern chief. Both raised concerns about the pace at which the legislation was being passed through Parliament without due deliberation. However, in the ultimate analysis, they supported the passage of the Amendment. Indulging in political hara-kiri was not how they had got where they had.

The self-proclaimed leader of the Dalits, Paresh Yadav's long-time bête noire in UP, angrily demanded a larger share of the reservation pie for scheduled castes, and sat down after predicting that the demand would only be met when a Dalit PM took office. The difficult personality of this leader, coupled with a disastrous term ruling UP, had led to his recent sharp slide to electoral oblivion, ensuring the first Dalit PM of India would not be him.

The leader of the Opposition – Karan Nehru's cousin – spoke in his trademark unsteady and unexciting monotone, which when combined with his fish-out-of-water body language, left you wondering about his qualifications to be the future PM, as he was destined to be with the reviving fortunes of the Congress in the north, thanks largely to Karan Nehru's efforts. The direct descendant of a series of Prime Ministers, he quoted each of his ancestors verbatim to prove his legitimacy to opine on the subject, and then finally announced that the Congress was the original party of social justice so it could not stand in the way of the passage of the Amendment. He wanted to be PM and that was all that mattered. Karan Nehru, sitting on the Opposition front row, three seats across from his leader, was visibly upset and did not clap at the end of his speech.

This was when Azim Khan stood up. Maybe it was just me, but I thought the entire Lok Sabha went silent in anticipation of what he was about to say.

'Mr Speaker, it is with deep regret that I speak in this august house today. Regret, because this Constitutional Amendment cannot be taken in isolation to the events that are taking place, just a stone's throw away, on Raisina Hill. If it weren't so, maybe we could debate the pros and cons of this unsatisfactory piece of legislation in a rational fashion, but I am afraid the Government is using the Amendment Bill as a political football that they wish to throw in the lap of the Rashtrapati Bhavan.

'I need not tell you, sir, that I am an avowed critic of any over-reach of presidential powers but this is not the way to counteract it. I am willing to submit that the majority of the public may support this Bill, but I also know that sometimes leadership requires us to do what we believe is right for the country despite what prevailing opinion may demand. That is the ultimate test we are being put to today.

'I cannot support this Bill because of the divisions it will cause in our polity, in our larger society, and imminently, in our very structure of governance. As a result my party's position as a partner in this Government becomes untenable and so our ministers will accordingly resign.'

Azim paused. There was shock writ across the Treasury benches. The Opposition cheered Azim's announcement, mainly because any cause of discomfort for the PM was something to celebrate. A Rajya Sabha MP sitting ahead of me shrieked in sheer joy. It was a minority government so Azim's decision made no practical difference in terms of its survival, as long as the Congress and BJP tolerated its existence, but from a moral standpoint it was a crushing blow to the Government's legitimacy.

'Finally, Mr Speaker, my party will not need to make use of the remaining minutes available to it in this debate and so I would like to yield it to the honourable member from Phulpur, my good friend, Karan Nehru. I think it is important we hear from someone who has faced the enemy in battle and can tell us how this Constitutional Amendment will affect our army as a fighting force. He has proved his credentials as a soldier and great patriot on the heights of Kargil. Let us hear him now on exactly that subject that so concerns us in this House today.' Azim took his seat saying, 'I yield to Shri Nehru of Phulpur.'

Azim's speech was like a bolt of lightning thrown into the well of the Lok Sabha, causing shock and confusion both in the Government and the Opposition. The visitors in the galleries tittered with glee. Parts of the House roared in approval, others jeered in derision, and still others had already turned their attention to Karan Nehru, who stood in his place, waiting to be heard, his gnarled left arm very much in evidence. It was high drama of the kind we did not dare expect any longer from our parliamentarians. It was exciting, it mattered and, by God, it was better than cricket.

I sat forward in my seat, straining to hear Karan speak. Sanjay sat next to me but we knew better than to ruin the moment by making any comment.

'Mr Speaker, I would like to thank the honourable member from Aligarh, my lifelong friend and partner in crime, who has so generously given me this time when, as he has just shown, he would have likely made much better use of it with his virtuosity of speech. I thank him too for his kind words and may I reciprocate these by saying that though he may never have had the opportunity to fight in uniform on the battlefield, I have always considered him the bravest man I know and will follow him till the ends of the earth.' Karan threw an eloquent salaam his friend's way and Azim acknowledged this by bowing his head in a way that showed even he was not impervious to emotion.

This was bloody good stuff; I almost didn't notice that an idiot on the bench behind was having a sneezing fit all over me.

'Sir, let me also say that as a Congressman I share my leader's position on this Bill. No national party that hopes to represent the interests of the downtrodden and disadvantaged millions could take any other stand. No, this is no mutiny on my part, in case those on the Treasury benches take solace from that fact. As a Congressman I understand my party's position, but as an Indian, as a soldier, I'm afraid I cannot see this Constitutional Amendment as anything other than a grave misjudgement.

'I will desist from getting into what politics is really at play here – we are all well aware of the events of recent months; you do not need me to narrate them. Nor do you need to hear from me the many arguments against this Bill. More qualified military men than I have delineated that position repeatedly in the media.

'I only ask each and every member of this House to think long and hard today about what we are going to do. I may no longer don the uniform of an officer of the Indian army but I will always be one in my heart – a conviction I know that I share with many fellow members of a common pedigree.

'So in the name of every officer and soldier, past or present, living or dead, I beseech this House to step back from inflicting this death knell to the Armed Forces of this country. The glory of our Armed Forces has always been based on the implacable belief that they stand united and equal against the enemies of our land. You are taking that away from them today and you know very well that social justice, as worthy a goal it may be, is no excuse for weakening an institution that so nobly and without complaint provides us the canopy of security without which nothing we do here would be possible.'

There was a rumble of discontent from the Government side but it passed as Karan Nehru, India's best known and most successful war hero, spoke for the men in uniform and had to be heard.

He took a sweeping look at the chamber before resuming to speak. 'Mr Speaker, I know I am running short of time so let me end by telling you about the defining moment of my life. It took place on the slopes of Tololing in Kargil, for which I have received much undeserved attention. I am known for my volubility but I have hardly ever discussed my experiences on that fateful day. It is appropriate that I do so today, briefly, and do it here.

'After I was shot, during the final offensive, it was my men, my brothers, who risked their lives to bring me down the mountain alive. I would not be before you, living and breathing otherwise. I will never ever be able to repay the debt I owe those men. It is a special kind of man who is willing to do that – not a better man than the rest of us, but one suited to the commitment to service for the country and his fellow soldier without question or hesitation. The same goes for the navy and air force. Caste and ethnicity have nothing to do with it. History has shown that valour shows itself in the most unlikely of places and people. The officer in particular is one who must provide leadership in the most trying circumstances and the Indian armed services have a very good system of finding those who are best suited for this role.

'Sir, unlike other government services, the bar that you have to cross to become an officer of India's Armed Forces must not and cannot be lowered for anyone, for any reason. The security of the nation is at stake and only the best may apply. I pray that you do not persist with this atrocity on the Constitution and the Republic. Generations to come will thank us for it.'

Karan took his seat to only pockets of applause in the House as many on the Treasury and Opposition benches did not dare show their approval for the tour de force peroration he had delivered in the face of majority opinion. The unambiguous approval of the Lok Sabha visitors' galleries though, gave me an inkling of what was happening outside Parliament.

This was a parliamentary debate that everyone was paying attention to. Sanjay and I were emotionally spent after listening to the two men.

But it didn't end there. As always there was more, much more yet to come.

A former maharaja of a prominent Rajasthan royal house who had served in the army had taken to his feet and begun his speech. He was a Rajput through and through, with an impressive turban and moustache to prove it. He sat in the Opposition and was perhaps one of the few MPs who could have said whatever he liked on the Amendment and not worried about re-election. Ancient feudal tradition still held sway in his fiefdom. If I remember correctly, he was said to be an incarnation of one or the other of the top tier of Hindu gods. So his subjects could not very well be expected to vote against their deity; democratic expression was not worth eternal damnation.

His patronizing tone of speech was asking to be mocked by the newly empowered castes who despised those born to position and wealth. That resentment burst forth as the former Maharaja made his views known on what he called the 'absurdities' of the proposed Constitutional Amendment. The ruckus was spearheaded by Shitij Yadav, who also happened to be an honourable member of the Lok Sabha, if you can believe it. Shitij possessed the most formidable vocal cords I had ever heard. He and his gang of troublemakers decided they did not want to hear from the former royal any further and started belittling his appearance and affected manner in the crudest possible fashion. One went too far and that was the end of the debate.

I will never forget the scenes that ensued and will probably never stop recounting an embellished narration of what happened. The story I am about to describe is a combination of what I saw, what Sanjay said he saw, what others claimed they saw, and what was replayed on the news. But mostly it is what I witnessed with my very own eyes and ears so if there is any fiction in the mix it's only a smidgen's worth.

It was a day when we as a country hit rock-bottom but had enough of a sense of humour to laugh about it.

Tempers began to boil when one of Shitij Yadav's men said and I quote, 'What would Rajputs know about warfare? They fought the Mughals by marrying their princesses off to them. That's why their forts are in such good shape.'

The jibe was received with laughter but it was a rather harsh historical judgement, indeed. Before I proceed further in my story I must clarify that the statement may have been true for some Rajput royals, but there was no way you could group all the Rajputs of the historical period in question under that generalization. For starters, Rana Sangha and Rana Pratap, both great warriors, would have been extremely aggrieved at the fact that their heroics had not been taken note of.

The disrespect to the Ranas' memory was soon avenged by a throng of Rajput MPs, most of whom happened to belong to the Opposition. They flung back insults pertaining to the cow-herding ancestry of the Yadavs, which riled Shitij's mob. If they couldn't take it, they really shouldn't have dished it out.

The Speaker tried to restore order but nobody paid him any heed. Not that it would have ultimately made a difference, but most of the top leaders on either side were not present to attempt a hosing down of their backbenchers. Karan and Azim had left the House after their speeches, otherwise I'm sure Mr Nehru would have been a leading participant in what was to follow.

Then the spat spread to a different part of the House. A Jat MP from Haryana had taken the opportunity during the disturbance to make a point to his neighbouring colleague, who was from a backward caste, on why he thought some ethnic and caste groups were just braver and more suited for armed combat than others. I was informed later that he had matter-of-factly stated that the Rajputs were not the best of fighters but at least they had a proven history of bravery, whereas the closest thing to a weapon that most of the backwards had come to wielding was a broom.

The backward caste MP, who unfortunately happened to be a Dalit, was understandably enraged and raised the alarm for reinforcements. The Jat MP couldn't comprehend why anybody should get fired up over a reality of life that God had ordained, but he wasn't one to turn away from a good fight. The Jat beckoned his own kith and kin, who brought along with them members of other martial groups who were also card-carrying members of the born-to-fight club. The battle lines were drawn and it was of no consequence any longer as to who was part of the Government or the Opposition.

It was all about caste and ethnicity. They had each reverted to their base identities.

Then the violence picked up. It started with a slap administered by a Sikh MP, naturally a Jat, to the insulted Dalit MP. A wave of violence engulfed the House. There were members wrestling in the aisles, heads being banged on the benches, a group free-for-all in the well of the House, loose papers floating in the air, torn dhotis and broken chappals strewn on the floor, and blood flowing freely in the House of the People.

What it all boiled down to was that the martial groups made common cause and went after any and all backward caste members they could find. After an initial battering, Shitij Yadav organized the more robust sections of the backward castes around him and counter-attacked very effectively. The neutrals tried to make it to the exits without getting caught in the crossfire; not that many were successful. The first usable weapon came courtesy of the chairs that the Lok Sabha administrators sat on at their table in the well of the House. After the chairs were smashed to pieces, their legs were used as wooden clubs. The accompanying table was unable to survive the stress of grown men savagely struggling upon it and gave way. It was cannibalized as well. Headphones, used for translations, became deadly projectiles and were flung across the chamber. No inanimate object in the chamber was safe from becoming part of the violent proceedings.

The backward castes were numerically stronger but the martial classes were individually bigger, it was true, and angrier. The MPs from the south and the east, along with the lady members, took their leave, washing their hands off the entire embarrassment. Smart people; I wouldn't blame them for harbouring thoughts of secession. That left the madmen of north and west India to bash each other's brains in. A handful of hardy women did remain behind and made their presence felt. One or two of the catfights were worthy of any of those wrestling programmes on television. Shitij Yadav, being a brute, was a good captain of his side. I saw him knock the turban off a Sikh and punch out a giant of a Maratha. But a captain without a competitive team does not make for victory. His men were clearly intimidated by their opponents, who were keen to showcase their superior fighting skills. The martial classes had a team but no cohesive strategy and single marauders would go into enemy territory, which was basically the Treasury benches, only to get themselves lynched by a group of backward castes on Yadav Junior's word. The well of the House was where the real toughies on both sides voluntarily came down from the relative safety of the benches to do battle.

The classic amphitheatre design of the Lok Sabha gave, in a farcical way, a gladiatorial feel to the combat. And from on high in the jam-packed visitors' gallery we stood transfixed, unable to take our eyes off the spectacle. Voyeuristic delight and stunned disbelief had captured our senses. Outrage would come later.

That men of standing, without the consumption of alcohol or drugs, could act like this, boggled the mind. The violence was fed by one of the oldest human fears, losing face. The martial classes wanted to prove that only real men like them were capable of defending the country while the backward castes wanted to overturn centuries of victimization by showing their oppressors that they were not inferior in any way. This congenital inability to look beyond caste identities – and they were supposedly the leaders of their communities – made them lose their heads and forget that the whole country could watch them in action.

The melee came to end when the Speaker of the Lok Sabha took the unprecedented step of permitting the entry of armed security personnel – with lathis but not firearms – into the House. By then the participants were running out of gas and, with cooling minds, had begun to remember where they were and what they were doing. There were still a few crazed stragglers who had to be physically dragged out of the House. One member tried to attack the police with a microphone stand and got a lathi on his ass, which did the job of subduing him.

We found out afterwards that every news channel in the country, and many international ones, had carried live the Parliamentary riot that lasted no more than fifteen minutes but made India a laughing-stock of the world. Even the famously rowdy parliamentarians of South Korea would have been impressed with our good form.

After it was over, and the House was empty I felt completely drained of energy and collapsed into my seat. It was then that the shame of my involvement in what I had seen hit me. General Bastard, Januha, the midget PM, me, even the ghost of my father – we were all conspiring to tear our country to shreds.

Chapter 11

THE CONSTITUTIONAL AMENDMENT was passed without further debate in the Lok Sabha and, soon after, by the Rajya Sabha. The Bill, which reserved twenty-one percent of seats for the backward castes in each batch of cadets selected after a competitive exam and interview for an opportunity to earn a permanent commission in the Armed Forces, was sent to Rashtrapati Bhavan for the President's assent.

General Bastard returned to centre-stage as further rumours of a constitutional crisis, and worse, brewed in officialdom. At the very last stage, the Constitutional Amendment had boomeranged on Paresh Yadav's Government, at least in the eyes of the middle class. The Government's public image took a real beating after the ruckus in the Lok Sabha, as well as the Nehru and Khan double-act. We were blamed for bringing Indian democracy to this sorry state and introducing the goonda raj of UP and Bihar to the heart of the nation's polity. Our message about the elitist officers of the Armed Forces was lost. The barbarism of the mob scene in the Lok Sabha had shocked a nation that didn't get easily shocked. People died by the hundreds every day on the streets – in accidents, murders, terror-acts and natural disasters – but nobody batted an eyelid. There was so much ever-present tragedy around them that people had turned inward and become oblivious to anything not directly related to their own existence. But the Lok Sabha incident had shaken them out of their cocoons and awoken them to a polity in crisis. And Shitij Yadav – who was captured on camera indulging in the worst of the violence in Parliament – had begun to embody in public perception the poison that had seeped into the political system. Paresh Yadav was too shrewd not to understand that his son was becoming an ever-increasing liability.

We had delivered to General Bastard, on a platter, the exact situation that he had been waiting for. The elected leaders of the country had shown themselves to be incapable of governing and the Great Saviour, President Dayal had the perfect opportunity to make his move for the good of the country. The prospect of a coup began to be openly spoken about and – what's more – many people no longer thought it such an unpalatable idea. Democracy was about to go out of style in modern-day India. People had lost patience with its plodding rate of progress and wanted results.

China had become the model country that middle-class India wanted to emulate. The United States was yesterday's aspirational story. Who needed a vote if the government left you alone to fill your coffers? We had orchestrated events to this time and place; that required true talent.

The economy was showing signs of going into a deeper recession and people were starting to get an inkling of a less than rosy future. Someone was going to be blamed for puncturing the optimistic halo that surrounded the much ballyhooed economic miracle, which had managed, with a few blips here and there, to survive even the most incompetent of governments since 1991. The midget PM was in grave danger of being held accountable for having spent budgetary resources left, right, and centre without giving a damn about continuing the reform process or even appointing a competent Finance Minister. Internal security was no better, with the Maoist Naxals causing mayhem in the ever widening red corridor, declaring that Parliament had lost the right to govern and predicting that their banner would soon flutter above Rashtrapati Bhavan – assuming they could manage to evict you-know-who. The jihadis from across the border had mercifully given us a short breather from their deeds of terror, but Kashmir continued to simmer with resentment, ignored by a Prime Minister who prioritized issues on a day-to-day basis. As a result you could forget about the government paying attention to issues of international importance like global warming and terrorism, India was looking firmly inward in the direction of Delhi and wondering who would be victorious on Raisina Hill. It was going pear-shaped for the Yadav Government and at the worst possible moment. The year was ending in a very unsatisfying manner.

Parliament adjourned after a session that would be talked about for years, perhaps for all time. The Lok Sabha had not suffered as much damage in its decades of existence as it had in that quarter hour of violence. The chamber required major renovations before the budget session and the Indian taxpayer would have to foot the bill. Lutyens and Baker must have turned in their graves. Nobody died from the injuries received in the brawl but some members were laid up in hospital for a while. The number of broken bones, lacerations and internal injuries sustained by members in so short a period was quite extraordinary. But I was heartened to learn, later that week, that many members from opposing sides had complimented each other on the fight they had put up. I know it sounds strange, but even such misplaced bonhomie was welcome in the prevailing environment.

A FEW DAYS before Christmas the rift between the President and the Prime Minister was laid bare for even the common man to see. It was not a pretty sight. General Bastard and the midget PM got into a verbal clash while waiting for the arrival of the President of Sri Lanka in the forecourt of Rashtrapati Bhavan. No points for guessing it was about the Constitutional Amendment. What was of more consequence was that they were caught in the full glare of the assembled media. Finally, General Bastard walked off in a huff. The Sri Lankan President alighted from his car to be met by a fuming and embarrassed Indian PM minus his head of state. The media went ballistic. Some news channels even hired lip readers to try and ascertain the exact words that had been exchanged. They need not have bothered; witnesses to the scene were more than willing to reveal the colourful language that was used. The prime ministerial oaths they said were of the ethnic variety while the former army chief's were from an international lexicon.

It was another national embarrassment; and another step closer to the brink.

That same evening General Bastard left for his Uttarakhand estate. His Press Secretary announced that the President would be spending the next couple of weeks in the hills to contemplate the present political situation in the country. No mention was made of the Constitutional Amendment. It was pretty clear to all that there was no way in hell this President was going to sign it.

If American Presidents' retired to their ranches to ponder important issues, ours had his estate. He was going to make his decision in a calm and deliberate fashion and without a doubt he was very pleased to keep the nation in suspense about what he would do. Januha accompanied him, which was a relief. Neena, to her great surprise, had been asked by her father not to accompany him on the trip. She had not wanted to go anyway, but she thought she would have to fight as always to stay behind; my presence being the usual sticking point. Her father's unexpected request only added to the trail of evidence that I felt signalled impending trouble.

Soon after his departure, the Election Commission announced that the election for President would be held in five weeks' time, on the first of February. Nominations for candidates would close in two weeks.

The timeline for the main protagonists was now clear-cut. Only the denouement was left to unfold. The problem for Dayal was that by withholding his signature from the Reservation Amendment Bill it was certain he could not get elected President. He could sign and have a shot at gaining the requisite support, but then would lose the backing of the Armed Forces for ever and would have to be satisfied serving as a constitutionally nominal head of state with no grander ambitions – that is, only if he got elected, since elections were never a sureshot thing.

He had a choice to make, and what a bloody choice it was.

THERE WAS A silver lining to all this. With the President away, I could enter Rashtrapati Bhavan without fear of bodily harm for a few days. And, having some influence with the mistress of the presidential residence, I decided that if we were going down, we would go down in style; no more doom and gloom.

I decided that Neena and I would throw a New Year's party at Rashtrapati Bhavan that would have the socially inclined begging to be invited. After all, there was really nothing to do while General Bastard decided how he was going to usurp political power. I spent a lot of my time trying to convince Neena about the party. Neena took some coaxing, but then reluctantly agreed and started to make initial preparations for it. It would only be a closed event for those who constituted our inner circle and those whom we trusted, she said. But I wanted to keep the guest list relatively young, or to be precise, a list I considered youngish from the vantage point of my almost three-and-a-half decades of existence. It would have been perfect if we could have used Ashoka Hall as the venue. But

Neena said there was no way we could ever get away with that.

To be safe we decided not to have the party inside the main building but under a large shamiana that would be set up on the grounds, on the golf course. Booze would be served – as it must have been before our hypocritical leaders had decided to stop serving alcohol at government functions, bowing to the Spartan views of Mahatma Gandhi, and thus rendering Rashtrapati Bhavan a dry zone. Well I was about to change all that – at least for one day. The oldies would be barred entrance and the rest of us, young turks, would go absolutely haywire.

The invitation list was drawn up. Naturally it was assumed that people would bring their friends along, which was fine with me as long as they were of a certain age group. That rule would be strictly applied and I made sure everyone understood it. Neena's vision of a select group was under dire threat. I arranged for a live band and singers, as well as the best catering money could buy. We were using government premises but there was no need to stooge off the taxpayer for food and entertainment. Neena got over her initial reluctance and as the end of the year approached she became as excited as could be. This was to be our first time hosting an event as a couple and I think that's what really enthused her.

Two days later, I had been divested of all my powers as host. Neena had taken charge and told me to restrict myself to paying the bill. I wanted to take issue with being pushed around and remind her that the party had been my idea but she was the one person I had never been able to out-argue, so I admitted defeat. The party had now morphed into such a different social animal from what I had wanted that even my mother ended up being invited.

Naturally General Bastard heard of the party, undoubtedly from one of Januha's spies, and demanded that Neena cancel the event. Neena told her father to bugger off and mind his own business; entertaining was her department and if he was not happy with her he could find someone else to be his hostess in the future.

The ultimatum did its job and there was no further overt interference from Uttarakhand. I was in love with the person who dictated to the would-be dictator! I do not know why but that thought made me feel quite good about myself. It must have something to do with a primitive sense of having bagged the alpha-female. Talk about being divorced from reality.

ON THE DAY of the party, boxes and crates of the best alcohol were driven into the Rashtrapati Bhavan. The caterers set up stations with every conceivable cuisine. The presidential kitchen had insisted on preparing the desserts and had outdone themselves with their Baked Alaska. No expense had been spared.

Rashtrapati Bhavan looked resplendent. Other than the subtle but elegant lighting, very little adornment was required – the presidential palace in the background and the ambience of the Raj were enough by themselves. The shamiana looked absolutely fantastic. There was music, there was drink and there was a thrilling scent of fun in the air. Guests started pouring in. Friends, old and new, rubbed shoulders with colleagues and relatives, close and not so close. There was a happy vibe, which made Neena happy, and so me. Osmosis was at work.

Hardly anybody left to go to another party as they normally did, in their self-important way, particularly on New Year's Eve. Our crowd was satisfied that they were in the one place that others would have given an arm and a leg to be. Their social wanderlust and insecurity were temporarily quelled. The crowd expanded and the dance floor started to attract attention. The beautiful thing about it was that Neena and I knew everybody, everyone was special and felt so for being invited. But it was not all fun and play, particularly for me as the host because I was required to make sure no one felt left out, particularly when so many people, important to my future survival, were in attendance.

I realized I had lost my private banker's stamina to effortlessly match every hee-hee with a ha-ha and had exhausted myself way before midnight. I ducked outside to the fairway for a short respite. Neena, who was in full party mode, was handling the hosting duties well enough. My absence was not immediately taken note of.

Away from the revelry, a sudden melancholy overpowered me. You could call it reality. Peering up at the mighty dome of the presidential palace I wondered how long it would stand before it too would meet its end like the rest of us.

'I was looking to catch you alone,' said a voice from behind me. I turned to spot Captain Chavan in full dress uniform. Even a homophobe like me had to admit he looked striking. A life spent in valour deserved its privileges.

'Chavan, what are you doing here?' He had accompanied his boss to Uttarakhand.

'Januha made up an excuse to ship me back. He doesn't trust me and hasn't been able to get rid of me yet.'

'What was his excuse?'

'He said he needed me to spy on this party of yours. By the way, great show you've put on tonight.'

'It isn't quite what I'd planned.'

Chavan pulled out a pack of cigarettes and offered me one but that was one vice I had not gotten to; it was one facet of my religion I followed scrupulously even if it had more to do with my fear of dying a painful death from lung cancer.

'Nothing ever is,' he said.

'Are there any cameras here?' I looked back towards the building and couldn't spot any electronic eyes.

'Yeah, but it doesn't matter anymore. I've been shut out from the inner circle.'

'Has the decision been made?'

'I think so. I chanced on the information yesterday when President Dayal, during one of the few occasions that Januha left me alone with him, told me that the Northern Army Commander and Western Army Commander would be visiting him in a couple of days. That can only mean one thing.'

'They are the most important, aren't they?' My knowledge of the army's command structure was rudimentary.

'They command an overwhelming majority of the army's manpower and firepower. No coup can take place without their consent.'

'Are they likely to dissent?' I asked hopefully.

'I doubt it. Your Constitutional Amendment has gone down very badly with the entire officer corps, particularly the top brass. The senior officers were soldiers of the old school who, after being continually maligned in public as a group, have begun to share grave misgivings about the civilian leadership.'

'It should never have come this far,' I said sadly.

'Nothing can be done about that now. But there is one last tip I can give you that may come in handy.'

'I'm all ears.' Whatever information he had fed me so far had been spot on.

'Tell your intelligence people to keep a close eye on every Special Forces battalion. They will be the leading edge of the sword when Januha makes his move. I have no doubt they will be responsible for wresting control of key institutions and for apprehending the senior civilian leadership. Also, the 9th Infantry Division in Meerut and the 6th Mountain Division in Bareilly, due to their proximity to Delhi, will naturally provide the foot soldiers to enforce the military's will on the capital. Their main job will be making sure the city and central police are quickly neutralized. But the Special Forces will form the core of Januha's strategy.'

Hearing Chavan clinically spell out what a military takeover would involve really hit it home. I was sure I would be amongst the very first to be either jailed, or worse. Perhaps it was time to leave the country.

'What about the rest of the country?'

'Local commanders will make their move once they are sure Delhi has been taken. Once Delhi falls, I suspect the rest of the country will tamely follow.'

'You're doing a good job of depressing me,' I said.

'Come now, there's still a party to enjoy before we deal with whatever lies before us. It's not a done deal to succeed, you never know what twists and turns of fate may happen yet. They still need everything to move like clockwork, if they lose the initiative in any way they will not be able to sustain it for long. India is a big country. Let's go back in.' He pulled me by my arm back towards the tent.

'Keep an eagle eye on the Special Forces, huh?'

'Count on it.'

We returned inside the tent with only minutes to go before we ushered in the New Year. The place was such a madhouse that Neena hadn't even noticed my absence. I was one of the soberest individuals in the party and that was an oversight I decided to remedy. I thought maybe if I drank enough I would be able to forget the doomsday story Chavan had just fed me, because as everyone around me counted down the last seconds to the New Year, I couldn't help thinking that they were counting off the minutes to the end of India too.

IT WAS ALMOST dawn by the time celebrations came to a close. The after-effects of the revelry were everywhere. More than one reveller had to be carried out by the staff and chauffeured home. Karan Nehru had managed to accomplish the feat of arriving with one lady, partying with a second and leaving for home with a third; like something JFK used to do as a young Senator about town. Shitij Yadav had come with Sanjay acting as his chaperone and had got through the party without causing much trouble, a few grabbed asses aside. The PM had been invited but had wisely abstained from visiting enemy ground. Dhillon Uncle got nicely sozzled and had a great time with his pals, even if he had to suffer a haranguing from his wife on the way out. Even Azim, a much mellower person when around his wife Radha, seemed to have gotten quite tipsy. It had ended up being the kind of unstuffy occasion I had wanted, with the young crowd outlasting the rest.

I had spent the initial hours of the New Year getting as hammered as I could, with no fear of becoming an embarrassment; the news Chavan had given me quite prevented that. I think I bumped into my personal spy Sahni at some point during the night and issued some orders to him regarding what Chavan had told me about the Special Forces but I could not be sure. I hoped I had not cornered somebody who looked like Sahni and scared the living shit out of him with ramblings about an impending coup.

I awoke the following morning in Neena's Rashtrapati Bhavan bed, with a throat as parched as the desert. Thankfully though, my head and stomach were in a tolerable state. I had found that my hangovers in winter were not that severe; the cold weather seemed to soften the blow. That probably explained why Russians have such a high capacity for drinking vodka.

I checked my watch. It was ten in the morning. Everybody who had attended the party was probably still asleep. I headed out of the room and into the corridor looking for a drink of water. Most of the doors in the family wing were locked shut, no doubt on Januha's orders, but I did manage to gain entry to the sitting room, where I had met General Bastard a few weeks earlier, and found an unopened bottle of mineral water with two glasses. As I was sitting and quenching my thirst the phone in the room began to ring.

I couldn't decide if I had any business picking up General Bastard's private line or whether I should answer it in case the extension in Neena's room was also ringing and it disturbed her well-earned rest. Finally I picked it up.

'Who's speaking?' asked the unmistakable voice of General Bastard.

'Why don't you guess, Mr President?'

'Sidhu?'

'Happy New Year, sir.'

'Where's Neena?' The ass didn't wish me back.

'Sound asleep.'

'I trust you had a fine time turning the most respected residence in the country into a debaucher's paradise?'

'You should have come, sir, you would have enjoyed yourself.'

'Some of us have more important things on our mind.'

I wondered if I should broach the subject on everybody's mind and then instinctively decided to go for it: 'So have you decided to sign the Constitutional Amendment yet or not?'

'What do you think?'

'I'm guessing you'd rather have your scrotum pricked by needles than sign the Bill into law.'

'I couldn't have put it better myself,' he admitted with a chuckle.

'Which then leaves you with two options.'

'Go on, Sidhu, don't let me stop your flow of wisdom.'

'Either fight the election or, if you are sure you can't win, forcibly bring the shutters down on Parliament.'

'Very good, Sidhu, but that's as far as our discussion can go. After all, you are the enemy. Be a good chap and tell Neena to give me a ring when she awakens.'

I retraced my steps to Neena's room and climbed back into bed. My body sensors were telling me there was much more sleep to be had. Neena, however, was not about to let me have any. She said, waking up and snuggling in close with me, that she wanted to start the New Year with a bang.

THE NEW YEAR brought no other immediate fresh activity. General Bastard was taking his own sweet time deciding on his next course of action. The news vacuum was filled with wide coverage of our party, which had the inadvertent effect of causing differences of opinion within various media organizations. The tight-ass editorial writers, mainly because I had not bought their silence with an invite, castigated us for desecrating the Rashtrapati Bhavan, but the more popular tabloid-oriented sections of the print media and television news channels glorified the grand show we had put on. The tabloid viewpoint beat the criticism of the op-ed scribblers hands down in the battle of public perception.

Abuse of privilege was a story that readers and viewers had heard of many times before but extensive video coverage and exclusive pictures from a star-studded bash at the Rashtrapati Bhavan was something novel and intriguing. In this new India of ours, style almost always trumped substance. And, if I may be allowed a boast, we had been nothing if not stylish that night.

During this period of limbo, Yadav Senior too made himself scarce, tired of routinely being asked questions to which he did not have answers. Yadav Senior, with Shitij in tow, made the rounds of his electorate reassuring his party's grassroots leaders that the show wasn't over yet. Uncertainty was the overriding sentiment among every strata of Indian society and it was affecting even the most loyal of the midget PM's supporters.

It stood to reason then that we, his staff, also were in a relative state of dormancy after the eruption of activity in recent weeks. Instead, Sanjay relied on work to occupy his mind. He pressed ahead on his quest to find a way to dismantle the shared loyalty of the Armed Forces officer corps by offering senior officers in all three services various inducements, including the prospect of becoming chief. But the reservation issue, as Karan had predicted, made it impossible for him to manufacture cleavages in the unusually united Armed Forces. I imagine it involved more of the latter.

For my part, I was trying to find some balance between the emotions of contemporaneous contentment with Neena and impending ruin for India when I was summoned by the Naik twins. The twins said they wanted to urgently discuss a matter that they considered of the highest importance. They specifically asked to meet with me instead of Sanjay, who instructed me to ask them what they wanted, give them a hearing and then get the hell out. He said they were bloodhounds and could sniff out the smallest of clues betrayed by an innocent. Sanjay also warned me that they were not beyond recording the conversation so I was to be very careful about what I said. I was going up against the princes of darkness and any mistake on my part could prove very expensive at this stage.

THE TWINS WERE staying at an impressive residence on the ultra-exclusive Amrita Sher-gil Marg, Delhi's very own Billionaires' Row, which supposedly belonged to a cousin but was their property in all but name. I was startled to be met by them, personally, at their doorstep. My father's adversaries did not feel the need to impress their sense of self-importance on me by making me wait even for a second. There was much fuss made. I was being treated like an honoured guest. I hadn't been prepared for this kind of reception. I'm afraid the firmness of my defences may have been softened a bit. It's a weakness most Punjabis display when met with warmth and hospitality.

The entire extended Naik family, who had collected in Delhi for the Christmas holidays, was presented to me, including the grandchildren. An attempt was made to forge a basis of commonality between me and their sons by drawing notice to our similar educational backgrounds; the obvious hint being that there was nothing to stop us from becoming good friends. The twins had three sons and two sons-in-law between them and these gents ran the family's numerous legitimate businesses, which had been bought or set up with the ill-gotten gains of the family patriarchs. It was expected that the second generation would bring respectability to the Naik name. The twins didn't need, from a financial standpoint, to indulge any further in wheeling and dealing but I think they couldn't stay away from Delhi's corridors of power – much like a real soldier always yearns for the battlefield. There was also of course always the unstoppable force of naked greed at work. No business could generate the revenue one government deal could produce with an equivalent investment of time and effort. Gaining a final revenge on my father must have been an added incentive.

I made the required small talk with the family. The wives of the twins were demure and considerably better looking than their spouses, which explained why the children looked quite unlike their dads. The grandchildren had none of the demon genes of their grandfathers, on a superficial level at least.

The Naik family was finally dismissed with a snap of the fingers and then the twins got to working on me, exuding a degree of energy that I wouldn't have expected from looking at them. The charm offensive had been executed without any shame or subtlety but had accomplished its goal nevertheless. I was their prey and they were not going to let anything distract them from softening me for the kill. No phone calls or employees interrupted us and I was made to feel as if they had nothing better to do than chat with me all afternoon. They were very, very good at this game. And I should know.

'So, Jasjit, we understand that congratulations are in order,' said Vijay Naik, the marginally more outgoing of the twins.

'You and your wife have reconciled. Well done,' added Pramod.

'Gentlemen, I'm not comfortable discussing my personal life with you.' I wasn't about to confirm the news on the off chance they were merely fishing.

'I understand you treasure your privacy, but you have nothing to fear from us,' said Vijay.

'We are the most discreet of individuals.'

Sincerity wasn't their strong suit and they had greatly miscalculated by employing it against me. I didn't like being taken for a fool. 'I'm sure you're very discreet when your interests are involved, but my private life is none of your business. Why don't we get to the reason for this meeting?' I was abrupt.

Pramod said, 'We can only broach that topic once we know that you have decided to become a more dutiful son-in-law –'

' – and have already made the first move in making up with the President,' Vijay finished for him.

The Naiks had a disconcerting habit of finishing off each other's sentences. They seemed to actually possess a common consciousness – the sort that twins are often said to share. They were a couple of freaks. So my night in Rashtrapati Bhavan and my telephonic exchange with the President had become common knowledge. 'Who told you?' I asked in resignation.

'We have associates at every level of government –'

' – including the household staff at Rashtrapati Bhavan. They keep an eye on everything that their master and mistress are up to without letting on.'

That meant the leak had been at the level of a bearer or chauffeur. I didn't see the need to be polite anymore: 'What do you want?'

'An alliance –'

' – for a prosperous future.'

I calibrated myself to the rhythm and weight of their double-barrelled manner of conversing. I couldn't see a scenario in which an alliance would be feasible. 'How would it work?'

'I don't think it's a secret that Dayal is about ready to grab power and when he does we will be in a position of great influence. Our friend Januha will be the defence chief and Prime Minister all rolled into one –'

' – and in a dictatorship there will be no need to be as careful in our functioning as we all have been up till today. We will have a king and his word will be law.'

'How wonderful for you! But I must remind you that at present you are in a democracy and such talk qualifies as treason.' They wanted something from me; and I wasn't going to make it easy for them.

'Was that democracy in action we witnessed in the Lok Sabha, sardarji? Any system is better than keeping up the sham we've had to live with for so many years.'

'The people want progress and don't care how it comes. Look at China.'

They had some nerve picking holes in the system that had made them their millions. I hadn't been able to figure out what precise role they had played in the Lok Sabha fiasco but there was no doubt that they, armed with Januha's dossiers, hadn't been innocent bystanders. So I was not prepared to sit back and listen to their hypocritical chatter about what ailed the country. Sanjay's instructions were jettisoned and I went with my instinct: 'You two jokers better start talking turkey because I'm close to losing my patience.' They were momentarily taken aback by my contemptuous response but they recovered swiftly.

Vijay flashed his dentures at me and said, 'You are your father's son, that cannot be denied –'

' – no question.'

They appeared unsettled by my confrontational approach so

I persisted with it: 'Thanks for the certificate. If your future is looking so rosy, why are you kissing my ass?'

'These military men don't understand business –'

' – but if the dictator were to have a son-in-law who shared our interests and understood our language…'

'Why would the son-in-law need your assistance?' I thought it prudent to speak of myself in the third person.

'Because, though he is married to the future ruler's daughter, the dictator-in-waiting still counts him among his most hated foes –'

' – and we could help the son-in-law make a permanent peace with the new ruler.'

This was getting interesting. If nothing else I wanted to find out what the twins really wanted from me.

'We cannot do this unless the son-in-law helps himself –'

' – he would need to make a gesture of good faith that we could bring before the dictator-in-waiting in order to win him over.'

I was tired of talking hypothetically. 'And winning him over would require precisely what kind of a gesture from me?'

'Handing over the PM's international accounts.'

Of course.

'Dayal will need to show to the country that he had valid reasons for sweeping half-a-century of democracy aside. Finding Yadav's loot will go a long way in solidifying the new government's grip on power.'

No shit, Einstein. 'I have no idea what accounts you are talking about,' I said. The entire room was probably wired; I had no intention of becoming the lead story on the evening news.

Pramod ignored my obvious lie and kept going, 'All the accounts needn't be handed over; two or three will be enough to hang Yadav. The rest of the funds we can distribute among ourselves, nobody need ever know. I'm sure you have the necessary power of attorney.'

'A finder's fee,' Vijay chuckled greedily.

I'm sure Januha would have been thrilled to hear that the twins were keeping their own interests up front as always. 'And then the three of us would go into business together,' I said.

'It would be an unbeatable combination – '

' – the sky's the limit.'

'But, of course, you would require me to hand over the details of these supposed international accounts of the PM right away to launch this grand partnership of ours?'

'Necessarily.'

'Better to do it now before the takeover. It will give you credibility in Dayal's eyes.'

I stood up and prepared to take my leave. 'To gain your unreliable assistance you expect me to simultaneously sell out my client, betray the memory of my father, and yet be less than truthful with my new associates about my former activities so that you can plunder away. I'd rather die. I can't believe people in the past have been dumb enough to fall for your tricks. Maybe greed does deaden the senses.' Let them record that.

They got angry and their masks of conciliation fell away. Vijay said, 'Your Government has been administered its last rites. If I were you I'd think about our offer seriously.'

'It's the best deal you're going to get. President Dayal will act without caring whether you are married to his daughter or not.'

'Gentlemen, this fight is not over yet. I am not in the habit of giving up before the last ball is bowled. If we do lose then I hardly think I will have to resort to using your services for making a deal with the new establishment. I have Neena for that. In the meantime, you will be well advised to think about your own welfare. I would suggest you leave the country very soon because I have inherited a certain bundle of documents that relate to your affairs and my father left very specific instructions on how to fix you. Your behaviour today is tempting me to put it into practice immediately. Good afternoon to you.'

It was always good fun to threaten cowards like the twins. The last I saw of the Naiks their mugs wore expressions of grave concern.

I left the Naik residence in better spirits than when I had entered it. It wasn't every day that I went toe to toe with the twins and came out intact, maybe even slightly ahead.

Chapter 12

AT FORTY-SIX MINUTES past four in the early evening of January 5, two powerful improvised explosive devices were detonated in the immediate vicinity of India Gate. It was a Sunday so people had gathered around the monument, a popular destination for families and tourists to visit for an outing and an ice cream. To make matters worse, India Gate was adjacent to Children's Park which was brimming with activity. The second bomb, which went off twelve minutes after the first, was the more deadly killer as many of the victims had run into its path while fleeing from India Gate. It was diabolical and sickening that anybody would target families and kids like that. Twenty-seven died, many of them extremely young. What made the attack even more significant was that India Gate was the only real war memorial that stood in Delhi, although the war it commemorated was a pre-Independence World War. Nevertheless it had come to be seen as a memorial for all those Indian brave who had sacrificed their lives for independent India. The Amar Jawan Jyoti, the eternal flame for the nameless and faceless unknown soldier, remained lit at India Gate in their memory. The terror attack extinguished it as well as the lives of many innocents.

What followed was complete confusion in the security apparatus of the nation; not one of the Yadav Government's strong points to start with. The National Security Adviser was a Yadav acolyte with a nervous disposition; he disappeared from sight after the blasts. Intelligence sources started leaking almost immediately, with customary utmost certainty, that the attacks were the handiwork of a Pakistani terrorist group with the backing of Pakistani intelligence, the dreaded ISI – They Who Must Always Be Named.

Pakistan, as expected, strongly denied the charges and advised India to look in her own backyard for the perpetrators, an insinuation to the Maoists, who in turn categorically denied any hand in the bombing. Since no real suspect was apprehended, the conspiracy theories took on a life of their own. Then PMO sources started briefing the press and claimed that the attack seemed like a 'professional and military type attack', hinting the unforgivable.

Rashtrapati Bhavan immediately retaliated at this insinuation, going as far as to issue a formal statement, castigating those who peddled such treasonous ideas, saying that the patriotism and loyalty of the Indian Armed Forces could never be questioned.

The safety and security of the country was now in question and everyone in Government was found cutting a sorry figure. The Opposition, particularly the BJP and Congress parties, had a field day shredding the Government to bits. The Armed Forces felt they themselves had been attacked – a bruised and battered India Gate gave symbolic voice to their hitherto silent disgruntlement. If it was Pakistan who had masterminded the attack, as many neutral experts believed, they had succeeded far beyond their wildest dreams in dividing India.

THERE WERE ELEVEN days left before the nomination process for the presidential election came to an end. Both sides were applying as much pressure as they could to gain a decisive edge before then.

'Any news from Sahni?' asked Sanjay. I had gone to South Block to get the latest updates and found him comfortably ensconced in Father's old office, despite not holding any official position in the PMO; but then he did not really need one.

'He confirmed that every spare unit of the Special Forces has gathered at their training centre in Agra. Januha spoke to them in person yesterday.' (I had realized latterly that I had, in fact, met Sahni at my New Year party and he had been able to decipher my instructions. He had been feeding information to me with machine-like efficiency in the days since. The man was worth every rupee.)

'So it begins. The IB is saying more or less the same thing. And the army commander for the Delhi area, Major General something or the other, is making suspicious visits to the Rajputana Rifles regimental centre in the cantonment area where there is always a large batch of soldiers. It's heating up.'

'Then why were the Naiks wasting their time with me?'

'The twins were probably working on their own initiative after hearing about the possiblity of a thaw in relations between you and the Rashtrapati. If they had got you to reveal your secrets, they would have seemed like heroes.'

'Possibly.'

'Or Dayal was getting cold feet and Januha wanted to give you one more try – only using bribery to extricate the PM's secrets this time. With the bank accounts in his hands, Dayal wouldn't wait a second longer,' said Sanjay.

General Bastard had started believing his press. His ego would not be able to withstand being vilified as the murderer of democracy. 'He wants to be a dictator but a dictator who is heralded by the people. He can't be sure of that right now,' I said. 'Januha must be pushing hard for it to begin.'

'Oh, he's frothing at the mouth all right.'

'The cost of this drama has risen with our enemies sensing

our weakness and people being blown up while on their Sunday afternoon stroll,' Sanjay said.

'At least India Gate is still standing.' I tried to look at the brighter side.

'I hope nothing worse happens.' Sanjay was worried.

'My nose is telling me that the coup isn't a fait accompli quite yet, there is more to do here.'

'Let's hope your nose is right.'

'Hasn't failed me yet.'

My mobile phone beeped announcing the arrival of a text message, and Sanjay's phone followed suit. It was from the PMO asking us to check the news. Sanjay and I turned on the TV and seeing the banner of breaking news, understood that the enemy may have slipped up at the very last moment.

And they had.

The crowds outside General Bastard's estate in Uttarakhand had been swelling since the New Year, as he'd shown no signs of returning to Delhi to sign the Constitutional Amendment into law. They were mostly passionate activists from various backward caste organizations who truly believed in their cause and were peacefully protesting their President's reluctance to support the social justice movement. No political party had supported the protesters overtly; the politicos had other problems on their mind. There had been a few untoward incidents but the police had brought them under control with professional calm.

That was before Januha had gotten involved.

The geography of the area around the Uttarakhand estate was such that the protesters came very close to the access road that led to the main gate of the tea estate at certain bends. General Bastard got in and out via helicopter so presidential movement had caused no problems.

But Januha was returning from his sojourn to Agra and his motorcade went screaming past; sirens blasting and flags flying.

The protesters thought the President was in one of the cars. A group of moronic troublemakers lobbed some bricks and one managed to hit the windshield of Januha's vehicle that he himself (control freak that he was) always insisted on driving.

Januha drove off the road into the trees and was lucky to get away with only a few scrapes and bruises, but his anger had been roused. The President was away in Dehradun city on a personal visit to meet some old friends. Januha was the senior officer present and free to do as he saw fit. What followed must have been difficult to comprehend for the millions who saw it on television, but I was not the least bit surprised. I had the advantage of being well acquainted with the monster in question.

The army functions best when indiscriminate force is required and that is why it is used only as a last resort in instances of civil unrest – emergencies involving militancy or large-scale riots being pertinent Indian examples. Januha retreated for a while behind the walls of the estate and everyone thought that was the end of it. They were so very wrong. He returned, in an open-top jeep, dressed in combat fatigues, with his crack team of Special Forces commandos and ordered them to clear the area of the protesters. The police tried to argue with them but they were told to stand down and so they did. They knew when to heed the command of a furious three-star general. All of Januha's moves were caught on camera by a gaggle of media, camped out there, waiting for just such a sensational event.

Januha, imagining himself in the middle of a battlefield, stood in the back of the open-top jeep and directed his troops. He was absolutely out of control, his deranged condition clearly evident in his manic gestures and screaming.

The operation started well, with the crowd backing away, but there were too many protesters and only a handful of soldiers. The trouble began with some pushing and shoving that then escalated into a mini-riot. Outnumbered and fearing for their lives, the soldiers reacted as they were trained to do and shots were fired from their automatic weapons. The shots must have brought Januha back to his senses because he was last heard shouting for his men to cease firing, but by then the damage had been done. Unarmed civilians had been mowed down. Their blood was on Januha's hands.

Sanjay and I watched the television in horrified silence as they replayed the pictures of the carnage, and as the estimates of the killed and injured kept rising.

General Bastard had been punished for trusting a loose cannon like Januha and had lost a golden opportunity to fulfil his ambitions in the process. We were going to ensure that it remained a permanent condition.

The India Gate bombing was relegated to an expired news cycle; it was just another episode in the cycle of terrorism. But Indian soldiers slaughtering Indian civilians in these circumstances! It was just insane – and vein-popping bonkers was exactly how you would describe the media reaction to it.

'Let's go see the PM,' said Sanjay and we both raced down to his office with renewed vigour.

We were back in the game.

THE MIDGET PM led the verbal assault on General Bastard by holding him personally responsible not only for the violent episode in Uttarakhand but also the prevailing environment of paranoia in the country. He said that the dastardly massacre of backward caste activists typified the mentality of most army officers with regard to their less fortunate countrymen. He asked for Januha to be court-martialled for mass murder and demanded that General Bastard immediately sign the pending Constitutional Amendment into law. If the President failed to comply with his request then Yadav Senior promised that he would lead a nation-wide stir until such a time as the law was enacted.

Every military installation and cantonment in Bihar and UP was surrounded by protesters of the most politically vicious and dangerous kind – criminals in the clothing of political workers, like Shitij Yadav. They brought a stop to all military activity in the area, particularly in Agra and Meerut. Each of these hot spots looked set to turn into another slaughter ground. Similar gherao demonstrations were organized in other states but nowhere was the confrontation as heated as it was in the PM's backyard. People-power and military-might were colliding in the Hindi heartland; and they threatened to take the whole country down with them.

I was told it was now my turn to lead the media blitz. There was no interview I refused or televised discussion I missed, since Januha was a subject I could be expansive on without Neena blowing a gasket. I donned the role of the outraged citizen and did not tire from repeatedly bringing up Januha's 'martial brutality'. I declared that this was what happened when the military did not stay within its bounds of conduct, my reference to greater matters of state being obvious. I quite enjoyed myself.

The Rashtrapati Bhavan did not bother to defend Januha, which was wise since there wasn't much to defend with, the television pictures having delivered a damning verdict. Januha was suspended from his post pending a military investigation. General Bastard had finally returned to the Rashtrapati Bhavan, after inspecting the site of the shooting and visiting the hospital where the wounded were being treated. He was brave to have gone there since he was not their most favourite person but he was able to win some brownie points with the patients, who were later interviewed, for displaying genuine regret. From what I saw on television, he looked quite shaken. But he breezed in and out of the hospital without saying a word to the media. That was a mistake – an experienced politician would have immediately admitted partial responsibility and then promised that those behind the carnage, regardless of their position, would not be spared. Januha should have been made to come forward and publicly sacrifice himself. Unfortunately for General Bastard, there were certain political survival tactics that you could only pick up and hone in the turbulent environs of the electoral arena.

One positive consequence of Januha's fall from grace was that the twins left town as quickly as their little legs could carry them. But before leaving they were kind enough to spill the bogus news that Neena was pregnant, father unknown. It took us a couple of days of denial after denial, before anybody believed us. One publication even began trying to openly guess who the father could be. Karan Nehru featured prominently among the candidates. Neena was horrified, while Karan could not stop beaming. I had half a mind to hire a Central Asian hit squad to take the twins out. It is truly amazing what you can arrange for in Dubai for the right fee.

HAVING BROKEN WITH my father-in-law in the most public manner so far, a reaction of some kind was to be expected from Rashtrapati Bhavan and soon enough Neena said that her deflated father had asked to see me. This was the first time he had initiated contact with me without some uniformed proxy relaying his wishes, so I imagined he was looking for a way to retreat and that was a relief; I reached North Court at the appointed hour.

This time instead of the family quarters upstairs I was shown into the presidential study where the head of state worked and received regular visitors like myself. Protocol was everything to military men, and I was now being dealt with like a legitimate caller – quite a change of tune, I had to say, and quite overdue too. The study was comfortably spacious with walls that were so white that they glowed, making me feel that I had walked into some celestial afterlife. The cream coloured furniture added to the effect, with the dark wooden desk providing the only contrast. Neena had made herself scarce, still traumatized from witnessing my last encounter with her father.

I was made to wait for less than ninety seconds before Dayal strode in. He nodded at me, no hand was proffered, and he pulled up a chair next to mine. So there was General Bastard, less than a foot away from me, dressed in a sherwani with a red rose in his buttonhole. Impeccably playing the part of President.

There was to be no small talk. 'You have a decision to make,' he began hurriedly. 'A lot has happened in recent days. Both you and I have done much that I'm sure we regret but it is time to let that go and think of what is happening to the country.'

What is it they say about patriotism being the last refuge of a scoundrel? 'Sir, why don't you make this easier by telling me what you want?' I had neither the time nor the patience to be patronized by him.

'I want to be elected President,' he said simply, his naked ambition revealed.

'After the Januha episode that is no longer possible,' I replied.

'Sidhu, I have never liked you, that is no secret I'm sure, but I'm a big enough man to admit I may have been hasty in forming a preconceived opinion of you. Do this for me, prove your loyalty to me, and we can start a new chapter. And if you won't do this for me, do it for Neena.' There it was – the ultimate trump card to be played in the game of power.

'Don't you dare involve her further in this cyclone of hate that you've sucked your beloved country into. Yes, I admit the PM could have handled the situation better, but he is who he is. What is *your* excuse?'

He stood up and I followed suit, though my vertical limits stopped well short of his. Despite my best efforts, I could not stave off the effect of his physical presence. 'If you cannot help with my goal then you are of no use to me, or my daughter. I will negotiate terms with those who have not been bought by Paresh Yadav.' He conveniently forgot that he had once been bought by the PM too. But something had changed – his words no longer carried the sting or fear they once had, he was a hollow man, an extinguished volcano, and I think he knew it.

'Suit yourself.' I could not find the requisite fire to say anything that would provoke an explosion in my nemesis. I was tired of all the fighting and arguing; tired of all the recriminations. I just wanted it to be over. General Dayal turned to go to his desk and I turned the other way to the door.

Neena was waiting for me outside the study and she bombarded me with more questions than I had answers for. 'So now what?' she queried after I had concisely recounted my meeting with her father.

'If this situation we're in continues to go as badly as it has, he's going to make you choose between him and me.'

'No, I told you before, I will not hear of it. I will kill myself before I do that. I cannot bear any more of this, Jasjit,' she said in such pure anguish that it made my insides squirm. And then she began to cry. Since I didn't have any words of reassurance I held her tightly in my arms; as though my arms would ward off the evil fate we seemed hurtling towards.

THE NEXT MORNING Azim asked me to visit his residence on Willingdon Crescent. I could defy the President of India but I dared not refuse Mr Khan.

It was a very cold day. Azim and I beat a hasty retreat indoors, as he found himself unsuitably attired to face the icy cold wind in the lawn. I hate the cold. I can function efficiently in the most extreme heat, but cold is my Kryptonite;

it makes me immobile and grouchy. Older residences in Delhi, particularly the Lutyens-era bungalows, were designed to keep the summer heat out, not so much the cold, but are notorious for failing on either count. In terms of degrees the temperature in Delhi never went below freezing but it sure felt like it did, because of the way the houses were designed. The high ceilings and the absence of insulation turned the bungalows into freezers during the worst of winter that normally lasted six to eight weeks on either side of the New Year. However, Azim's study was toasty warm thanks to an effective radiator heater. Nifty gadget; I made a note to buy one.

'The President has sent a message to us in the Opposition. He claims to have lost his hunger for power and wants his troubles to go away. He is willing to make peace with the Government as long as two of his demands are met. First, the PM must go and second, the Constitutional Amendment should be buried.'

'That's all? He might as well ask for the PM to bend over.'

'Look, he is chastened and we must take advantage of the opportunity.'

The mist of emotion cleared from my mind and I understood what Azim was talking about. If General Bastard wanted the Opposition's help he must have been feeling really isolated after Januha's departure and quite devastated by the public's censure. The insecurity would be only a passing phase and we would have to move quickly to take advantage of it. I now better understood that my meeting with him had just been a final gambit, a last-ditch effort to cling to a dream that had drifted beyond his grasp. Yet even in his dire circumstances he had still found a way to be petty with me about the whole thing.

'Before any decision, we need to assess the situation. You go first,' I suggested, banker to banker.

Azim stretched his arms and said, 'All right. The PM

and Dayal have fought hard for weeks but now the strain is showing. Their followers do not share the leaders' hate-fueled zeal and have gone about as far as they can. In the case of the President, his military alliance has started splintering since Januha's moment of madness. The air force and navy have washed their hands off of the coup plan. Even within the army senior brass there is a small but growing faction that is getting cold feet. But the President still has the allegiances of the army chief, the vice-chief, the Western Army Commander and the Northern Army Commander; more than enough support to seize power. Whether he can maintain his hold after the coup is another question because the public does not see him as the noble warrior anymore.'

'And the PM?' I prompted.

'The PM has also emerged severely damaged from this episode. He may have hardened his support base among the backward castes of UP and Bihar but the upper castes and minorities are now completely alienated. It was the upper caste vote that had finally overcome their suspicions of him and given him the extra seats that made him the clear choice for Prime Minister. In the next election, the upper castes are certain to organize against him and vote tactically to coalesce their support behind his closest rivals. He will never regain his present position of political supremacy. The Constitutional Amendment stopped the coup, which is what it was designed to do, but in the process it also brought the end of the Yadav premiership closer. The coalition allies in Government are angry that the PM allowed his ego to escalate the battle with the President beyond all bounds. The current tense situation in UP and Bihar has convinced most of the parties in Government that the PM must go and are only waiting for him to make one more mistake before they pull the rug from under his feet. They are already looking for new partners in the Opposition with whom to form the next government. So you can say both the

Prime Minister and the President are running out of time in which to reach a result in their favour and even if they do, it will be a victory without joy.'

He had laid it out as perceptively as it was possible to do. I could see the chess pieces of General Bastard and the midget PM sitting on the board. We were in a position to alter the moves from either side of the board.

'What do you hope to do?' I felt as if my body was going to explode from an overdose of tension and exhilaration.

'After I spoke in Parliament during the vote for the Reservation Bill, many senior army officers reached out to me. They – honourable and sensible men for the most part – were as horrified with Dayal taking the reins, as the rest of us. Many of these generals have vowed to do anything to restore order. The India Gate bombing has everybody worried about what else our enemies have planned if we keep distracting ourselves with this silliness. With a little work, I think I can get a slew of generals to send in their resignations on this issue, saying a pox on both the Rashtrapati Bhavan and Paresh Yadav's Government. The air force and navy are too limited in size for it to matter whether they follow the army's lead or not. If we get really lucky, these resignations could set off a chain of resignations amongst the rest of the officer corps. Mass resignations are not beyond the realm of possibility. It would be the most splendid of all ironies – Gandhian tactics of protest being made use of by the military! Overnight the Indian army's brain trust will be empty; the country's borders defenceless against an external attack. No Prime Minister can survive that kind of a debilitating blow! After that, with a little media management, Dayal would be shamed off his high horse. His moral authority will be nil.' Azim was going a bit overboard now.

'Generals do not voluntarily resign their posts, not in India, not anywhere,' I pointed out.

Azim smiled, 'I know, but it would be wonderful to behold, wouldn't it?'

'If only. What else have you got in your arsenal?'

'Toppling the PM will solve everybody's problems. Dayal will lose an excuse to take over and the army will settle down.'

'Can you manage it?' I queried.

'With your help I can,' said Azim to my horror.

'No,' I said before he could say another word.

'Do you trust me, Jasjit?' he asked, breaking it down to the core issue.

I tried to look away from him but failed; Azim Khan had me pinned in his gaze and there was no escaping it. What path would he make me follow him down? The answer to his question was obvious, but I was afraid where it would lead. He had a magnetic effect on me. For a man in my business that was dangerous.

'You know I do,' I replied reluctantly.

'Thank you. Then let me tell you why you need not be overly loyal to Paresh Yadav. I've known this for sometime but I did not tell you because it was not my place. Now, forgive me, but I must. Do you know why your father went to Bareilly the day he died?'

There it was, it all came back to Father and his death, where it had all begun. I remembered Dayal had said something to taunt me but I had not thought much of it since. I shook my head and he proceeded with his disclosure.

'He had gone there to finalize a transaction that covered up a scandal of such magnitude that it had the capacity to damage the PM grievously, to the extent he may have had to resign in disgrace.'

'Tell me.' I needed to know.

'Master Shitij Yadav had been in Bareilly a week prior to your father's visit and he'd taken a fancy to an unfortunate young lady at a local college he'd visited. She was found raped and murdered in an open field the next day. She was last seen at his side. She was Muslim and turned out to be a relative of a senior Maulana of the Barelvi school of Islam, with the reach to finish any support Paresh Yadav may have left in the minority community. Your father went to Bareilly to pay the family off and keep it quiet. He succeeded all too well.'

Azim let it be known very clearly that he did not hold Father in high standing.

'I appreciate your telling me this.'

'You're welcome. I shared this with you because I want you to think about your life and where you're headed. Do you want to end up like your father, cleaning up the filthy messes of these ingrates till the day you die? Or do you want more? Give me something to work with, Jasjit, and I promise this will be your ticket out from this life. Trust me,' he urged.

It was a compelling offer, despite his disparagement of Father. 'Why don't you use the rape and murder story?' I asked.

'That story has been buried too deep, your father made sure of that. Even General Dayal and his goons tried real hard to dig out the truth, but couldn't. The presidential nomination deadline is upon us, I need a killer blow in hand as leverage right now. You are in a position to save our country from a great fracture, Jasjit. I haven't known you long, but I'm glad that I met you and I know with every fibre of my being that you, my friend, will do the right thing. You aren't going to make a liar out of me, are you?'

He made a valiant attempt to awaken my better angels. He need not have bothered. I found out right then that I did not have any. Giving away the details of the Prime Minister's offshore bank accounts would only have implicated me. I needed room for deniability. So instead I went ahead and told him everything about the Israeli arms deal that connected both the main players and my father.

But Father was dead and it was time to move on. At least the source of the leak in this case would be in some doubt.

The secrets I had not given up to threats of instant death and worse, I had voluntarily ceded to this man. Why? Sure, it was a spur-of-the-moment decision, but in many ways it was also a cool, calculated choice. I realized it was the only path left to me if I wanted to get out of this imbroglio in one piece with Neena still at my side. It helped that Azim, the only man left standing, was a man I could trust; and he was providing me an honourable exit strategy.

Deep down, of course, I understood that the real reason for my opening my mouth was that I really did not want to end up like my father – crushed into nothingness after a final ignominious cover-up, because he had allowed himself to be treated like nothing more than an errand-boy by the likes of Paresh Yadav and his ilk. I loved and admired my father, but there had to be a limit and I had reached mine.

It was time to start thinking for myself and to break out of the mental shackles that I had been restrained by for so long. The hell with the midget PM, the hell with the shit that was Shitij, and, definitely, the hell with General Bastard for instigating it all out of an inflated opinion of himself! I was going to take sides all right – my own. If the future of the Indian republic was safeguarded at the same time, well and good; I'd be sure to take credit for that later.

I just hoped Azim could pull off what he had planned or I would have much to answer for.

Once done, there would be no denying I had broken the code I had been born into and lived by all my life; there could be no coming back from that.

AZIM, WHO WENT immediately into non-stop backroom negotiations with my information about the Israeli Arms deal had given me a single chore – to find Karan Nehru because he was nowhere to be found. Karan had gone underground and no one knew where the heck he had disappeared to. There was nobody at his house, the wife and kids were in Allahabad for the winter vacations – which perhaps explained his brazen escapades at the New Year's party.

Karan's mobile phone was switched off. None of his recent lady friends could shed any light on his whereabouts. I began to worry and put trusty old Sahni on the case. It took his people a whole day to locate him. He was holed up in a suite at the Imperial Hotel. Only Karan Nehru would choose one of Delhi's most high-profile and centrally located hotels in which to have a tryst. He was booked under the name of, you guessed it, Jasjit Singh Sidhu. As if I did not have enough trouble with the press already! The hotel staff said that he had left specific instructions not to be disturbed for any reason at all. All food and drink orders were to be left outside his door and the dishes retrieved from the same place. He had not been physically seen by the staff in more than a day.

I was aware Karan tended to go on a binge every now and then, though never before in Delhi. But the pressure had been intense in recent days and he had been put to the test in the aftermath of the Lok Sabha debate. He had borne the brunt of the scheming cabal that surrounded the insecure Congress President, who had murmured retribution for his mutinous conduct; and then there was the expected backlash from zealous votaries of social justice, some of whom had gone so far as to issue death threats. (Azim had similarly been besieged by anti-Muslim virulence, but unlike Karan he was used to being targeted by the forces of hate and employed his usual policy of disdainfully ignoring them.) Karan had manfully faced up to the consequences of his actions but one-man armies need to unwind too and maybe he just needed to freak out a bit; I knew that feeling well.

Not getting a response to my calls from the reception of the hotel to his room I asked the desk manager to open the door to Karan's suite for me. It was the middle of the afternoon and Azim was getting testy about valuable hours being wasted, so I traversed the corridors of the overly Raj-nostalgic hotel and then went into his suite alone, not knowing what I would find.

Inside, every curtain had been drawn open and sunlight streamed into the room with full force, making me shield my eyes. The windows hadn't been cracked. I could smell a narcotic presence in the air; a more precise identification of the drug was not within my competence, never having craved to smoke as much as a cigarette in my life. Karan lay on his stomach, passed out on the bed, wearing only pink and white striped boxers. The covers of the bed lay in a crumpled heap on the side. Empty bottles, half-eaten plates of food, overflowing ashtrays, and small plastic sachets containing who-knows-what made up some of the tapestry of mayhem before me. The only order in the room's disorder were Karan's clothes that had been placed, neatly folded, on the back of an armchair. I had new respect for military training.

All of my attempts at awakening Karan from his beauty sleep proved futile. Running out of any other ideas I reverted to the tried and tested. I dragged Karan out of bed with some difficulty, and threw him in the shower. The jet of cold water did the job and Mr Nehru returned to the living with a scream of protest:

'*Motherfucking behanchood gandu...* Don't you know who I am?' He used all of Delhi's choicest curse words and rounded it off with Delhi's favourite phrase of self-importance. A true blue Dilliwallah.

'I'm afraid I know you only too well, old chap,' I remarked, accompanying it with my most charming smile, which was sure to irritate a man in Karan's state; and it did. To his credit he didn't take a swing at me.

'Sikhu, what the hell are you doing here?' He had taken to routinely calling me by that infuriating moniker, which I tolerated only because he was who he was.

'Delivering urgent summons from Azim.'

'What's happened?'

'It appears that positions have changed. We are all batting against the Yadavs now.' I gave Karan a towel and he stepped gingerly out of the shower.

After taking a minute to digest my news he asked, 'You too?'

'Turned everything upside down. We have walked through the looking glass, my friend.' I told him about my confessional statement to Azim.

'There was an inevitability about it, you know. Never saw how you could like the Yadavs, particularly Shitij the pig.' He dried himself and slumped down on the pot. 'What time of the day is it?'

'Late afternoon – three-thirty.'

'Wednesday?'

'Thursday.'

'Ah.'

'Needed a break, did we?'

'Hell no. I'm in love, Jasjit.' Nobody fell in love more frequently and with more goofy intensity than our Karan Nehru.

'In love with whom?'

'Didn't you see her? She was lying next to me on the bed.' He got up from the pot and cringed as his head dissented at the sudden movement. I felt his pain.

Crossing over to the other side of the bed, Karan pulled at the covers that had fallen to the ground. A sharp tug at the comforter and a naked female body rolled out.

At first I thought it was a corpse until I saw, to my relief, that there were signs of life. She was just dead weight; sex, alcohol and drugs combining to make one heck of a sleeping potion.

'What do you think?' he asked, standing over her like the great white hunter.

It had to be said that the comatose lady's body was undoubtedly compliment-worthy. 'Nice body,' I commented neutrally, already fearing Neena would somehow get wind of this.

'Forget that, don't you recognize her?'

Karan directed my sight upwards, or downwards to be more precise, as her head was at my feet. Lying naked before me was Urvashi, the single-named superstar heroine who had reigned over Bollywood for the last half-dozen years with hit after hit.

I admit I was impressed but there were more pressing things at hand: 'I'm very happy for you, Karan, but cover her up, will you? The desk manager is out in the hallway and he could walk in any minute.'

I left the room quickly, assured the worried desk manager that everything was fine, and waited for Karan in the coffee shop downstairs, as he roused and saw off his lady love. When he finally emerged, two hours later, no telltale physical after-effects of his binge remained other than the tale his eyes told.

Karan Nehru was ready to go to war.

Chapter 13

AZIM KHAN WANTED the Yadav clan to be softened before he put his plan into practice, so he let Karan loose to do what he did best. Karan Nehru, with guns blazing, was really something to behold. He was fighting the battle of the just and righteous; it showed in his media performances. Karan Nehru ruled the nine pm news bulletins for the next week. He ripped into the Yadavs in a way that could only have stemmed from genuine loathing. In his fiery and unrestrained representations on television he portrayed Paresh Yadav as a Prime Minister responsible for pushing through an important act of legislation through Parliament, solely for the purpose of settling a personal feud with the President, whom Karan did not find free of culpability for the constitutional crisis either. But he did say that General Bastard was not the devil incarnate that some had been trying to trick the nation into believing these past few months.

Karan's most venomous assault was saved for last and was targeted at the PM's weakest spot – his son. Karan had gone public with his criticisms of the PM right after the Government's candidate for President had been announced; a puppet if ever there was one.

The media forgot about everything else and unilaterally focused on the political tremors that Karan left in his wake. The agitation for the President to approve the Constitutional

Amendment lost momentum with attention moving back to Delhi. The tensions in UP and Bihar melted away. Very soon after, the army was allowed to go about its business without any bother. The PM, the driving force behind the agitation, was being targeted and all his key functionaries – especially Sanjay who had organized the marches on the army installations – were called back. Karan had taken a lot of the pressure off General Bastard's back by diverting it on himself.

Januha was expediently sacrificed, on Neena's insistence that he be once and for all removed as Military Secretary and not merely suspended. Rashtrapati Bhavan released a press statement saying the President had taken this action after an army board of inquiry on the massacre in Uttarakhand had found his chief aide's actions indictable on numerous counts of command misconduct and prima facie criminal behaviour. He asked that the case be brought to court-martial in the speediest time-frame possible and justice be done. In close succession to this, General Bastard, in his first live interaction with the media in weeks, said that he would give the text of the Constitutional Amendment a thorough study, with the aid of legal advice, before deciding on what to do with it. He said he was not going to pre-judge the issue. It was a seemingly impromptu remark at the end of an event.

Dayal was playing ball with Azim and Karan, but he would not be elected President. We needed Neena, quietly supported by Chavan, to be at General Bastard's side to keep him from misbehaving and doing as he pleased; something he had got used to doing when he still believed he was going to become emperor of the country. He did not enjoy being told what to do but the results were immediate and he could not argue with them. By the time Karan kicked off his full frontal assault on the Yadavs, the President rarely made it to the first page of the newspapers anymore. Though Neena was running the show at Rashtrapati Bhavan now, I still stayed out of her father's way.

But I did get to see more and more of Neena, and that suited me just fine.

Once he had captured everyone's attention with his initial salvos against the PMO, Karan started describing with great specificity why he believed the constitutional crisis had been manufactured by the PMO itself to silence the President (to whom also he was continually careful not to give an unqualified clean chit) after uncomfortable questions began to be asked by the Rashtrapati Bhavan on the corrupt and incestuous way the PM was running his government. The President had been universally respected at the time so his criticisms could not be easily dismissed by the PMO; and so they personally vilified him.

Karan described the talk of a coup as a hoax perpetrated by the PM as a key part of this campaign to besmirch the image of the President. He said he was ashamed of his own part in this bastardization of the democratic process. A fitting choice of words, I thought. His diatribes in Hindi were even more stinging and damaging than his statements in English.

He called the controversial Constitutional Amendment the greatest legislative travesty to be visited upon the national security of the country, creating catastrophic instability within the security apparatus of the country, and allowing for a terror strike to take place in the heart of Delhi. The Amendment, he alleged, was pursued for no other reason than the sake of a power-hungry leader's need for petty retribution. He claimed the entire episode had divided the country along civil and military lines, as well as according to caste and ethnicity. Karan declared that, even after taking into consideration the reality that we as a nation had been plagued with a poor run of leaders, Paresh Yadav had to be the most destructive and evil Prime Minister that India had ever seen. He had to be ousted before it was too late.

Karan's diatribes were brilliant and inspired, breathing fire and using facts only when he saw fit. He had thrown a whole new light and interpretation on events that the public had been fed in a certain context by the media. There was no defence against his accusations because there was just enough truth in them to give the charges force; Karan's recent rebellious truth-speaking in Parliament made him a credible source. His passionate and convincing performances had seriously jolted the PM's hold on power.

The PM's coalition partners began to make ominous noises. The Opposition parties rallied around Karan, even his own Congress party got over its complexes, and started egging him on – they knew a star when they saw one. But Karan kept them all at arm's length and kept his eye on his goal.

The next person on his hit list was Shitij. The weak spot had to be exploited and there was much to be exploited there.

Karan agreed to be interviewed one-on-one by Rahul Kapur, an Anglophile television personality who considered his work only half done until he had pushed his guest into saying something truly outrageous and controversial. Karan was Kapur's wet dream come to life. The live interview set off a chain of events that changed all our lives forever. I watched it at the Rashtrapati Bhavan with Neena – General Bastard had taken to sulking in his room. I suppose the thought of returning to the Vice Presidency was not appealing:

Rahul Kapur (*cufflinks and Rolex sparkling under the set lights*): 'Mr Nehru, today's newspapers quoted you as saying that you had touched only the tip of the iceberg with what you had said in the last two or three days. Could you possibly have more to say?' (*RK baring his teeth in a predatory smile*)

Karan (*in a blue kurta and lounging in his chair as if he were chatting at a bar*): 'I have two words for you – Shitij Yadav.'

RK (*now drooling*): 'The *PM's* son?'

(*Karan nods in confirmation*)

RK continues: 'Pray don't stop, the floor is yours, sir.' (*RK sets himself in his famous listener's pose with hand under chin and right shirt sleeve cufflink clearly visible*)

Karan (*emphatically*): 'The man, as we now all know, is a menace. He has surrounded himself with the scum of the earth and poses as great a threat to the proper administration of this country as any son, daughter, son-in-law, daughter-in-law or any other despicable relative of a PM has ever done.' (*Karan wears a pained expression*)

RK: 'So the PM is the worst leader we have ever had and his son is a menace? Aren't you going too far?' (*RK uses his favourite interviewing technique of first provoking his guest and then leaning forward on the desk aggressively, daring him to answer*)

Karan: Shitij Yadav is in the pocket of the Naik brothers of Geneva and does whatever they order. He needs them because they cover his gambling debts that have ballooned to stratospheric levels and he is afraid that his father may find out. To keep the bookies at bay, he uses his influence to keep the police off their tails, and countless other such favours at the expense of the taxpayer. We already know his proclivity for violence as we saw in the Lok Sabha and during the BCCI elections when he became the board President by bullying and buying his way in – the bookies were absolutely thrilled when they heard of his election, by the way. His love for violence takes other forms, as well. I have personal knowledge of how a clean-up operation was launched by the PMO after he beat a defenceless young lady to within an inch of her life after being raped! It's amazing what you can get away with when you have enough money and power. Shitij Yadav sits in on many of the important meetings that the PM takes. How long do you think it'll take for an intelligence agency like the ISI or CIA to compromise him and blackmail him for state secrets, if they haven't already? Do you still think that I've gone *too far*,

Rahul? (*The last inflection mimics RK's Anglo-speak at the end; it doesn't go down too well with the interviewer*).

RAHUL KAPUR MAY not have liked Karan's mocking tone but it certainly went down very well with Neena. As for Mr Nehru's allegation of a rape cover-up, it was an altered, restrained version of the truth, since he did not go all the way and allege murder; but Karan was pointedly trying to allude to the Bareilly incident and only the Yadavs knew of what he spoke. They wouldn't know for sure though whether he was on a fishing expedition or specifically referring to what had happened in Bareilly, since there had been numerous other incidents of Yadav Junior roughing up women over the years that had been hushed up as well. By not alleging murder, as per Azim's advice, Karan had left reasonable doubt in the mix, hoping thereby to get a paranoid reaction from the PM and his beloved son. The man who had handled the cover-up was dead and I doubt the father and son had confided in anyone else, possibly not even Sanjay. They might very well have been without counsel on the subject. I could guarantee they would not risk confiding in me at this juncture, so I was going to put my acting skills to good use and play the oblivious bystander in their presence as they stewed in their own shit.

Therefore, all in all, Karan's performance was a triumph on multiple levels. I particularly loved the way Karan had managed to include the twins in his mudslinging. Most of that information had naturally come from me.

The Rahul Kapur interview was immensely damaging for the Yadavs; more so than anything Karan had said before. Moral turpitude was something the Indian people had learned to expect from their leaders but they would not stand for their PM and his or her family acting like gangsters – Sanjay Gandhi had figured that out the hard way.

THE KITCHEN CABINET was called into an emergency session at the PMO. I had been keeping Yadav Senior at bay so far by saying that there was no need for me as their personal spokesman to respond to Karan as he was a summer storm, mostly bluster and little fury, and that it would pass; that there was no need to give him more attention than he deserved. Karan's ruthless salvo at Shitij made that an impossible story to stick with.

But now the situation was critical and valid explanations were being demanded. I sat quietly among his brood.

Yadav Senior was fuming. I got a good sense of his agitated mental state from the amount of blood-red paan juice that was dripping from both corners of his mouth. It made for quite a contrast since he normally ate his paan in a relatively neat manner. Karan had completed his mission objective.

'This is simply disastrous,' said the midget PM. 'We need someone out there in the media to take him on. Jasjit, *you* have to take him on.'

I didn't like the look of how this was shaping up. Karan was a thousand-pound gorilla. There was no way in hell I was going to get in the ring with him. And he'd have to demolish me just to prove to the Yadavs that we had really fallen out. I wanted to avoid public humiliation if I could. And, anyway, I was on the other side now.

'Karan will tear him to pieces,' Kumar spoke up, coming to my rescue.

'I'd have to agree,' said Shitij. Though I was relieved, I was also slightly hurt that their opinion was so categorical.

'What else can we do?' asked the midget PM, who was looking more haggard by the minute. The silence that followed his plea was deafening. 'Is it *that* hopeless?' he said hollowly.

Sanjay began to explain the predicament: 'The problem is that much like the slapping incident in Chandigarh, what

Karan has spoken about is basically true – even if he did exaggerate the significance of the charges for the purpose of creating hype. Shitij *has* major gambling debts, he *was* seen with the Naik brothers when they were here and there *are* enough witnesses waiting in the wings to confirm his unfortunate treatment of those women. A horde of journalists must already be checking up on these leads and they will get to the bottom of the truth. It's just a matter of time. Therefore, like we did for the Chandigarh thing, it might be best to keep mum. Shitij's participation in the Parliament melee is still fresh in everyone's minds, making them predisposed to believe the worst about him.'

'The walls are crumbling around me and you want me to sit tight. Sanjay, inaction is not an acceptable strategy anymore,' said Yadav Senior.

'A misstep will only make it worse,' I replied unhelpfully.

'What else could Karan tell the media?' Sanjay steered the lagging discussion forward.

'The international accounts,' said Shitij, finally daring to speak up.

'He doesn't know anything about them,' I entered the fray. If they only knew the Israeli deal had been busted wide open and Azim had put together a dossier on it which he would soon use to bring the Government down. The game was up, and I think Yadav Senior sensed it.

'Karan has said what he had to, that was enough,' surmised Sanjay.

'I wish he would just disappear…' muttered the midget PM as he massaged his temples with the tips of his fingers.

I watched Shitij sit up and pay close attention to what his father had just said.

'That would only increase your problems,' said Sanjay, very aware of what the PM was implying. I sat frozen in fright.

'You're right, of course. Forgive me, I was overcome by

despair for a moment. I never thought one man could cause so much havoc. The things we are compelled to do for family even when they are not worthy. I have been saddled with a burden who it seems will be my undoing.'

The midget PM was more heartbroken than angry, and was in the process of making peace with the reality of what was to come. Shitij almost disappeared into his chair.

The finish line had come into view.

IT WAS NEARLY a quarter past midnight by the time Neena and I finished having dinner with Azim, Radha, Karan and Pooja. We were celebrating the imminent rescue of Indian democracy from the equally alarming evils of despotism on the one hand and populism on the other.

During dinner, Azim had said that now that the Government was tottering and an alternative coalition taking shape, he had fixed an appointment to meet the PM the next day, when he would tell him he had lost the trust of Parliament and that he should resign. What he did not say, in front of the ladies, particularly Neena, was that he would carry the dossier on the Israeli arms deal with him to make sure Yadav Senior complied. Karan had earlier used the dossier to dictate to Dayal that he would make no attempt to stand for President, as he was still threatening to do, with the nominations still two days away from closing. The acting President had abused Karan to high heaven but had finally agreed.

It had been a truly memorable evening: a great dinner, at a great restaurant, in a great hotel, to celebrate a great triumph. We rose from our table and leisurely approached the porch area of the spanking new Gautam hotel, all pretty high on life and wine.

Karan, impatient and restless as always, had had quite enough of the slow pace at which we were advancing down the lobby towards the porch – the ladies distracted by the window installations of the hotel's high-end shops, and Azim discussing with me his plan of action for the next day.

Karan cannoned through the exit and asked the valet to announce that his vehicle be brought around. He liked to cultivate an image of being a man of the people, and chatting up valet attendants was his way of perpetuating that image, at least in his own mind. He did this now, while standing behind the lectern which held the microphone that the valets used to call for the chauffeur-driven cars that were parked in the basement. Whatever Karan was saying to his audience they seemed glad to hear him – so much so that other hotel guests gravitated towards Karan.

This was when a dark-grey sedan with black tinted windows pulled up right in front of Karan and a man got out of the front passenger seat pointing a revolver at an unsuspecting Karan Nehru, no more than fifteen feet away. Two shots were fired in quick succession. We saw Karan fall to the right; and someone screamed, probably Pooja, fearing the worst. We were almost near the glass doors of the porch when the shooting happened and therefore got an unimpeded view of the event. That is until Neena's security men got into the act and pulled us to the floor. After which a couple of these brave-as-hell army men ran out to engage the shooter. They need not have bothered since the shooter already lay immobilized, having been shot in the groin.

The shooter's car began to make its getaway, which is also when Karan's chauffeur arrived on the scene and, having helplessly witnessed what had happened, instinctively rammed his BMW into the side of the much smaller car, making a harshly metallic and monstrously loud impact. I momentarily flashed back to how my own kidnapping had begun in an eerily similar manner.

Azim lunged to where Karan squirmed in some discomfort on the ground. Azim helped him to his feet, and carefully inspected his friend from head to toe, which was when he discovered entry and exit holes in Karan's kurta millimetres from his abdomen. The bullet had passed clean through the loose cloth of the flowing garment, across his body, without as much as grazing him.

My eyes were transfixed on the pistol in Karan's hand.

Simultaneously, the sordid episode took a real sharp twist when the identity of the man lying unconscious in the backseat of the getaway car became known – Shitij Yadav was removed from the tangle of the wreckage with great difficulty. Karan had to be physically restrained from inflicting further damage to the person of the comatose Junior Yadav.

Karan explained later that he had been leaning against the valet microphone stand and had lost his balance in sheer fright when he saw the assailant pointing a gun at him. The first shot missed through sheer providence, but toppling to the ground behind the valet stand is what, Karan had no doubt, saved him from the second shot because the shooter had closed in and was certain of hitting his target. Shitij Yadav and his assassination squad had gotten their intelligence wrong on two counts: First, he should have been aware that Neena and her crack security men would be present. Second, (and there was no way he could have known this) Karan had got so many death threats since he had made his anti-reservation speech in Parliament that he had procured for himself a deadly 9mm semi-automatic concealable pistol with a lightweight plastic frame which he carried in an ankle holster – fearing that too much security would cramp his 'carefree' lifestyle.

After the assailant saw Neena's advancing security men he began backing up to his car, which is when Karan grabbed his pistol, crawled around the valet stand to his left, a feat for a man with his disability, took aim and brought the shooter down. He single-handedly neutralized his would-be assassin, and so we let me him crow all he wanted. What was left unsaid was that had the pistol and Neena's security been absent that night, as is reasonable to assume under normal circumstances, all the shooter would have needed to do was walk a few steps around the valet stand and nobody would have been able to save Karan from certain death.

The country learnt of the very precise details of what transpired that night from the ultra-sophisticated surveillance system that had been installed at the hotel. Not surprisingly, a copy of the relevant recording made its way to the media within the hour and Karan's near-death experience was repeatedly aired for the voyeuristic pleasures of all. Footage of an unconscious Shitij being removed from the assailants' car was the other recurring favourite of the television channels, and was posted everywhere on the Internet.

Shitij, apparently, had decided to remove the man tormenting his father and threatening his position from the scene, thereby also hoping to regain his father's lost respect and love. He could have sent his men to do the job and need not have personally gone along but Shitij's need to see the end of the man who had publicly labelled him a rapist and a menace to society had been too compelling to resist; besides his fetish for violence was overpowering. In acting on his urges, Shitij, who suffered extensive injuries but lived, proved Karan's observations about him as correct and destroyed any chance his father might have had of clinging to office.

The Yadav Government was at an end.

SHITIJ'S ACTIONS HAD left the ruling coalition in tatters, so we wouldn't need to use the Israeli arms deal against the PM, much to my relief. I would still have to explain what I was doing supping with Azim and Karan, but that was hardly a shooting offence. Besides, I doubted either of the Yadavs were giving me a moment's thought in the state they were in. It was only Sanjay I feared.

And I was right.

A day-and-a-half after the attempt on Karan Nehru's life, I got a call from Sanjay Kumar. He wanted to meet; just the two of us. We decided to have a drink at the Habitat Centre, the only club that had deigned to grant membership to Sanjay Kumar and where he naturally felt most at home. Government servants and businessmen would kow-tow to him like ass-kissing supplicants when they needed their work done but making him a member of their clubs – Delhi Golf Club, Gymkhana and the India International Centre being the capital's most exclusive triumvirate – was something they couldn't stomach. Class prejudice was alive and well among my brethren – i.e. Delhi's pompous elite. If I knew Sanjay, he'd bear it with a smile and then get his revenge when the time was ripe – turning the Delhi Golf Club, which leased its land from the government, into a grazing area for cows would no doubt go down well with the voters back home.

I asked after Yadav Junior's health: 'How is the piece of shit?'

'He'll live. Bones will heal, but there may be brain damage.'

'I think that in his case that may have happened at birth. How is the PM taking it?'

'Not well, obviously. Both his personal political future and his political legacy in the form of his son have imploded in one crash. Just a matter of time before he resigns. If he was in his senses he would have given up the fight already.' Sanjay's analysis was brutal.

'Couldn't agree more,' I echoed.

Then Sanjay changed the subject. 'I know what you have been up to,' he disclosed abruptly. I felt a blade pierce my heart. I should have known better than to think that this business would end tamely. I decided I wasn't going to try lying to him – that would have been futile and stupid, but I knew I didn't need to blurt out a confession either.

'And what exactly are you referring to?'

'You know, helping Karan Nehru and Azim Khan.'

'I didn't have a choice really.' There was a reason we were speaking about this over a drink and not at the end of a gun's barrel. I decided to play it cool.

'There's always a choice. Once you make it you must own it,' said Sanjay.

'And never regret it,' I added.

'What info have you given them?' he enquired.

'More than enough to finish the job,' I confessed a second time.

He nodded as he caressed his glass. 'It was plain to me that once you fell back in love with your wife it was just a matter of time before you defected. I'm just glad you didn't join our President's team.'

'I just picked the neutral corner; I joined the ones who wanted the national nightmare to be over, and who also happened to be men I could consort with without hating myself.' I had said too much.

'Maybe. I'm still convinced you risked it all for love,' Sanjay insisted. 'A man can do anything for love, Jasjit. You may not believe it from looking at me but I understand what it feels like to be passionately and irrationally in love. My wife is Muslim and when we eloped, it meant that we were saying goodbye forever to our comfortable lives in Kanpur. Our families didn't understand and we didn't hear from them for years until *after* I had made a name for myself. They came crawling out of the woodwork then; our religions didn't seem to matter to the worthless users anymore. Such is life.'

Sanjay was a constantly amazing package of surprises to me. I took it as a good sign that he was opening up to me. Although I realized that it wouldn't matter what secrets he confided to a condemned man. 'Marrying outside our religions is something we have in common,' I ventured.

'Along with having the sense to make good use of these

exceptional women. Our party's Muslim vote is largely dependent on my close links with the Muslim leaders and ulema – a relationship that my wife had been responsible for tending and strengthening year after year. In your case, Neena has raised your profile to a national level. I could get you elected from any part of the country you wanted.'

We were back to talking about politics after a lengthy detour. 'That is what I would call the height of optimism. Have you shared the news of my treachery with anyone?'

'I don't see any reason to, not yet anyway. The President is no longer the monstrous threat he was a few weeks ago – Januha can be thanked for that. And while we were distracted with the coup machinations, your friend Karan Nehru pummelled our boat with his torpedoes leaving this Government on its last legs. Now Azim Khan is busy finishing the job with the ruthlessness of a paid assassin. What good would be served by having you hanged for simply giving a helping hand? Of course, even though the PM is distracted right now he may still see the papers or watch the news and ask what you were doing socializing with his enemies. I'm sure you have a very convincing alibi prepared, but it might be prudent to recruit a third party to back up your story in case of such an eventuality.'

Really? And I wonder who this unnamed third party could be? He had clearly made me an offer of protection. The intial ingredients for a deal were there, but I had to be careful not to seem overly eager. That would not do at all. 'What will become of the Constitutional Amendment?'

'We did our best and showed our commitment to social justice. Let the next government handle it. Their bungling will seem very sweet from our new responsibility-free seats on the Opposition benches.'

'And may I ask the cost of your discretion regarding my activities?' I returned to the matter at hand.

'The PM has been shown up as a weak fool. If his exit is as inglorious as it seems likely, there will be no way he can recover.'

'Which opens the opportunity for a younger, hungrier leader...' I understood what he was proposing.

'It won't be easy. A challenge to the leadership of a major political party inevitably leads to a split, which is what I want to avoid. It will be counter-productive to my larger ambitions.'

Kumar was coming into his own as a political leader right in front of my eyes. 'I wish you all the best in your pursuit of the Prime Ministership, Sanjay, I have no doubt you'll get there. What do you need from me exactly?'

'The wholesale takeover or a split of a party the size of ours is an expensive operation,' he said straightforwardly.

'How much?' I asked.

We had moved into my area of expertise. He put a number forward and I agreed to it without a second's haggling. Considering the damage he could cause, I would have paid twice what he had asked for.

'That was easier than I thought,' he said, betraying his nervousness, once the deal was finalized.

I looked at Sanjay and smiled broadly as I felt the weight of the last few months slip from my shoulders. No price was too high for freedom; I, who had made my living pricing the intangible, knew that. 'You are doing me a service, old chap,' I said, shaking his hand. 'And I am just paying you what I think is a fit price for that service. Welcome to the free market, Mr Kumar.'

Epilogue

A POLITICAL FIRESTORM, the likes of which few had ever seen, followed Shitij's attack on Karan. The Yadav Government was brought down before the week was out, with General Bastard, shorn of ambition and enraged that his daughter's life had been put to risk, feeling confident enough to take a prominent role in the digging of its grave, which perhaps distracted him from obsessing over the approaching reality that his own days as President were numbered. He called in Yadav Senior's coalition partners and threatening to dismiss their Government if they did not find a new leader and fast. It was an un-constitutional move but who cared about the Constitution anymore? It could have been used for toilet paper after we had been through with it.

Yadav Senior resigned without complaint; Shitij's involvement in the murder attempt on Karan had taken the last of the fight out of him. Karan wisely kept silent on the matter, letting the pictures on television speak for themselves. A new minority government was installed with outside support being provided by the two national parties, the saffronites and the dynasts, on a day-to-day basis. It was a strange agreement but we were living in strange times. The Government trudged along over the succeeding months mainly because the entire political establishment was exhausted after the titanic battles of the previous six months and was even less inclined than before to deal with another general election.

The Constitutional Amendment regarding reservations in

the military was quietly returned to the Cabinet by the newly-elected President, without signing it, for the executive and legislature to reconsider. The new President, an experienced politician, proffered the advice that the politicians restructure the reservation proposal to include all Indians who were economically backward regardless of caste. It was not an outright rejection and was a ploy designed to confuse the issue, in which he succeeded.

The new Government did not want to rock the boat by confronting Rashtrapati Bhavan, having already seen where that route had led their predecessors, and agreed to set up a commission to look into the President's suggestions. The Constitutional Amendment was buried deep in the maze of the bureaucracy. Some noise was made by the usual suspects, Sanjay Kumar chief among them, but it was half-hearted at best. Everybody was busy licking their wounds.

Led by a bunch of eunuchs who were insecure as could be of their tenure, the new Government, astonished even me with how brazenly they went about satiating their greed. You see, the moderating and guiding hands of old – my father's, and then mine – were missing.

General Bastard was his usual cocky self for about a week after the new Government was formed but he soon found the thought of returning to the lesser position of Vice President heart-wrenching. He made all kinds of noises about not being able to serve in the secondary role again but when the hour arrived the lure of office – any office – was hard to resist and he continued as the Veep, the Presidency lost to him forever. There was some talk about bringing charges against him for what he had taken part in over the previous six months but nobody wanted to dig up that mess again and Dayal was left alone. He increasingly spent time at his Dehradun estate and lost active interest in Delhi and me. Thank God.

The army chief General Das was sacked by the new PM and

was succeeded in the post by the Western Army Commander, General Balbir Singh Kohli, who according to Azim had valiantly defied Dayal even under tremendous pressure and held up any coup attempt with his intransigence, buying Azim and his allies enough time to come up with a solution. Yes, yes, he was a Khatri, but a warrior, and no Jat Sikh, not even Dhillon Uncle, was anything but overjoyed when his appointment was announced. During his tenure he did the impossible and managed to restore the trust that was lost between the civilian leadership and the military brass through his no-nonsense, transparent approach.

I handed over all control of the Yadavs' foreign accounts back to them, visiting them after Shitij had sufficiently recovered, mentally and physically, at the hospital and was cooling his heels there as he awaited imminent arrest – you see, in our democracy the murderous sons of former PMs are not immediately dragged off to prison. We did not discuss anything other than the financial dealings that we had been involved in. Despite everything, I liked Paresh Yadav, and as a man, considered him my father-in-law's superior by many degrees. We parted ways amicably.

And what of Messrs Khan and Nehru? Would they fulfil the hopes and aspirations that the country placed on their sturdy shoulders? Time will tell, but they were certainly India's future and I for one would watch them closely every step of the way, because, just like everyone else in this country, I have a deep need to be inspired by the words and deeds of a real leader; someone to inspire us and push us to find the best within ourselves.

With all due respect to my friend Mr Nehru, Azim Khan was that man for me. But would India recognize his greatness, or would we get distracted by that radioactive name of his, that transmitted so much of so little value? The answer to my question, when it arrives, will say more about us as a country than it will about Azim, I think. I shall wait and watch; India has a way of surprising even the most cynical amongst us.

After the shooting, Neena moved out of her father's lodgings and we set up our home together. General Bastard was not happy with the inconvenience this brought to his life but he held his tongue as he knew there was no way that I would ever live under the same roof as him. I have made my peace about sharing Neena with her father, it definitely still grates but I have learnt to handle it within myself. Neena is my love and there can be no one else, I know that now. This realization has helped me through the toughest of times. We've made it so far.

As for me, I lead the worry-free and decadent existence of those who never need to work a day in their life again. I travel, golf, socialize, and give my thanks that I made it through my living nightmare. Sahni, my private spy, took his company public and asked me to become a director on its board. I could not refuse after everything he had done for me and I lend a hand whenever he needs help, which is not often.

After the newly installed powers-that-be found their footing they came calling on me, to fill Father's shoes. I did not hesitate to send them packing. But as time goes by, and the memory of unpleasant events fades, I have begun to itch for a return to the game. Money obviously isn't the issue, it goes deeper than that.

I could take up Azim on his unexpected offer to join his party and become a neta, firmly coming out of the shadows once and for all, but I know that would be mere vanity at work. To be another mediocre, powerless politician does not appeal when you have lived the life I have and know where the real decisions are made – in the shadows. It is the shadows that provide my natural habitat.

Okay, fine, I'll cut the coy bullshit and give it to you clean. Power is a commodity and the Delhi Durbar is where it is traded. Despite everything that I have been through I cannot imagine a life that involves doing anything else. So when I do make my comeback, God save the son of a bitch who gets in my way because I have been taught by the best and have forged my destiny in the crucible of the darkest days of our republic.

There is no denying what the twins said.

I am my father's son.